PRAISE FOR LISA SCOTTOLINE'S

"... Scottoline is one of the hot new writers of legal/crime fiction snapping at the heels of John Grisham and Scott Turow."

—*Cincinnati Post*

"Still hot . . . Lisa Scottoline proves herself equal to the task of maintaining a winning formula that is both fresh and entertaining. . . . Scottoline's heroine is a tough cookie with a marshmallow heart, and she talks like a cross between Mike Hammer and Erma Bombeck. . . . [A] hard-edged, humorous sensibility defines the book's mood and runs through it like a river of hope. . . . *Legal Tender* is a page-turning thriller festooned with red herrings and a comic sensibility that is quite rare in the cloak and dagger department. . . . Lisa Scottoline is a welcome breath of fresh—and funny—air."

—*Milwaukee Journal Sentinel*

"This smooth tale moves."   —*San Jose Mercury News*

"Don't miss former practicing attorney Lisa Scottoline's latest."

—*American Woman*

"Bright, funny, and fast-reading."

—*Ellery Queen Mystery Magazine*

LEGAL TENDER

LEGAL TENDER

A ROSATO & ASSOCIATES NOVEL

LISA SCOTTOLINE

HARPER

NEW YORK ● LONDON ● TORONTO ● SYDNEY

HARPER

LEGAL TENDER. Copyright © 1996 by Lisa Scottoline. All rights reserved. Printed in the United States of America. No part of this book may be used or reproduced in any manner whatsoever without written permission except in the case of brief quotations embodied in critical articles and reviews. For information address HarperCollins Publishers, 195 Broadway, New York, NY 10007.

HarperCollins books may be purchased for educational, business, or sales promotional use. For information please e-mail the Special Markets Department at SPsales@harpercollins.com.

FIRST HARPER TORCH PAPERBACK EDITION PUBLISHED 1997.

FIRST HARPER PAPERBACK EDITION PUBLISHED 2016.

ISBN 978-0-06-240013-0 (pbk.)

16 17 18 19 20   IND/RRD   10 9 8 7 6 5 4 3 2

For my editor, Carolyn Marino,
who has always encouraged me to be tall.

And for Kiki and Peter.

LEGAL
TENDER

ONE

I edged forward on my pew in the gallery so I wouldn't miss a single word. My ex-lover's new girlfriend, Eve Eberlein, was about to be publicly humiliated by the Honorable Edward J. Thompson. I wanted to dance with joy right there in the courtroom. Hell hath no fury like a lawyer scorned.

"Let me remind you of something you have plainly forgotten, Ms. Eberlein," Judge Thompson was saying between discreetly clenched teeth. A bald, gentlemanly judge, his legendary patience had been tested by Eve's attack on the elderly witness. "This is a court of law. There are rules of conduct. Civility, manners. One doesn't check common courtesy at the door of my courtroom."

"Your Honor, this witness is not being candid with the court," Eve said. Her spiky brunette cut bounced in defiance as she stood before the dais, in perfect makeup and a red knit suit that fit her curves like an Ace bandage. Not that I was jealous.

"Utter nonsense, Ms. Eberlein!" Judge Thompson scoffed, peering down through reading glasses that matched his robe. "I will not permit you to cast aspersions on the character of a witness. You have asked her the same question over and over, and she's told you she doesn't remember where the Cetor file is. She retired two years ago, if you recall. Move on to your next question, counsel."

"With all due respect, Your Honor, Mrs. Debs was the records custodian at Wellroth Chemical and she remembers perfectly well where the Cetor file is. I tell you, the witness is lying to the Court!" Eve pointed like a manicured Zola at Mrs. Debs, whose powdered skin flushed a deep pink.

"My goodness!" she exclaimed, hand fluttering to the pearls at her chest. Mrs. Debs had a halo of fuzzy gray hair and a face as honest as Aunt Bea's. "I would never, ever lie to a court!" she said, and anybody with any sense could see she was telling the truth. "Heavens, I swore on a Bible!"

"Ms. Eberlein!" Judge Thompson exploded. "You're out of order!" He grabbed his gavel and pounded it hard. *Crak! Crak! Crak!*

Meanwhile, Mark Biscardi, my ex-boyfriend and still-current law partner, was fake-reading exhibits at counsel table. He was downplaying the debacle for the jury's benefit, but was undoubtedly listening to every syllable. I hoped he remembered my prediction that Eve would crash and burn today, so I could say I told you so.

"I object, Your Honor!" shouted plaintiffs counsel, Gerry McIllvaine. "Ms. Eberlein's conduct toward this witness is an outrage! An outrage!" McIllvaine, a trial veteran, had been standing out of the crossfire, keeping his mouth shut until it was time to grandstand for the jury. All the courtroom's a stage, and all the men and women in it merely lawyers.

Then, suddenly, I began to focus on the jury box. Most of the jurors in the front row were scowling at Eve as Judge

Thompson continued his lecture. Two jurors in the back, retirees like Mrs. Debs, bore a prim smile at Eve's comeuppance. Eve had alienated the lot, and it would taint their view of the defendant's case. Unfortunately, this was a high-stakes trial and the defendant was a major client of my law firm, Rosato & Biscardi, alias R & B.

Damn. I sat up straighter and looked worriedly at Mark, but he was stuck playing with the trial exhibits. He and I had started R & B seven years ago and watched it grow into one of the most successful litigation boutiques in Philadelphia. I cared about the firm so much I couldn't even enjoy watching Eve screw up something besides my love life. Something had to be done.

I stood up in the middle of the proceedings, calling attention to myself without a word because of my height, a full six feet. It's a great height for a trial lawyer, but as a teenager I stood by so many punchbowls I got sick from the fumes. I grew up to be taller, blonder, and stronger, so that now I looked like an Amazon with a law degree.

"Ouch!" said the lawyer sitting next to me, as I trounced solidly on his wingtip.

"Oh, excuse me," I yelped, almost as loudly as Judge Thompson, still scolding Eve, with the jury's rapt attention.

"Shhh," said another lawyer.

"Sorry, so sorry," I chirped, struggling out of the crowded row like a boor going for Budweiser in the second inning. I noticed out of the corner of my eye that one of the jurors, the Hispanic man on the end, was being successfully distracted. "Oops! Sorry about that," I practically shouted.

Once out of the row, I strode past the bar of the court to counsel table, where my ex-beloved was sweating armholes into his English pinstripes. As Mark turned to see what the commotion was, I leaned close to his dark, wavy hair and breathed in his expensive creme rinse. "You're screwed, hombre," I whispered, with some pleasure.

"It's her first time out," he hissed back. "She made a mistake."

"No, *you* made a mistake. I told you she isn't a trial lawyer. She can't connect with people, she's too cold. Now hold up an exhibit so we can fight in peace."

Mark grabbed an exhibit and ducked behind it. "What's happening with the jury? This is killing us."

I snuck a peek sideways. Most of the jurors were watching me and Mark by now. I wondered if any recognized me, infamous radical lawyer Bennie Rosato. I could only hope my hair looked less incendiary than usual. "The jury's wondering whether we're still sleeping together. Where's the client, Haupt? He's the cheese, right?"

"Yeah, Dr. Otto Haupt. Guy with the steel glasses in the front row. How's he taking it?"

I checked the reaction of the aforementioned, but his expression was a double-breasted blank. "He's a suit, not a face. And no more excuses for your new girlfriend. Deal with her."

"What do you want me to do, spank her?"

"You wish." He'd tried it with me once but I'd laughed myself silly. "Keep her at second-chair. Don't let her take any more witnesses."

"She needs to work on her people skills, that's all."

"I hate that expression, 'people skills.' What does that mean? You either have a heart or you don't."

He flashed me a photogenic smile. "Why are you here, Bennie? Do I need to take this crap from you, now? In the middle of trial?"

"It's the least you can do, I'm about to save your ass. Grab the glass next to that file." I picked up a pitcher of water from counsel table. It was heavy and cold, and there were even some ice cubes left. Perfect.

"Why am I doing this?" He reached for the glass.

"Don't you remember Leo Melly, the transvestite who wanted to march in the Columbus Day parade? From the old days, when you fought for things that mattered, like the right to wear puce in broad daylight?"

A glint of recognition flickered through Mark's gorgeous brown eyes and he hoisted his glass. "Way to go, Bennie. Just don't mess up the patent application, it's an original."

"Brace yourself." I reached for the glass but it popped out of my outstretched hand and tumbled end over end like a fumbled football. *"Whoooops!"* I squealed, lunging for the glass, but missing it so expertly that I bobbled the pitcher, too. Ice cubes and frigid water gushed out like a mountain waterfall, raced past the errant glass in an icy torrent, and landed with a noisy splash in the middle of Mark's lap.

"Argh!" Mark shouted, springing to his feet. "Wow! That's cold!" Eyes wide, he jumped away from counsel table, crunching the ice cubes in a frantic jig.

"Oh no!" I cried, then dropped the glass pitcher on his foot. "Oh, it slipped!"

"Yeeow!" Mark grabbed his toe.

"Oh, I'm sorry! I'm so sorry!" I flapped my arms like a baby seal and tried to look helpless, which isn't easy for me. I haven't been helpless a day in my life.

Meantime, chaos was erupting at the front of the courtroom. A juror in the first row pointed in surprise. The back row, mostly older women, burst into giggles. Eve had turned around, her lipsticked mouth hanging open. Judge Thompson tore off his glasses, his lecture abandoned. "Bailiff! Deputy!" he barked. "Get some paper towels! I won't have my tables stained!"

"Yes, Your Honor," said the courtroom deputy, who was already hurrying over with paper towels. He shot me a dirty look as he mopped up the water pooling on counsel table and dripping onto the dark blue rug.

"Can I have a few of those?" Mark asked. He snatched a handful of towels and dabbed his crotch, which triggered another wave of tittering from the jurors in the back.

Judge Thompson sighed audibly. "Let's break for the morning recess, ladies and gentlemen. Ms. Howard, please escort the jury out, since the deputy is otherwise engaged." *Crak!* He eased out of his chair and left the dais shaking his head.

"It's your mess, you clean it up," snapped the deputy. "Better make sure there's no water marks." He dumped the pile of paper towels on the table and walked off toward the court reporter, who was flexing her fingers.

The courtroom emptied quickly, the lawyers laughing and talking as they filed out. Plaintiff's counsel snapped his briefcase shut and left, walking past Dr. Haupt, who lingered by the door, his Teutonic features betraying only the slightest bit of annoyance. My acting had been so good I fooled even him. So be it. It wouldn't be the first time I looked like a jerk for the cause.

"Thanks a whole lot, Bennie," Mark said. He swabbed the huge, wet stain spreading like bad news across his crotch.

"Sorry, partner," I told him, surprised to feel a tiny twinge of regret. Ice cubes melted into the rug, and Eve stepped over them delicately to reach us.

"You okay, honey?" she asked softly, and rubbed Mark's back with a concern so touching I almost gagged.

"It's water," I pointed out. "He'll live."

"You could have been more careful," she said, frowning. "I was just getting into my cross."

I almost laughed. "Do you really believe this was an accident, child? I dumped the water to—"

"That's enough, Bennie," Mark interrupted, holding up a wet paper towel. "I'll handle this."

"Oh really."

"I'll handle it."

"You'd better. I have to go, I have a new client. Lots of luck, kids." I turned to avoid a puddle, then took off, banging through the heavy mahogany doors. As they closed I heard Eve's laughter, followed by Mark's. Masculine, heartier.

I remembered his laugh, I remembered it all.

Now what I had to do was forget it.

TWO

The goose egg made by the initial blow was tinged a virulent pink and a deep gash contorted the teenager's strawberry blond eyebrow. His left eye had hemorrhaged, the white turned a crimson red, and that side of his face was mottled from bruise and trauma. Luckily, the skin on his forehead wasn't split, so I guessed the weapon was a billyclub, not a service revolver. Somebody on the force must have liked young Bill Kleeb.

The judge had sent the case to me, since Kleeb and his girlfriend, Eileen Jennings, had filed complaints of police brutality, my expertise. Philadelphia had coughed up $20 million in lawsuits for police misconduct in the past two years, and most of the money went to clients of mine. My cases ran the gamut from police assault, excessive force, and false arrest to the officially "mistaken shooting," like the grad student who was shot by an off-duty cop because the student was wearing a knit Eagles cap, the same as a robber seen fleeing in the area. The cop, who had been drinking, temporarily forgot that everybody in Philly wears Eagles caps, especially when the team's in the playoffs.

That case had made headlines, as had the complaints I filed against the 39th District, where a cadre of Philly's finest confessed to fencing stolen goods and falsifying evidence in drug cases, thereby sending over one hundred people, including a sixty-year-old tailor, to prison for twelve years. No matter that the tailor was innocent. He won two mil from the city, for which he paid my nominal fee and made me a custom suit. I liked my work, it had a purpose. The way I figured it, my hometown didn't need me to tell it we had a problem in the department, it just needed me to remind it once in a while. For this I charged only a nuisance fee. My fee to be a nuisance.

"Now tell me again, Bill. Why didn't you ask the cops for a doctor?" I took inane notes during the interview so I wouldn't stare at his battered face, a part of the job I never got used to. I scribbled on my legal pad, DOCTOR, DOCTOR, GIMME THE NEWS.

"I said I didn't need no doctor. They put ice. It was good enough." His hair was a greasy blond, and splotchy freckles spread across his small nose and onto a swollen upper lip. Bill had the kind of teeth only poor kids have anymore, irregularly sized and spaced. Amazingly, none had been knocked out during the melee.

"You should have gotten it checked. Anytime you lose consciousness."

"I'll remember that."

I wrote, I GOT A BAD CASE OF LOVIN' YOU. "How's your ribs? They all right?"

"Fine."

"Does it hurt to breathe?"

"Nuh. See?" He blew a cone of cigarette smoke into the air.

"Impressive. No kicks to the stomach? No feet, clubs, anything?"

"I'm fine," he said crankily, and I began to feel ticked off. Maybe it was the way the morning had gone so far.

"If you're so fine, Bill, why did you allege the police used excessive force against you? And why do you want to plead not guilty when we have an offer that gets you out of jail free?"

"It's Eileen, my girl." He shifted position in his blue prison jumpsuit. "She . . . uh . . . wants us to do the same complaint. . . . Together, like."

"But it doesn't make sense for you to plead not guilty. Eileen's the one who started the trouble, she's the one with the record." For smalltime prostitution, but I didn't need to drive home that point.

"She wants us to be, like, a united front."

"Well, you're not. You're two different people, you have two different situations. That's why you have separate lawyers. Eileen's in more trouble than you. She had the weapon."

"It was only a taser gun."

"Electricity applied to the chest of an arresting officer. You think that doesn't count?"

He ran his tongue over his swollen lip. "Eileen, she's got quite a temper. She'll be pissed if I don't go along."

"So what? Who wears the nose rings in this family?"

Bill winced as he dragged on his Salem. Cigarette smoke and cheap disinfectant thickened the air in the interrogation room. The lattice cage over the door window was furry with dust, and a chewed-up Styrofoam cup lay on its side on the filthy table. I've seen this same Styrofoam cup in every precinct in Philly. I think they move it around.

"Take the deal, Bill. If you plead guilty, you walk. If you

plead not guilty, you go directly to jail. It's one of the fine iro-
nies of our criminal justice system."

He still wouldn't meet my eye.

"Okay, let's get off that subject for a minute. Give me some
background. You were demonstrating for animal rights when
they arrested you. You don't think Furstmann Dunn should
test its vaccine on monkeys, is that the story?"

"They got no right. We got no right. We don't own them,
we're just bigger."

"Got it." Some of us, anyway. I couldn't help noticing my
latest revolutionary was a tad on the short side. "Are you a
member of PETA or any other animal rights groups?"

"I don't need no authority over me." He sucked on his
Salem, holding it down like a lollipop.

"I take it that's a no." I wrote, NO. "So it's you and Eileen.
Are you two married?"

"We don't need no authority—"

"Another no," I said, making a note. NO 2. "So it's you and
Eileen against the world. Romantic." I had felt that way with
Mark, when I was younger and entirely delusional.

"I guess," he said lazily, the "I" sounding like "Ah." I
couldn't place his accent even though I know every Philly accent there is.

"Where you from, Bill? Not from here."

"Out western PA, out past Altoona. The boonies. I was
raised on a farm, that's how I come to know animals. It was
the 4-H ruined me." He laughed, emitting a residual puff of
smoke.

"Did you graduate high school?"

"Yup. Then I booked it to York and worked at the Harley
Davidson factory for a while. That's where I met Eileen. She

was workin' in the lab, Furstmann Dunn's lab. That's where they were testing the vaccine. She took pictures of them tor- turin' the monkeys. She saw the way they treated 'em. They *abused* 'em."

It didn't sound like a word that came naturally to him. "Ei- leen tell you this?"

"They use electrodes, you know."

"On the monkeys?"

"On minks. For mink coats. Stoles and whatnot."

"Minks? Why are we talking about minks?"

"I don't know. It was you brought it up."

I wrote down NOT MINKS. Was he just dumb, or was a con- versation with an anarchist necessarily confusing?

"It's all part of the same thing," he added. "It's all wrong."

"Bill, can I give you some advice?" I try to run the lives of all of my clients, to redeem the job I'm doing with my own. "If I were going to protest animal experimentation, I wouldn't pick on Furstmann Dunn, because they're working on an AIDS vaccine. People want to cure AIDS, even if it takes a few chimps to do it. Why don't you go after the fur companies instead? Then people can get behind you, agree with you."

He shook his head. "Eileen, she don't care if people agree with us or not. She wants to put a stop to it. It was her idea to call the TV stations and the radio."

"You did make quite a commotion, didn't you?" I said, feeling an unaccountable tingle of pride. They'd had every- body there, even the national TV news. Part of the fussing was a spontaneous counterdemonstration by a group of gay men. A tough issue, but I was undefeated in not judging my clients' politics. I didn't defend what they said, just their right to say it without a nightstick to the noggin.

"Got a whole lotta press, too. Eileen liked that." Bill took another drag on his cigarette.

"You shouldn't have resisted arrest. They had a whole squad there, and it was just two of you. You don't strike me as a fighter." I glanced at Bill's arms; white, thin, flabby.

"Nuh, I'm a lover, not a fighter." He smiled crookedly.

I bet he wasn't much of either, but I found myself liking him. I flipped through the file in front of me, which was almost empty. Bill had no priors, even in the counties, which was why the D.A. had offered me such a sweet deal. The poor kid had thrown one punch his whole life, and it had landed him here. "I don't get it," I said, closing the file folder. "Why did you hit the cop?"

"Because he was beatin' on Eileen. I was tryin' to get him off her. He twisted her arm, so she'd go down, like." His eyes flared. "All she did was holler on him."

"Except for the taser, remember? She threatened the cop with it, and the CEO of the company. She trapped the man in his Mercedes."

"Okay, so she was trying to give him a dose of his own medicine. It coulda been worse. She wanted to blow him up in that fancy car of his."

"Blow who up? The CEO of Furstmann?" My chest tightened. I'd never gotten used to murder cases, even when my legal argument was sound, so I gave that work up a long time ago. "Bill, did Eileen say she wanted to kill the CEO of Furstmann? Did she mean it?"

"She's tough, Eileen is." He looked down at his cigarette. "That's why she don't want to plead guilty to the charges. Make 'em prove we done wrong. Go to jail, like a protest. Maybe do a hunger strike."

I set down my ballpoint. "Bill, answer me. Did you talk about killing the CEO with Eileen?"

He looked away, avoiding my eye. "She said she wanted to, and I told her not to. She said she wouldn't do nuthin' 'less we talked about it first."

"Would she tell her lawyer she wanted to kill the CEO?"

"Dunno."

I leaned across the table. "Not good enough, Bill. The murder of a CEO, with you as an accomplice, you could get the death penalty. The D.A. here asks for death in every murder case, she wants to prove her manhood. You understand what I'm saying?"

He stabbed his cigarette into the logjam in the tin ashtray.

"Killing that CEO wouldn't solve anything, no matter what your girlfriend says. There are twenty other suits waiting to take his place. They got the same cars, they got the same degrees. They line 'em up, they call 'em vice presidents. You're smart enough to know that, right, Bill?"

He nodded, stubbing out the smoldering butt.

"I want you to promise you won't do anything that stupid, not on my watch. Look at me, Bill. Tell me you're not that stupid."

His good eye met mine. "I'm not."

"No. Say it after me, 'I'm not that stupid.'"

"I'm not that stupid." He half smiled and a yellow eyetooth peeked out.

"Excellent. Now you're going into that courtroom this morning and you're going to plead guilty, you with me? I got you the best deal going, and you're gonna take it."

"I can't. Eileen—"

"Forget about Eileen. You'd be a fool to do what she wants. She'll take you both down, not just her, and you're my lookout. You're the one I'm worried about."

He shook his head and sighed. "You got kids, lady?"

"Yeah, I got kids, Bill. You."

THREE

Inside, Philadelphia's new Criminal Justice Center looks nothing like a courthouse. Playful bronze stars, curlicues, and squiggles are inlaid into the lobby floor, and it says SANDY BEACH—SEA GULLS—SALT AIR—COOL BREEZE—DANDELIONS—MOSSY BANKS in a continuous loop in the hallways outside the courtrooms. ARSON—PROSTITUTION—COLD-BLOODED MURDER would be more appropriate to a criminal court, but reality can be no fun at all.

In the swank arraignment courtroom, on the black designer pews, the pushers sit with the crackheads, the pimps sit with the hookers, and the lawyers sit with the clients. Nobody but me sees any parallels here, I'm pretty sure. I sat at the counsel table next to a nervous Bill Kleeb, watching Judge John Muranno climb the few steps to the gleaming walnut dais and settle into his leather chair between flags of the United States and the Commonwealth of Pennsylvania. Muranno, a short, stout judge with a bulbous nose, wore his permanently martyred expression, which earned him the nickname Pope John.

"Mr. William Seifert Kleeb, are you present in this courtroom?" Pope John intoned, though Bill was plainly sitting before him. It was the opening call-and-response of the colloquy, a mass written by lawyers and judges to safeguard the defendant's constitutional rights, so we could either plead him out or try him, where he would be convicted if he was poor or black and especially if he was both.

"I'm here," Bill said, half rising. I shoved him up the rest of the way.

"Mr. Kleeb, is this your signature?" Pope John waved the written form.

"Yeah. Yes."

"Did you review this form with your counsel?"

"Yes."

"Are you presently under the influence of drugs or alcohol?"

"Nu-uh."

"Are you presently under the influence of any type of medication?"

"Uh, no."

"Have any threats or promises been made to you to induce you to sign this paper?"

"No."

Pope John proceeded to recite the charges against Bill, and I watched the reaction of an increasingly restless Eileen Jennings. She was five foot two, with long matte-black hair and a killer body, even with one arm in a sling. She fidgeted in her chair at the other defense table. Her eyes were dark and round, with a gaze that didn't rest anywhere too long, but was always roving. They narrowed as Bill answered Pope John's final questions. She'd been around enough courtrooms to know what came next.

"Do I understand correctly, Mr. Kleeb, that you are pleading guilty to the charges against you?"

"Yes, sir," Bill answered.

"No, he isn't!" Eileen shrieked, springing from her chair. Her public defender, a harried-looking young man with a nascent beard, yanked her back down by her good arm and tried to calm her. I touched Bill's elbow to steady him, and he kept his eyes straight ahead the way I'd told him to. The gallery started talking among themselves and there was some laughter.

Pope John continued as if nothing untoward was happening, since it wasn't in the missal. "Mr. Kleeb, do you make this plea freely, willingly, and of your own volition?"

"Uh, yes," Bill said, more quietly than before, and Eileen jumped to her feet again. Every vein in her neck bulged as she struggled in her lawyer's grasp.

"Bill, what are you doing!" she screamed. Two bailiffs hurried over and it took all three men to push her back into her chair, and she cursed as one jostled her broken arm. The gallery grew noisier and the same man in the back laughed crazily.

Pope John cleared his throat. "If there is another disruption of these proceedings, the Court will be compelled to place the defendant in restraints."

"That won't be necessary, Your Honor," said the public defender. Eileen began stage-whispering to him frantically, even as the bailiffs stood above her.

"Mr. Kleeb," the judge continued, talking over the noise, "the Court accepts your plea. You are released on your own recognizance. I see from your case file you have not been here before, and I do not expect the Court will see you here again. Thank you, Mr. Kleeb."

"Yes, sir." Bill eased into his seat, without looking at Eileen or me. His forehead was damp and his hands clasped together as if he were still cuffed.

"Miss Eileen Jennings, are you present in this courtroom?" Judge Muranno was saying.

"I plead not guilty!" Eileen cried, rising again, and this time her lawyer gave up. They obviously had no rapport, so I guessed she hadn't told him about the CEO. "I had the right to protest the torture of those animals and those *pigs* beat me, Your Honor! They broke my arm and they beat me up! They had themselves a fine time!"

The faces of the arresting uniforms remained impassive as they sat in the row behind us, chrome badges lined up on their blue shirts. I knew most of them, and only two would've kicked the crap out of Eileen for fun. Noticeably absent was the cop she had tazed into a hospital stay. I heard he'd be out in a day and was considering a counterclaim.

"Miss Jennings," Judge Muranno asked, "are you represented by counsel?"

"No, I have a public defender," she said, and her lawyer winced. He looked all of twenty-three, since the P.D.'s office got them out of law school and burned them out fast. Each P.D. handled as many as thirty-five cases a day and often didn't get the file until showtime.

"You are represented by counsel," Pope John said, and read the charges, taking Eileen through another version of the liturgy and turning the other cheek at each insolent response. He accepted Eileen's not guilty plea, set a trial date that everybody knew was illusory, and banged the gavel, *Amen*, for the bailiffs to take her to State Road.

Eileen didn't look back but Bill watched her leave, and as soon as the door closed behind her, he stood up like a shot. "I have to go," he said, his voice trembling. He kept his face turned away as he shook my hand.

"You did the right thing," I said, but he didn't respond, just turned and hurried past the bar of the court. "Bill?" I called after him, but he bolted out the courtroom door in front of Eileen's lawyer, who held a stack of red accordion files under a pinstriped arm. I grabbed my briefcase and hustled after the public defender, catching up with him in a hallway that thronged with the disenfranchised, waiting to be arraigned. SANDY BEACHES, my ass.

"Are you really Bennie Rosato?" the P.D. asked, as I fell in stride beside him.

"No, she's even taller. You've got quite a handful in there."

"I'll say." He threaded his way through the crowd, turning his shoulders sideways. "Congratulations on that verdict, I followed it in the papers. Man, ten cops on one guy, up in the Northeast. The Police Advisory Board is a joke, isn't it?"

"Listen, about Jennings—"

"I'd been wanting to meet you. I remember when you came to speak at my law school. Last year, at Seton Hall?"

I pushed past a fragrant circle of hookers. "Have you talked to Jennings at any length?"

"Jennings?"

"Eileen Jennings, your client."

"She's not my file, I'm just filling in."

"Whose file is she?"

"Abrams, he's on trial." He checked his watch. "Damn. I was supposed to be upstairs ten minutes ago."

"I want you to know I think Eileen Jennings is dangerous."

"Are you kidding?" He dodged a herd of cops. "She was all talk, no action."

"But what about the taser?"

"Hah! The chief wants me to cop it from the evidence room for the Christmas party."

A family passed between us with toddlers in tow, and I waited to ask, "Do you know if she has a gun, or any explosives?"

"This isn't my file."

I grabbed his arm. "You got the *file*, so take some responsibility. You have to find out if she's really dangerous. Do you understand?"

"I'll make a note, okay?" He wrenched his arm free and hustled off, disillusioned and disappearing into the mob at the elevator bank.

I stood there and let the crowd flow around me. The P.D. wouldn't make any note. Even if he did, it would get lost in the sea of notes, in the sea of files. The files, of course, were people. Black and white, crazy and sane, tall and short, even the ones shuffling around me at this very minute. Most of them on a first-name basis with handguns, child abuse, knives, crack addiction, and boxcutters. They were flooding in, choking the hallways and corridors, people that were downgraded to files and finally to statistics, the life bled from them, and the humanity.

For a second I felt stunned, thinking there was nothing I could do about it, no matter how hard I tried. Not even if I was right about Eileen, not even if I was wrong. Because there were twenty others waiting to take her place, itching to take aim. They lined 'em up, like the vice presidents. And they would be met with equal and opposite force, one that had arms as well as the law. There was a war on, truly, a pitched battle. And as clearly as I perceived it, I still didn't know which side I was on. I was in the middle, at sea.

Rowing furiously, and not knowing either shore.

FOUR

walked to clear my head, striding down Benjamin Franklin Parkway under the colorful, oversized flags that hung from the streetlamps. They billowed like spinnakers in the stiff breeze from the Schuylkill River not ten blocks away, rattling the chains that fastened them to the poles. It made me wish I was out on the river, sculling. The water would be choppy in the wind and there'd be whitecaps, little ones that kept things exciting. Maybe tonight, I promised myself, as I headed to the chrome monolith known as the Silver Bullet, there to find my best friend Sam Freminet and drag him out to lunch.

I hit the building's marble lobby and grabbed the first elevator, only to feel a familiar constriction in my gut as it headed skyward to my old law firm, the huge and insanely conservative Grun & Chase. We used to call it Groan & Waste, as in our young associates' lives, but I hide those bad memories away. Groan & Waste didn't own me anymore. Nobody did.

"Where's that Looney Tune? He in?" I said to the young receptionist when the doors opened on Sam's floor. She had no idea who I was, but knew exactly whom I meant.

"He's in. Should I tell him who's here?" She was reaching for the phone, unsure whether I was a lawyer or a trouble-maker, when in fact I was a little of both.

"Bennie Rosato, his favorite Italian," I said, and breezed past her questioning glance. I've gotten that look as many times as I've heard how's the weather up there, because I don't look Italian at all. With some cause.

I charged by the costly Amish quilts and large-scale oils on the walls, past secretaries with files in hand to give their conspiratorial giggling some ostensible business purpose. I didn't recognize any of them; all the secretaries I knew were smart enough to leave. "Hey, ladies," I said anyway, because I have a soft spot for secretaries. My mother used to be one, or so she says.

"Hello," answered one, and the rest smiled. They assumed I was a client, since no Grun lawyer would greet a secretary.

An associate scurried self-importantly by, but I didn't recognize him either. Of fifteen of us associates, only Sam had stayed and made partner. Since then he'd ascended the classes of partners to the tippy-top of the firm, becoming the youngest three-window partner ever, which is the tax-bracket equivalent of a five-star general. If they'd known Sam was gay and not merely eccentric, they would have set him on fire and billed somebody for it.

I reached Sam's sunny office and closed the door behind me. "Honey, I'm homo!" I called out.

"Benniieeee!" Sam looked up, blue eyes bright behind neat rimless glasses. Tall and slim, he had a handsome face, with a straight nose and fine cheekbones, framed by reddish-brown hair that was trimmed every four weeks. "How are you doing?" he said, coming around the desk to give me a warm hug.

"I need cheering up. How are you?"

"I'm looney, as usual, and up-cheering is my specialty. Siddown." He waved me into a leather sling chair and mock-tiptoed back to his desk. "Be vewwy, vewwy quiet. We'we hunting wabbits."

I laughed and flopped into the chair.

"See? It's working already."

"I knew it would. That's why I came." My gaze wandered over the framed cartoon cels hanging on the walls amid Sam's double Yale diplomas. Slumped on a glass-topped table against the far window were stuffed toys of Sylvester the Cat, Foghorn Leghorn, and Porky Pig. Pepe Le Pew had fallen into a porno-graphic clinch with the Tasmanian Devil. "I see Pepe's out of control again."

"Per usual. That skunk's a regular JFK."

"Don't say that about my Pepe."

"Pepe has no idea what matters in life. Daffy does. He's a duck with priorities."

"Like what?" I asked, though the answer was staring me in the face. A statue of Daffy sat on the desk, roosting atop a mountain of dollar bills and a sign that read BIGGER BETTER FASTER CHEAPER. "Money?"

"Yes, money, and don't say it that way. Daffy is happening, Bennie. Daffy is God."

"He's too greedy."

"You can never be too greedy, *chica*. Do you know why I'm the best bankruptcy lawyer in these here parts?"

"Because you're morally bankrupt?"

"Only partly. The reason is, I understand money. Where it went, where it should have been, how to get it back. I have a sixth sense for it. You, on the other hand, maintain the absurd belief that love is more important than money. What kind of lawyer are you?"

"A dinosaur."

"Extinct."

"So be it. But Pepe Le Pew is my man."

"'Ah, ze l'amour. Ah, ze toujour. Ah, le grand illusion,'" Sam said. "'Scent-imental Romeo,' 1951. You can be bought, too, you know."

"Bull."

"*Si*, my little liberal. You're a sucker for a loser, any kind of loser. The more lost, bruised, concussed, and cussed-out, the better. Same way with me, when I spot a bankruptcy. We're the dogcatchers of the profession."

"Thanks."

Sam pouted, sticking out a lower lip. "I'm not cheering you up anymore, am I?"

"It's okay."

"What's up, doc? You still feeling bad about Mark?"

I sighed in resignation. "It's annoying, isn't it? He dumped me a month ago. I should be getting over it." I felt like kicking something, but most of the office furniture was glass.

"That's not so long, Bennie. You were together for, what, six years?"

"Seven."

"You're going to hurt awhile, expect it. Eve is so lame. She was here last week with Mark, annoying the crap out of me. So smooth and plastic. She's Lawyer Barbie."

I didn't want to dwell on it. "Why'd you call me last night, Samuel? I got home too late to call back."

He hunched over his desk. "I'm worried. I heard a nasty

rumor. There's an associate defection in progress, did you know that?"

"At Grun, somebody going for the barbed wire?"

"No, at R & B."

"What? At *my firm*?"

"That's what I heard," he said, nodding. "A partner of mine in litigation got a call from one of your associates. The kid said he'd be looking for a job soon, and another associate was looking, too."

"Who? Who were the associates?"

"They didn't say. What's going on, Bennie? Can you afford to lose two associates?"

"No, not with the cases I have coming in. Damn." We had only seven associates, with Mark and me as the only partners. "It can't be true."

"Why not? You know how these things go, especially lately. Half the firms in the city are breaking up. Look at Wolf, and Dilworth. It's like teen suicides, coming in clusters."

"Why would any associate want to leave R & B? They make almost as much as I do."

"They're ingrates. Socialism doesn't work, autocracy does. Ask Bill Gates. Ask Daffy Duck."

I rubbed my forehead. "We were trying to do it differently. Not like at Grun."

"What a bunch of bull. You should've stayed here. We could be working together, having fun. You could've been my resident beard. All you had to say was 'light chocolate,' and everything would've been different."

I flashed on the day. I had gotten The Call from The Great And Powerful Grun. A gaggle of associates flew to my office to prepare me for The Visit, tell me The Question he'd ask, and

The Answer I was supposed to give. "Say 'light chocolate,'" I said, remembering aloud. "'Light.'"

"You knew he was going to offer you a Godiva chocolate—"

"And ask whether I wanted dark or light—"

"You were supposed to say 'light.' His favorite. But no, my Bennie had to say, 'I don't eat chocolate, Mr. Grun.'" Sam shook his head so mournfully I burst into laughter.

"What? I *don't* eat chocolate."

"You couldn't eat the freaking piece of chocolate? It would have killed you to eat it? You would have *choked*?"

"Exactly," I said, though I didn't explain. Sam knew my history anyway. I had swallowed so much crap already it would have lodged in my throat and cut off my air, throttled me with the terrible need to please, to say yes, whatever you need, at whatever cost. I stood up and started for the door. "I'd better get back to the office. I want to see what's going on. Thanks for the tip."

"Wait, I heard you were on the noon news, defending that animal rights group that started a riot."

"It wasn't a riot and they're a couple, not a group. Two kids, one confused, one not so confused." I meant Eileen, the latter. I'd have to address that problem, but at least for now she was in jail.

"Well, this time I'm on the cops' side. Furstmann Dunn may be close to an AIDS vaccine."

"I know—"

"Tell your clients to come with me when I take groceries to Daniel. He can't even swallow because of the thrush, I have to buy him baby food. Tell that to your clients."

"Client. I got the good guy."

"Good guy? Screw him!" Sam reddened in anger. He had

a low flashpoint, especially since he'd made partner. Mark always said it had gone to his head, but I'd disagreed. "Let him represent himself! Better yet, let one of his lab rats represent him, then see how well he does. I hope the cops beat some sense into him!"

"Calm down, you don't mean that."

"I do, too. I'll beat that kid myself! Me and every fegola I know. We'll hit him with our purses!"

"Good-bye, honey." I leaned over the desk and stole a smooch.

"I hope they broke his knees! I hope they snapped his dick right off!"

"Th-th-th-that's all folks," I said, and slipped out.

FIVE

I opened the arched wooden door to R & B's townhouse and experienced a familiar feeling. I was home. Mark and I bought the house as a brick shell with money from his family and remodeled it into law offices as we paid back the loan. I'd sanded and polished the hardwood floors; Mark had put up the dry-wall. We painted the walls and baseboards a golden yellow, and I decorated the offices comfortably, with soft chairs, pine side tables, and gentle watercolors.

"Hey, Bennie," said Marshall, from the half-window above the reception desk. Her dark blond hair was gathered into a French braid and she wore a cotton dress that hung on a frame too fragile to bear any responsibility at all. In fact, Marshall was R & B's receptionist, administrator, and bookkeeper, and ran the little office behind the reception window like Stalin.

"Why aren't you at lunch, lady?" I asked.

"We're too busy. You got a zillion calls." She handed me a yellow stack. R & B, it said at the top of our internal stationery, in a hip font. Mark was in charge of hip, I could only do homey.

"Then go home early, will you? Leave at four and I'll get the board covered." I didn't want Marshall defecting, too. Besides the fact that she ran the place, I felt comfortable with her in a way I didn't with the associates, from whom I kept a professional distance.

"You sure? I might take you up on that. I have to get fitted for a bridesmaid dress." She rolled her blue eyes.

"Pink or turquoise?"

"Turquoise."

"Lucky break."

"You got that right."

The phone rang, and she reached for it as I wandered down the hall with my messages, scouting for associates. The hallway was empty, so I strayed casually into the law library, which doubled as our conference room. Nobody was there either. The round, egalitarian conference table was bare, surrounded by thick federal reporters, their gold foil volume numbers running in shiny rows. Maybe the associates were out to lunch. Or on job interviews.

I left the library, went back down the hall, and climbed the spiral staircase to peek at the upstairs offices. Each one was the same size, none smaller than Mark's or mine, and each associate had been given a thousand-dollar office allowance to decorate it. Between our sexy caseload and permissive management, R & B attracted the best and the brightest from the local law schools—Penn, Temple, Widener, and Villanova. Our associates were all Law Review or close to it, and we paid them like the demigods they thought they were. What could they possibly have to complain about? And where the hell were they?

I walked down the hall, checking office after empty office. They'd put all sorts of crap up on the walls, and I hadn't uttered a peep. Bob Wingate's office was a memorial to Jerry Garcia; Eve Eberlein's was redone in feminine chintz. The only businesslike office belonged to Grady Wells, a Civil War buff. It was furnished simply and the walls were covered with antique battlefield maps in wooden frames. Grady kept a map chest with skinny drawers in the corner, but he wasn't in his office.

Nobody was in, anywhere. I considered snooping to see if there were any résumés lying around, but decided against it. I was committed to our individual liberties. Also, I might get caught.

I headed into my own messy office, kicked my pumps onto the dhurrie rug, and moved some papers so I could curl into the cushy maroon wing chair behind my desk. A client once told me that my sloppiness was the mark of a true outlaw, but he was wrong. I was just a slob, nothing political about it.

I unlocked a rickety desk drawer and pulled the file of computer printouts that listed the associates' hours. Whoever was working the hardest could be the most unhappy. I read down the list of associates, ignoring the administrative hours, looking only for billable time. Fletcher, Jacobs, Wingate. Most of the associates were billing two hundred hours a month. Hard time, so everybody should be miserable. Even Eve Eberlein showed a hundred and ninety hours so far. I tried not to think about which activities she considered billable.

I flipped backwards to the previous months. The times rang true except for Renee Butler, who'd put in a rugged April on trial in family court. Renee had been Eve's roommate since they graduated from Penn with Wingate, but the two women couldn't have been more different. Renee was black, slightly overweight, and committed to her practice of domestic abuse cases. She was all substance to Eve's pure form. Was Renee one of the associates who wanted to leave? Was there a way to find out?

Of course.

I tossed the time records aside and crossed the room to the unmatched bookshelves against the wall. Law reviews and treatises were mixed with clippings and reprints, and I forgot where I'd put the legal directory. Damn. I scanned the cluttered shelves.

Eureka! I yanked the directory off the shelf, found the listing, and called. "Meyers Placement?" I said weakly, when a woman picked up. "Uh . . . I may be out of a job soon and I need to talk to someone."

"Hold please," she said, then the phone clicked and another woman came on, with a professionally soothing voice. "May I help you?"

"Yes, I'm calling from R & B, Rosato & Biscardi? I need to find a job, I think."

"To whom am I speaking?"

"I, uh, can't say. I'd die if my boss found out. She's a real bitch."

A surprised laugh. "Well, you can send us a confidential résumé. Address it to—"

"Am I the only one from R & B who called you? Or have you gotten a call from Renee Butler?"

"I'm not at liberty to give out that information."

"But I'm not the only one, am I? I won't send my résumé if I'm the only one." I was hoping she'd see her exorbitant fee slipping away.

"No, you're not the only one."

"Is it Jeff Jacobs or Bob Wingate? I bet it's one of them."

"I can't confirm either of those names."

"I know Jenny Rowland's miserable here. She says it sucks."

"I really can't reveal our clients, dear. I do have three résumés from R & B, but that doesn't mean we can't place all of you."

Three résumés? Three associates wanted out? That was almost half the crew. My heart sank. I didn't listen to her sales pitch, just waited until she stopped talking, thanked her, and hung up. *Three?* What was going on?

I felt stricken. I'd talk to Mark about it as soon as he got back. A firm our size couldn't sustain that sort of blow, not now. Mark's commercial business practice was booming; my First Amendment practice, representing media clients against defamation suits, was finally at the point where it subsidized the police misconduct cases. Mark and I were bringing in a million in billings a year and paying ourselves a hundred thousand each, not to mention feeding thirteen mouths. Doing well and doing good, with a genuine rock 'n' roll esprit. Until now.

I looked back at my desk, piled high with messages, correspondence, and briefs. I'd better stay ahead of it if we were heading into crisis mode. Damn. I pushed my worries to the back of my mind and set to work, ignoring the sounds of the associates as they got home. I heard them laughing and joking, then the ringing of phones and the song of modems as they got back to work. Two of them, Bob Wingate and Grady Wells, were arguing a point of federal jurisdiction in the hallway, and I cocked my head to listen. Sharp, sharp lawyers, these. I liked them and was sorry that three were unhappy. Maybe I'd try to talk them out of leaving. Right after I spanked them.

At the end of the day I shook off my work buzz and went downstairs. I could hear from the commotion Mark had returned. The whole firm usually met at the end of the day in the library, and I gathered he was holding forth down there, regaling the associates with war stories from the Wellroth trial. Did you hear the one about the water pitcher?

But when I reached the library's open door, I saw it wasn't our usual in-house confab. Mark was sitting at the conference table with Eve, and next to her was Dr. Haupt from Wellroth and a bluff older man I recognized as Kurt Williamson, the company's general counsel. I veered left to avoid interrupting them, but Mark stood up and motioned to me.

"Bennie, come on in," he said expansively, but there was an edge to his voice I didn't like. His jacket was off, his silk tie loosened. "I have some good news for you."

"Good news? About the trial?"

"No, on another matter. Other *matters*, in fact. Kurt is sending us two of Wellroth's largest new matters, including the structuring of its joint venture with Healthco Pharma. A major, major deal." His eyes were sending nasty signals, which I read as a so-there after this morning's debacle.

"That's wonderful," I said, though what I meant was, that's lucrative. "Mark is a terrific lawyer, Kurt, and I know he'll do a great job with it."

"He has so far," Williamson said, nodding. "His opinion letter gave us a whole new perspective on the joint venture. Did you see it?" He leaned over the table and handed a thick packet of papers to me.

"Nice work, creative work," I said, skimming the opinion letter for the second time. No opinion left R & B without my review because of the malpractice exposure; I'd seen it when it was a research memo prepared by Eve and Renee Butler. I flopped the memo closed and handed it back to him. "Very creative."

Eve smiled tightly at the praise and so did Dr. Haupt, or at least I think he did. The fissure in the lower half of his face shifted like a fault line.

"I agree," Williamson said. "One of the problems with the pharmaceutical business is controlling the product once it's developed, as you can see from our present dispute over Cetor. Developing a successful product is a complicated process, often involving interlocking patents. Interdependent patents, more than a dozen."

"That many?" I said, though he didn't seem to require any response to continue. Corporate clients love to talk about their business. Listen or somebody else will.

"Even more. In the joint venture, the rub is which company will control the patents should a successful product be developed. Mark's idea was that half of the interdependent patents should be held by each party. All the patents would be rendered useless except in combination with the others."

"Really," I said, though I remembered it from the memo. "So the patents would fit together."

"Like keys to a lock."

"Amazing," I bubbled, though the simile had been mine. I had edited out the metaphor the memo had used, comparing the patents to keys to a treasure chest. It was too cute for an opinion letter, where the language is supposed to be so bland nobody could remember it, much less hold the firm liable for anything.

Williamson stood up, smoothing his bumpy seersucker jacket. "Well, I really must be going. The Paoli train calls, and so does my wife."

Mark and I laughed in unfortunate unison. We always laugh at our clients' jokes, but we try not to be so obvious about it. "I'll walk you out," Mark said, rising to help Williamson gather his papers. Dr. Haupt rose, too, and Eve put the file back together, working smoothly.

"Thanks again, Kurt," I said to Williamson. I shook his hand as he left, and he mock-withered in my grip.

"Still rowing, are you?" he asked, smiling. "I haven't sculled in ages. I'm getting older."

"You too? What a coincidence."

Williamson laughed as Mark gave him one of those elbow touches that qualify as business intimacy, and Williamson let himself be cuddled out. Dr. Haupt followed silently, leaving Eve and me alone in the conference room. I decided to be nice to her. "Congratulations on the new business, Eve."

She continued gathering the papers, but she was frowning. "They're sexist, even Dr. Haupt. He didn't even acknowledge me."

"Hey, Eve," called a boyish voice from the door. It was Bob Wingate, the Deadhead with gaunt cheekbones, sunken brown eyes, and an alternative pallor. Dressed in a Jerry T-shirt and khakis, he ambled into the library and climbed onto the window seat. "How goes the Wellroth trial?"

Eve masked her pique. "Great, just great," she said, and I chose not to contradict her.

"Cool." Wingate nodded. "Did Mark let you do a witness?"

"Sure. I cross-examined two of them and argued a motion at the end of the day. An evidentiary motion."

"Damn," Wingate said, scratching his longish hair. "I worked my ass off all day on one brief. When's he gonna let me have a trial? I've done almost fifty depositions in two years. I think I'm ready, don't you?" He bumped his black high-tops against the wall, making scuffmarks on my paint job.

"Wingate, stop with your heels," I said.

He looked at me like an injured child. "When am I gonna get some trial experience, Bennie? I'm ready. I can do it."

"Ask Mark. You didn't want to work for me, remember?"

"It wasn't you, it was your cases. And he always puts me off."

"Then keep after him."

Wingate sulked in the window seat as Eve sat down, fiddling with her charm bracelet: a gold locket, a silver key, a tiny heart. I wondered if Mark had given her the bracelet; he'd never given me anything so expensive.

"I thought that went very well, didn't you?" Mark said, returning like the conquering hero. "Eve?"

"Fine," she said, smiling. "It went great."

"What went great?" asked Grady Wells, drifting into the library, dressed in a gray suit and Liberty tie. Above his broad shoulders was a pair of gold wire-rimmed glasses, an easy smile, and thatch of curly blond hair no amount of water could civilize. It was the only unruly thing about Grady, a tall North Carolinian with Southern manners and an accent that fooled opposing counsel into thinking he was slow-witted. Nothing could be further from the truth.

"We're talking about the Wellroth trial," Wingate said. "Eve did two witnesses. Meantime, what are you dressed as, Wells?"

Grady looked down at his suit. "A lawyer, I think."

"But isn't this your Ultimate Frisbee night? The last night of the season? The big party?"

"I have to miss it. I'm meeting a client."

Wingate snorted. "Maybe there is no ultimate night of Ultimate Frisbee. Maybe every night is the ultimate. You're the golden boy, Wells. You tell me."

"Renee!" Mark said, beaming as Renee Butler arrived,

wearing a loose smock of Kente cloth. "Come in and cele-
brate. Wellroth is sending us some very significant new business, including an antitrust case. I want you and Wells to
work on it. It'll be a monster."

"If you need me," Renee said.

Mark turned to Grady. "Wells, how about you?"

"No thanks," he said, with a confidence afforded by his
credentials. A Duke grad, he'd clerked for the Supremes and
before that had been an editor of the *Harvard Law Review.* It
was a coup R & B got him; he chose us because he had a girlfriend in Philly at the time.

"You don't want even a piece of it?" Mark asked, but Grady
shook his head.

"Antitrust is drying up, anyway," Wingate mumbled. "It's
been dead since the eighties."

"Hey, everybody!" called Jennifer Rowland, from the door.
A petite Villanova grad, Rowland effervesced constantly, like a
Dixie cup of 7-Up.

"Come in, Jen," I said, and moved over to let her squeeze
in with our two remaining associates, Amy Fletcher and Jeff
Jacobs. The library was so small that at the end of most work-
days it looked like the stateroom in a Marx Brothers movie, but
I didn't mind it. I enjoyed hearing about the day's legal problems, and the associates enjoyed airing them. Well, now we
had a real problem. I decided to deal with it. "You know, gang,
I'm glad you're all here, because there's something we should
discuss. I've been hearing some rumors."

Mark's head snapped around. "Rumors? What about?"

"About Wells?" Wingate said. "Is he really a Republican?"

Mark cut him off with a hand chop. "Wingate, if you were
funny it would be different. But you're not, so shut up."

Wingate flushed red, and I cleared my throat. "Rumor has it that some of you are circulating résumés."

"Résumés? You're kidding," Mark said, looking as surprised as I was. He was undoubtedly pissed I hadn't spoken to him privately, but I wasn't about to wait. Suddenly his dark eyes began scrutinizing the faces around the table. "Who's looking for a new job?" he asked. "Who?"

"Mark, that's not the point. It doesn't matter who's looking. I didn't bring it up because I expected somebody to tell us."

"You mean you're not trying to out anybody," Wingate said tensely.

"No, I'm not. But I wanted to tell you, and I speak for Mark, too, that we would hate to lose any one of you. You've all been working very hard and that takes a toll. So if you're unhappy about your hours or about anything else, just come to us privately and tell us why. Maybe we can fix it, and nobody has to leave R & B. Now, that's all I'll say about it, unless you have questions."

Jennifer Rowland raised her hand shyly. "Bennie? I was wondering about something."

"Of course. Anything."

"We've been hearing some rumors that you and Mark . . . you know." She looked awkwardly from Mark to me, and since it was my role to be graceful in defeat, I spoke.

"Well, Jenny, it's true that Daddy and I did, in fact, break up. But it wasn't your fault and we love you the way we always did." The associates laughed and so did I, though it killed me. Mark reddened and glanced at Eve.

But Jenny was waving her hand, trying to silence everybody. "No, actually, I knew that you and Mark broke up. What

I heard was that the firm was breaking up. That you and Mark were dissolving the firm."

Mark went white, and so did I. "Jenny, of course that's not true," I said, but Mark was already on his feet.

"People, I think this has been enough of a therapy session for one night. Everybody out of the pool." He clapped his hands together to get the associates moving. "Come on, everybody out."

"Wait a minute, Mark," I said. "They have a right to ask, a right to know what's going on. It's their jobs."

"Bennie, stop." He held up his hand. "I know what I'm doing."

The associates were already leaving. Amy Fletcher and Jeff Jacobs left together, with Jennifer. Wingate popped off the window seat and hustled to the door behind Eve and Renee Butler. Grady was the last to go and glanced back at me, his large gray eyes full of intelligence, and something else. A trace of sympathy. There, then gone.

I shut the library door and faced Mark.

SIX

"It's over, Bennie," Mark said.

"I know, I noticed we weren't sleeping together."

"Not us. R & B. The firm. It's true."

"*What*?" I couldn't believe what I was hearing. My face felt red, my throat, thick. A fist of pain and anger formed in my chest. "What are you talking about?"

"I want to go out on my own."

I told myself to stay calm and control my tone. I didn't want us to start screaming at each other. It hadn't gotten us anywhere but apart. "You're already out on your own."

"I want to start over, make a new firm. I need a fresh start." He shoved his hands deep into the pockets of his suit pants. "It's too hard, with you and Eve in the same firm."

"Slow up a minute. This is my business you're talking about, my livelihood. The stuff with Eve is personal. I know the difference."

"Then what happened today, with the water pitcher? Eve thinks you did it because you're jealous of her. She doesn't see how she can stay, with you here."

I gritted my teeth. "Then let her go, it's my firm. You know and I know today was about business."

He folded his arms as he stood on the opposite side of the conference table. "She should be up for partner in a couple of years. Will you make her one?"

"I'll decide that then, but I doubt it. I don't think she's qualified, not after what I saw today."

He laughed abruptly. "Bennie, who stands on principle. Always."

"Absolutely, and why not?" I said, fighting to check my temper. "Eve's a fine corporate lawyer, but she can't try a case to save her life. She's not as good a trial lawyer as anybody in her graduating class—Butler, Wells, or Wingate."

"Wingate? He's a slacker. He doesn't have the brains, even if he did have the energy! I can't introduce him to a corporate client—"

"Lower your voice," I told him, in case the associates could hear.

"Eve's smart, Bennie. That idea for the joint venture, it was hers. You saw the memo."

"So? We've turned down lots of smart kids for partnership."

"I'm telling you, she's good."

"Maybe in bed."

His lip curled. "That was unnecessary."

"But that's why you want to give her special treatment, isn't it? Where does that leave the other women? Or the men? She doesn't have the talent, period. No matter who she's sleeping with."

He shook his head. I shook mine. Silence fell between us as we both fumed.

"I'll take my clients," Mark said quietly. "Wellroth and the other drug companies. You take your practice, the defamation clients and the excessive force cases. We divide the assets and the receivables down the middle. I made copies of the computer files, on disk. Also the standard form file, since we wrote it together, and the billing system. Eve photocopied the case files for the drug clients."

He'd had it all planned out. All of it with Eve, behind my back.

"We split up the associates. Whoever wants to come with me and Eve can, and whoever wants to come with you can. I found some new office space on Twentieth Street. It's sunny and bright. The lease starts in two weeks."

"You're moving in two weeks? Good. Go."

Mark stood stock still. The picture came suddenly into focus, and I went ballistic.

"No, *I'm* moving? *You're throwing me out?* Mark! You own the building, so you're taking my firm! I sanded these floors!"

"Bennie—"

"Is there anything else I should know? Is there anything else you want to tell me?"

"You brought it on yourself."

"Screw you!" I shouted, without caring whether the associates heard. "Where do you get off?"

"Where do *I* get off? Okay, so since when do you represent animal rights activists, Bennie?"

"What's that have to do with it? You've been planning this for months, you hypocrite!"

"Today was the last straw. Do you care that Furstmann Dunn and Wellroth are owned by the same parent? You didn't do the conflict check, did you, before you rode off to save the day!"

I was so mad I could scream, and I did. "I defended that kid against criminal charges! His brutality suit will be filed against the police department and the city! There's no conflict of interest, Furstmann's just the location!"

"Of course you didn't check it, you didn't care. Dr. Haupt told me after lunch, he got a fax during the trial. They messengered it down to him, Bennie! You were representing the group that was picketing *his* company! My *partner*! How do you think that looked?" Mark raked his hair back with a furious swipe. "It's a miracle we got those new cases! Whether you want to believe it or not, it was because they like Eve!"

"But where's the conflict? My client has no interest adverse to them!"

"Don't be so technical, would you? He's ruining their image! It's a public relations nightmare. They're a quiet German company. They play it low profile. They don't want the attention."

"That doesn't make it a conflict! You do whatever they say, whether it's right or wrong? March to their tune?"

"So there! That's your attitude and I'm supposed to keep you?"

Keep me? It knocked the wind out of me, like a jackboot to the diaphragm. "*Keep* me?" I said, my voice hushed. "I pull my own weight here. My billings are equal to yours. *Better*, last year."

He rubbed his chin and sighed. "I have to look to the future, Bennie. I want to develop this drug company business. Look what's happening with Wellroth and their joint venture. There's money in it."

"Money, again."

"Is money a dirty word? I shouldn't make more than a hundred grand?"

"You used to say you didn't need even fifty grand."

"That was then, this is now. You may not want a future, but I do. You may not want kids, but I do."

I took another deep breath. I knew this fight, every punch and counterpunch. I did want kids, just not yet. I couldn't, not with my mother getting worse. I looked away, out the window. The sun was going down. People were walking home after work. The day was over. R & B was over. I thought of the river, running through the city, not two miles from where I stood.

"Bennie?"

I turned and went for the door. I wasn't going to fight anymore. All that was left between Mark and me was a business deal, and he had a right to end it. Let him go, let it all go. I'd do it on my own. I walked out of the library, closing the door behind me.

My oars cut the water with a chop. I reached out and pulled them into my stomach with one slow, fluid stroke, as controlled and even as I could make it. Gliding back on the hard wooden seat with its greasy rollers, knees flattening against the oily rails.

The black water resisted but only slightly. There were no whitecaps. The wind had died down and everything had gone still. I was rowing on a mirror of smoked glass.

The surface of the water reflected the decorative lights outlining the boathouses along the east bank, then the streetlamps along the drives as I pulled away from civilization. There were no lights at all in the middle of the river, where it was pitch-dark.

The oars hit the water with a splash, and I pulled them through it, imagining its sleek blackness as tar, making me slow down each stroke and concentrate. Feeling the scull lurch forward slightly with the next stroke, and the next. Keeping it slow, and languid, and black. Right down the dark water, suspended there. The only thing connecting me to the river, connecting me to anything, was the handle of the oar, rough and splintery under my calloused hands. I was holding on to the stick that held on to the world.

I feathered the oars and took another long stroke. Scooted under the arch of the craggy stone bridge, where it felt cooler, shadier, even now at midnight. Moving through the widest part of the river so the few cars on either side seemed far away, their headlamps like pinpoints, not strong enough to cast any brightness down the road.

I heard another splash and felt a spray of cold water on my forearm as I hit the stroke too hard. Easy, girl. I reached far out and over my toes for the next stroke, stretching, extending every inch of my body. A powerful stroke but still controlled, always controlled. I tried stroking like that for the next ten.

One, two, three, not power strokes, just for technique. Not thinking about anything but technique. The stroke, the control, the timing. The speed of the scull and the *slip*-sound it made as it sliced through the water. The creak of the rigging. The fishy rankness of the water and the green freshness of the trees. The shock of the cold spray, the jolt of the lurch forward. The city was far away. The city was gone. Four, five, six strokes.

Soon the sound of my own breath, coming in short, quick pants, and the slickness of the sweat as it sluiced down between my breasts and under my arms. I was working hard and

I wasn't a college kid anymore. There were beads of sweat on my knees, but they evaporated as the boat picked up speed, floating just high enough in the water because the stroke was working so well. I'd finally found the rhythm and I couldn't go wrong. Seven, eight, nine, ten.

In the middle of the river, in the middle of the night.

SEVEN

I decided against crying when I got home. It never did any good and my eyes puffed up like pet-store goldfish. Instead, I showered, toweled off, and got ready for bed. Bear, my golden retriever, lay on the floor, watching me pad from bathroom to bedroom and back again. Her wavy coat was the exact color of a square of light caramel, and she was big-boned, like me.

"Bedtime, girl," I said, and she jumped onto the mattress, circled twice, and settled on a spot in the middle. It had always driven Mark crazy. Now it wouldn't. Things were looking up.

I climbed in beside Bear, nudged her over, then switched off the light. She yawned theatrically, and I smiled, scratching the rich folds of soft fur on her neck. She drifted almost immediately into a slumber marked by a breathy snore, but I kept scratching. I wouldn't be sleeping for a while.

In the bedroom underneath mine, in the apartment below, my mother was in bed and not sleeping, either. I'd checked on her before I came upstairs, and she was tossing and turning. I read to her until she fell asleep, but she was awake again by the time I got out of the shower. I could hear her through the floorboards. Talking to herself and others she imagined.

But I didn't think about that either. Something would have to be done. I would have to do it.

But not tonight.

"She's not eating at all?" I asked Hattie, standing to pour us a cup of fresh coffee the next morning. Hattie Williams was the black home-care worker who lived with my mother and took care of her. She rose early and even at this hour was dressed in black stirrup pants and a TAJ MAHAL T-shirt glittery with mosques. Hattie was very short, very wide, and her straightened hair was an unlikely shade of orange, but none of that mattered to me.

"Skipped lunch and dinner yesterday," she said. "Not even her soup."

"Did she drink anything?"

"Only a little water, and she won't be still." Hattie shook her head. "Too scared to go out for her walk again. That's three months she ain't seen the sunshine, and she been talkin' to herself more. Did you hear, last night?"

"Her little chat with Satan? When's that boy gonna straighten up and fly right?"

But Hattie didn't smile, as she usually would. The skin around her eyes, though remarkably unwrinkled for her age, was a shade darker than the rest of her face and looked even darker this morning. I wanted to make her laugh, at least for the moment.

"At least the TV stopped bossing her around, Hat. I was really beginning to worry. What if we had to get rid of it? Then you couldn't watch *Loving*."

"Now that's enough. That's enough now, hush." She waved me off with the most begrudging of smiles, so I replaced the coffeepot and sat down at the kitchen table in my mother's junky apartment. The table was fake Early American, the napkin dispenser a cloudy acrylic, and the cups and saucers tannic-tinged melamine. It was all the crap from our old house, I'd moved the bulk here at my mother's insistence. Cost me two thousand dollars to move two hundred dollars worth of chemistry.

I sipped my coffee and shook my head. "Why can't I make a decent cup of coffee? Every morning it's the same thing. What do I do wrong?"

Hattie drank her coffee and paused. "Too much water."

"What? Monday you said I put too much coffee."

She laughed, tickled. "You can go in front of a jury, you can go on the TV news. You can even go argue in front of the Supreme Court of the United States. I got the feather to prove it." She meant the white quill the Supremes give to lawyers who argue before them, sort of a consolation prize, in my case. "But you can't make coffee that don't taste like cardboard."

We both laughed, then stopped abruptly. "Hattie, don't look at me like that. I know what you're thinking."

"It's time. I can't get her to take her Prozac, half the time she thinks I'm poisoning her. Puts up such a fuss, damn near wakes the whole city. It makes her anxious, nervous. She paced all mornin' yesterday. She's upset all the time on account of that damn Prozac."

I'd noticed it, too. "Let's stay with it for just a while longer."

"No more stallin', you." She set her plastic cup down with a clacking noise. "Even her doctor said we got to get goin', and that was two, three months ago. She's worse every day."

I thought of my mother's doctor, a soft-spoken young man

with a prematurely graying beard, so thoughtful and intellectual as he explained electroshock therapy in his office that day. He could afford to be cool, it wouldn't be his mother at the end of the extension cord. "But they don't even know why it works," I said. "The doc told us, he admitted it."

"What's the difference why? Who cares why? It works." Hattie leaned forward and pressed her ample breasts against the table. "The doctor said every other day for a coupla weeks, that's it. He said she'll start to get better fast. She already signed the form for me. It will help her."

"*Electroshock?* How can that help her? Shoot a hundred volts into her brain?"

"It's not like you're makin' it sound."

"Yes it is, it sure is. The electricity induces a brain seizure, a grand mal seizure. Sometimes they start the seizure and it doesn't stop. And sometimes the patient dies."

Hattie's broad features creased into a skeptical frown. "I read the form. One outta how many die?"

"Who cares how many? What if she's the one?" It didn't sound convincing, even to me, but this wasn't about odds and numbers and scientific theories. This was about my mother. "Besides, she'll lose her memory."

"Child, what's she got to remember anyway? She lives in a nightmare world. She's afraid all the time. She can't go on like this. She'll starve."

My stomach turned over. "No. Give her one more day, then we admit her to the hospital and they put in the feeding tube. It worked last time."

"And how many times you think your momma can take that, in and out the hospital? She needs shock treatments!"

"Hattie, I'm defending a kid who believes you shouldn't do

that to an animal. A monkey. A mink." Whatever. "They think you don't have the right."

"This ain't about rights, Bennie. She got her rights now and she dyin'. Dyin'," she said softly, and I could hear Georgia in her voice, a lilt that appeared only when she was tired or angry.

I sensed she was both, and looked at her face anew. The dark circles, the downturn to her eyes. Her cheeks had grown puffier, she'd gained weight. Her blood pressure problem had reappeared, its presence announced by the tall brown bottle of Lopressor on the table. My mother's care was taking its toll on her, and it tore at me inside. I had a choice: Hattie or my mother.

I got up from the table, it was all I could do. Bear, resting on her side, raised her head from her paws, her round brown eyes questioning. She would stay all day with Hattie, who would watch the soaps, make homemade soup, and change my mother's diaper. Come Sunday, Hattie would take the bus to Atlantic City, there to stand before the slot machines at the casinos, pushing the button and watching the spinning bars. Letting the clanging, jangling, and clattering obliterate every other thought. I understood it completely.

I walked to my mother's room with Bear's toenails clicking at my heels. I opened her door and stood there, letting the familiar scent of tea roses waft over me. It was my mother's favorite perfume, and we doused the room with it to please her and mask less pleasant odors. She wouldn't let us open the window, so the air in the room remained heavy and close behind the drawn curtains.

I looked down at my mother in the soft light. She lay under her old chenille coverlet, having finally fallen asleep around dawn, and she made a tiny figure in the bed. A figurine in a roomful of figurines. Ceramic birthday angels, muted Hummel figures, a prized Lladro. She had collected them in the days when she still went out, days I didn't even recall.

Her black hair had gone gray but was still wildly wavy. Her bony, hawkish nose was belligerent even in sleep, as was her pointed chin. Only her last name tied me to her, for I had none of her features and all of my father's. I assumed, since I'd never met the man. Never even saw his picture. My mother didn't like him much and refused to marry him. At least that was what she told me as a child, though I'd come to suspect differently.

And as long as I could remember, she had been bitter, resentful. Then the resentment turned to a rage and the rage burrowed inside her and ate her up. That's how I saw it as a child, even though they called it "bad nerves," then a "nervous breakdown." Later science entered the picture and the doctors decided my mother had an "electrolyte imbalance," as if all she had to do was drink Gatorade. We went through medication, Pamelor, then Elavil, but she wouldn't take either. She was getting older and harder to handle. We ran out of medication just about the same time we ran out of patience and money.

Though one uncle had sent the funds that supported us, the relatives who had been helping slipped away as I grew older, attriting for various reasons that all amounted to the same reason. Some died off, and at one point I wondered if that were the only way out. But before I knew it I was coping with it, getting two jobs after school and applying for aid for her. Meeting with the doctors, even as a seventeen year old, and eventually giving up on them because they had nothing to offer her, and changing her diaper myself.

Then I found Hattie and could breathe, for the first time. Went to college on scholarship, close by to Penn, then to law school, on half-scholarship. Graduated and made the money to keep alive the figurine in the bed. A little old Italian lady, but tough; like an aging hen, wasting, exhausted, but still fighting. I used to think she was fighting death. Until I realized she was fighting life.

"Bennie, Bennie, come quick!" It was Hattie, standing in front of the television in the kitchen. Bear turned, too, ears lifted at the alarm in her voice.

"What?" I closed my mother's door.

"Look, on the TV. Isn't that your law firm?"

I ran to the TV and froze at the image on the screen. A black body bag was being wheeled out on a steel stretcher and loaded into a black coroner's van. The scene changed to the brick townhouse, then a close-up of the plaque that said Rosato & Biscardi. I turned up the volume, but somehow I couldn't hear the news. Couldn't bear to hear it.

"Mark." Hattie pointed. "Somebody killed him."

EIGHT

MOBILE CRIME DETECTION UNIT, it said on the boxy white and blue van parked in front of the townhouse. Police sawhorses and squad cars blocked the cobblestone street. A group of reporters pressed against the yellow crime-scene tape. I ducked the cordon and pushed my way to the door, showing my ID to the cops who tried to keep me from Mark.

By the time I got there he was long gone, they'd taken him for an autopsy. The thought of it made me sick. I couldn't respond, couldn't speak sensibly when the uniformed cop started asking me questions. Mark. I'd walked out on him. I'd cursed him. They would be the last words he heard from me.

"Come along, Ms. Rosato," the uniformed cop was saying. "The homicide detectives want to speak with you." He hustled me into the townhouse as the press cameras clicked away.

It was a madhouse inside. Marshall was standing near the reception window, crying and hugging Amy Fletcher. Wingate slumped in a RIDIN' THAT TRAIN T-shirt on the sofa, his face wan, sitting next to Jennifer Rowland, whose cheeks were tearstained. Renee Butler was talking with Jeff Jacobs in the library, and looked at me oddly as the cop tugged me down the hall. I felt a strong arm pull on my shoulder from behind.

Grady Wells. "Are you okay, Bennie?" he asked. He was wearing his gray suit and print tie, and his eyes looked slightly red behind his glasses.

"Grady, Jesus."

He tried to pull me out of the cop's grasp. "I'd like to speak with Ms. Rosato for a minute, Officer."

The cop yanked on my elbow on the other side. "Not now. Detective Azzic wants to see her."

"This is firm business, which has to go on despite your investigation."

"The detective's been waiting—"

Suddenly Grady wrenched me free from the cop and hustled me back past a stricken Marshall. We banged through the door to her office behind the reception desk and Grady locked it behind us. "Bennie, listen," he said. "Mark was stabbed to death last night. At his desk."

"My God." I sank down next to the telephone console.

"Now listen, they don't have the murder weapon, they don't have anything. They've been calling your apartment all morning. They want your fingerprints, they want to talk to you. Where have you been?"

"My mother's."

"What about last night?"

"I was the last to leave, I think. I locked up."

"The murder took place around twelve o'clock, I heard the assistant M.E. talking. Where were you at midnight?"

"On the river, why?" I felt bewildered, almost dizzy. I was

rowing when Mark was killed. I should have been here with him. I could have stopped them, whoever it was. "Who did this? Did they break in?"

"No. There was no forced entry and nothing was taken. The police think you killed Mark, Bennie. You're the prime suspect."

"*What?*" It came as a jolt, like an aftershock after the main quake. "Me?"

"The police want to question you, but you can't go in without a lawyer. Let me represent you. I can do it."

It was happening too fast. Mark, gone. Now this. "Grady, I don't need a lawyer. I didn't kill Mark."

Boom, boom, boom! came a pounding on the door.

"Bennie, listen. Think," Grady said, touching my shoulder. "You were the last one with him. You locked up, so whoever got back in either has a key or was let in by Mark."

"That doesn't mean I—"

"They're questioning the associates, taking them down to the Roundhouse. They already questioned me, I was in early. Every associate told them about the fight you and Mark had. Wingate, especially, he heard it all. The cops know Mark left you for Eve and also that he wanted to dissolve R & B. You're the one with the motive, and if you've got no alibi, we have a problem."

I closed my eyes. How had this happened? My heart beat faster.

Boom, boom, BOOM!

"Wait a minute!" Grady shouted at the door. "Bennie, let me represent you. You can't be questioned without counsel."

"I can represent myself."

"With the cops? Are you nuts? You cost the police department a fortune, heads rolled because of you. No, they're loaded for bear out there. I'll table my other clients, and when the cops charge you—"

"*Charge* me?" I said, panic constricting my throat. "How can they charge me? What evidence do they have? I didn't do it!"

"Bennie, focus," he said, grabbing my arm. "You need help now, you're in trouble. I haven't done many murder cases but I know the facts inside out, and I can handle myself in any courtroom. I wouldn't be a fact witness, anything I'd testify to, any associate could testify to. So hire me. I'm here and I'm ready."

The doorknob twisted back and forth, jarring me into clarity.

"We don't have a lot of time, Bennie. Say yes. Now."

In a blink, I became the client, not the lawyer. I tried to listen to Grady argue with a uniformed cop, but I was disoriented, shaken by Mark's murder and the police presence. The last time I'd had a uniform in my office was when I deposed him. Now it was me they were after. Everything was turned topsy-turvy. The world stood on its head.

"There's no reason to question her at the police station," Grady was saying, trying to persuade one Officer Mullaney, a martinet with a mustache.

"It's not my decision, Mr. Wells. It's up to Detective Azzic. He asked me to remain with Miss Rosato until he takes her downtown."

"Ms. Rosato has clients to deal with, many of whom will have questions about the firm and their cases. She can't be out of the office for the morning. She's the only principal left in Rosato & Biscardi."

"Those are my orders. Bring her down."

"Tell Detective Azzic he'll have one hour to question her today. See you at the Roundhouse." Grady took my arm and led me out of the waiting room.

"Bennie," Marshall cried, distraught, and almost collapsed into my arms as we hustled by.

"I know," I told her, fighting the lump in my throat. I rubbed her back.

"It's awful, it's just awful," she said, sobbing. "As soon as I opened the door, I knew something was wrong."

"You found Mark?" I asked, shocked.

"What did you see, Marshall? How did you know?" Grady asked, prying her off of me.

"The coffeepot . . . was left on." She mopped her eyes with a handkerchief and fought for control. "It was all burned, it stunk. And the Xerox was on . . . and the computers on the first floor. Everything. I thought someone pulled an all-nighter, so I went upstairs." She wiped her nose. "Mark . . . was lying across his desk. His face was to the side and I thought he'd fallen asleep. You know, at his desk like he does?"

I knew. I remembered.

"So I called to wake him up, but he didn't move. That's when I saw the . . . blood." Her tears welled up again. "There was blood all over the back of his shirt!"

I tried to visualize it. Mark over his desk. His white shirt. His blood spilling out. It was sickening.

A criminalist bumped into me with a dusting kit. The hallway and library swelled with police personnel. A police photographer was climbing down the spiral staircase from the upstairs offices, maybe coming from Mark's office. I still couldn't believe he'd been murdered here, in this house. "I have to see for myself," I said, only half aloud.

"Bennie, wait," Grady said, but I turned on my heel, barreled past the associates and police, and headed up the spiral staircase, squeezing by the people going downstairs. Up the down staircase, my whole life, but this time I was driven. I reached the second floor, ducked the tape, and hustled down the corridor.

"Miss!" called a uniformed cop behind me, but I ignored him and slipped into Mark's office.

The sight took my breath away. I leaned on the doorjamb for support. There was a large blackish pool of blood in the middle of Mark's desk. It soaked the papers and the leather blotter we'd picked out together. It spilled over the side of a desk I'd refinished as a gift. It tainted everything it touched, defiling it. Mark's lifeblood.

Grady came up behind me. "It's okay, Bennie."

"No it isn't. Nothing about this is okay," I said, more harshly than I intended. I stared at the pool of blood and flashed with a rising nausea on the murder scenes from my old practice: an anonymous alley, a ransacked apartment, the drafty shell of an abandoned house. This crime scene was different. A place of business, of law, of rules and statutes. Mark's and mine.

"He must have been working," Grady said, bending over Mark's desk to read his papers. "It's a contract, an agreement to dissolve R & B. It looks like he was editing it when he was killed. There's a noncompete. You agree not to solicit the business of any drug company within a ten-mile radius for the next two years."

"Boilerplate. He knew I'd never take his clients." I couldn't tear my eyes from the desk. Blood buckled the papers covering it. Fingerprint dust smudged its perimeter, in clumps dark as stormclouds.

"I was up here before and nothing looked out of place to me. Does it to you? Anything odd? You would know better."

I tried to survey the office without emotion. Bay windows cast bright light behind the glossy modern credenza. Against the wall stood teak bookcases, with Mark's textbooks and other reference books neatly shelved. A matching teak file cabinet sat next to the bookshelves, with a CD player on top. "It all looks the same," I said numbly.

Grady looked out the windows and across the street. "Maybe someone in one of the other townhouses saw what happened."

"We're checking into that," said a gruff voice.

I turned around, and standing in the door was a detective I hadn't met. He was built like a fullback and evidently stuffed into a lightweight navy suit, with a white shirt and puffy polyester tie. "I'm Detective Azzic," he said, extending a hand with a stiff cop-smile. His face was broad-featured, Slavic, with brown eyes that slanted curiously upwards. "Frank Azzic."

I shook his hand. "Bennie Rosato."

"I know who you are. The tape is there for a reason, Ms. Rosato. This is my crime scene."

"It's also my law firm."

Even the cop-smile vanished. "I know you don't have much respect for law enforcement, but we have our rules, and we have them for a reason."

"Don't give me this, Detective, not now. I have no quarrel with the police when they enforce the law. It's when they fence stolen goods I lose my sense of humor."

"I'm Grady Wells," Grady said, stepping almost between us. "I'm representing Ms. Rosato in this investigation. She's very eager to assist you in finding her partner's killer."

Azzic snorted. "Is that why she broke into a secured crime scene? In most cases, physical evidence is found at the scene of the crime. She could contaminate the evidence, drop fibers and hairs, or even destroy evidence."

I didn't like the insinuation. "Let's get to the point, Detective. I understand the police think I killed my partner, which is absurd."

He turned to me calmly. "Maybe it is. Where were you last night after eleven o'clock?"

"Detective," Grady said, "I'm instructing her not to answer that question. And if she's in custody, you haven't Mirandized her."

Detective Azzic chuckled. "Down, boy. I don't see any custody situation here. I'm just asking a coupla questions. Maybe we can eliminate the ride downtown here and now, then it won't matter who drives."

I doubted it, but answered anyway, "I was rowing."

"Rowing?" His sparse eyebrows rose and he looked as surprised as a homicide detective can ever be. "Like in a rowboat?"

"Like in a scull."

"At night? In the dark?"

"I like to row at night. It's the only time I can find."

"Did anyone see you?"

"Not that I know of." Grady shifted unhappily at my side.

"How did you get to the boathouse?"

"I walked."

"Detective," Grady broke in, "I think this questioning is unnecessary. Isn't that all the information you need?"

The detective folded his arms. "No, I think we need to continue the interview down at the station."

"What time?" Grady shot back, and if he were disappointed it didn't show.

"An hour or so. Give me some time to get my papers together. I have to get the original of Mr. Biscardi's will."

"His will?" I asked, and Grady flashed me a discreet let-me-do-this look.

Detective Azzic looked at me, cocking his head. "You didn't know Mr. Biscardi had a will, Ms. Rosato? Wasn't he your boyfriend and business partner?"

Grady shot me another warning glance. "Please don't answer that, Bennie. I'd like to see the will, Detective."

I clammed up and got my bearings. Mark was murdered. I was a suspect. It made sense that Mark had a will, but we'd never discussed it. I'd never really thought about it, he was a young man. I felt suddenly alarmed.

Detective Azzic slipped a hand inside his breast pocket and retrieved a packet of papers for Grady. "I had this copy made before I bagged it. The will is dated July 11, three years ago, but I guess you didn't know that, Ms. Rosato."

I didn't take the bait, but watched Grady's eyes tense behind his glasses as he read. There were ten pages or so, but he skimmed them rapidly. His face betrayed nothing as he snapped the papers closed and handed them back to Detective Azzic. "Thanks," he said.

"Interesting, huh?" the detective asked, looking from Grady to me.

Grady hustled me to the door. "We'll see you at the Round-house, Detective."

"What did it say?" I whispered, when we hit the hall.

Grady was about to reply when we turned the corner and ran smack into Eve Eberlein.

"Oh!" She stood back from us as if shocked. She'd obviously been crying, her eyes were swollen and she wore no makeup. Her short hair was a mess and her chic dress was wrinkled. "What happened, Bennie? What happened?" she said, her voice pained and confused.

I knew just how she felt. I felt a terrible twinge inside. We shared the same loss. "I don't know," I answered, before Grady took my arm and lifted me almost bodily down the hall.

"I'm sorry, too, Eve," Grady said. "Goodbye. Take care."

I glanced back for one last look. In front of Mark's office stood Detective Azzic. He was watching me as he lit a cigarette and blew out a jet of smoke. His eyes narrowed behind the smoke, his expression grim and knowing.

NINE

We stood in the two-car parking lot behind the office while Grady dug in his suit pocket for his motorcycle key. The bike was a vintage black and maroon with a duct-taped leather seat and tarnished chrome pipes engraved with *Norton*. I didn't relish riding it to the Roundhouse, but that was the least of my worries right now.

"What did the will say, Grady?"

He found his key, swung a leg over the bike, and settled in the ripped seat. "Get on the bike, please."

"First tell me what the will said."

"Kindly get on the bike, Bennie. I'll talk to you about it when we're away from the office. The press is right out front. I don't want them finding us in the middle of the conversation."

"I can't wait. Tell me about the will."

"Is this how it's going to be?" He frowned at me as he straddled the bike. "Are you going to fuss with me about everything?"

"You're the one who was yanking me around the office."

"I was defending you. I'm your lawyer."

I couldn't get used to the way it sounded. "Grady, get real. I'm your boss and I have crow's feet older than you."

"I hate to disagree with you, but I'm your boss now. I'm barely five years younger than you, and I have to call these shots as I see them. So I'm advising you, as a purely legal matter, to get on the bike. Before I become angry."

"Do you even get angry?" I'd never seen it around the office.

"I do, surely." He nodded.

"What happens then? You throw things? Curse?"

"Never," he said, without further explanation. He pushed back his hair and shoved his head into a black Shoei helmet. All that remained of his face were glaring gray eyes and a determined jaw. "See the extra helmet on the back? Kindly put it on."

I looked at the helmet, a shiny white orb that looked like a lightbulb. "Why do you have an extra helmet?"

"In case I meet a woman with better manners than you."

I folded my arms. "I'll put it on if you tell me about Mark's will."

He sighed and pushed his helmet up over his hairline, then readjusted his glasses. "What do you think the will said, Bennie?"

"I don't have a clue. Mark has no family left, just a stepbrother in California—"

"He didn't count as much as you," Grady said, an edge to his voice. "The will doesn't set the dollar amount, but Mark left you everything he had. The townhouse, the corporate accounts, even his personal accounts. Stocks and municipal bonds, mutual funds. The will expressly provides that you inherit R & B and continue it if he dies."

My mouth dropped open. I was amazed at Mark's generosity, and his love. Then I realized why the police suspected me. If I'd known about the will, the only way I could keep R & B would be to kill Mark before he dissolved it. I imagined the Commonwealth's case taking shape, the facts gathering like thunderheads before a storm. Homicide investigations had a momentum of their own, particularly in high-profile cases. The pressure to produce a suspect invariably led to a quick arrest, just in time for the evening news. And until a charge came down, innuendo damaged as surely as indictment.

"I'm in deep, aren't I?" I said, thinking aloud.

"Not if I can help it." Grady tugged his helmet back on and kick-started the motorcycle, which rumbled to life in a throaty way. "Put on your helmet," he shouted.

I took a deep breath, then put the lightbulb over my head.

I walked into the grimy waiting room in the Homicide Division on the second floor of the Roundhouse, Philly's police administration building, and was immediately confronted by that horrific photo gallery. It hadn't changed much, even over many years. WANTED FOR MURDER, it said on both walls, above about fifty 8 × 10 head shots. Each man's expression was slack with the oddly flat effect only the deepest rage can bring to a human face. I couldn't help noticing that none of the faces was white and none was a woman. The only whites were the detectives and women were nowhere in evidence.

Except for me. I stood next to Grady, and as conspicuous as I was, was pointedly ignored by the ten-odd detectives in the shabby squad room, which was painted an ugly blue. I recognized some of them as witnesses from past lawsuits, and they milled frostily around battered steel desks arranged in jagged rows. Water-stained vertical blinds blocked out the sun, one window was completely closed off by dingy gray file cabinets. I took it all in as if it were a room I had never seen. In a way it was, now that I was the murder suspect.

The phone jangled at the desk in front of us. "Homicide," a detective barked in a raspy voice, picking up. He was a stocky redhead and sipped coffee from a mug that said STUDMUFFIN. "Nah, he's out. This is Meehan."

Meehan. The name sounded familiar, then I realized who he was. He'd lost a lot of weight, but the voice was the same. I heard it last year, in that assault case in the Northeast. The defendants had been uniformed cops and Meehan had been a witness to the beating, one of three cops who stood by. He wasn't charged and had evidently been promoted. I met his eye as he listened on the telephone, and he regarded me only coldly. I could expect nothing else. I'd embarrassed him on cross. Grady had been right. I'd have no friends here.

"Ms. Rosato." Detective Azzic appeared and motioned for us to follow him.

"We're coming," Grady said. I squared my shoulders and walked with him into the squad room, past the small adjoining room whose open door was labeled Fugitive Squad. Inside, two detectives sat before state-of-the-art computer screens. It was the only place in the Homicide Division that looked as if it were in this decade.

"We're in Interview Room C," Detective Azzic said, opening its door.

Interview Room C was the way I'd remembered it from the old days, as small as the waiting room and just as filthy. A two-way mirror hung on the wall opposite a table with an office chair tucked under it. Another chair, a heavy steel one, was bolted to the floor on the other side of the table.

"Have a seat," the detective said, easing his large frame into the chair in front of the desk. He waved for me to take the steel chair, and I did. Grady stood by me, and we were joined by a tall, thin-lipped detective whose brown jacket hung loosely on his bony shoulders. He introduced himself as Detective Mayron and leaned against the wall, his crepe sole resting flat behind him. The cops usually questioned in twos on murder cases; one to watch while the other did the talking. I used to tell clients it was so they could play bad cop, bad cop.

"Mind if I smoke?" Detective Azzic asked, shaking out a Merit from a short white pack.

"Yes," Grady said, and Azzic paused before lighting up. "You kidding?"

"No. I'd prefer you didn't."

Azzic half smiled and dropped the pack into his breast pocket, keeping the one cigarette out, unlit. "So, Ms. Rosato, we asked you here because you may have information that would help us understand what happened to Mr. Biscardi."

"She won't be making any statements, Detective," Grady said.

Azzic looked up at him. "It would help if she could explain what happened last night between her and Mr. Biscardi."

"I appreciate that, but as I said, she's not going to do it that way. She's not making any statements. Kindly ask her a question."

Azzic leaned close enough for me to smell the nicotine clinging to his jacket. "Ms. Rosato, many witnesses help themselves more by just telling the story without the lawyers getting in the middle."

I almost laughed. "I am a lawyer, Detective, and I'm already in the middle."

Grady's fingers dug into my suit so hard I felt it through my shoulder pad. "She's represented, Detective. Please ask your first question."

"All right. We'll do it your way, to start with." Azzic crossed his legs and the steely edge of a gun in an ankle holster popped into view. He flopped his pant leg over it, but it didn't dispel the intimidation factor and wasn't meant to. "Ms. Rosato, you're certainly familiar with the criminal law and police procedures, but it's my duty to tell you your rights. You'll have to suffer in silence."

"Go right ahead."

He went through my Miranda rights. I'd found them routine when they were read to my clients, but they took on an uncanny significance now that I was the one sitting in the chair bolted to the floor. I strained to relax and played a game with myself, trying to place Azzic's accent. It was blunt, working class, with that pronounced *o* indigenous to north Philadelphia. I guessed Juniata Park or maybe Olney.

"Let's pick up where we left off," Azzic said. "What was your fight with Mr. Biscardi about?"

"It wasn't a 'fight,'" Grady interjected. "It was a discussion."

Azzic nodded almost graciously. "What was your discussion with Mr. Biscardi about?"

I cleared my throat. "Mark wanted to dissolve the partnership."

"But you didn't want him to."

"Bennie—" Grady said, but I waved him off.

"I was surprised, but I had no choice. The partnership was dissolvable at will by either partner."

"You weren't happy about it, were you? You and he had started the firm together, and you were seeing each other for many years until he took up with Ms. Eberlein."

Grady squeezed my shoulder. "Detective, I'm instructing her not to answer that question, if that is a question. Please move it along."

Azzic sighed. "You shouted at Mr. Biscardi during this discussion, didn't you? You were angry."

Grady squeezed again. "Asked and answered, Detective. There was a discussion about the partnership's dissolution and they disagreed, but both parties decided to move on. Next subject or I'm afraid we'll have to leave."

Azzic rolled the unlit cigarette around his fingers. "Ms. Rosato, did you know you stand to inherit twenty million dollars as a result of Mr. Biscardi's will?"

"What?" I blurted out, shocked. *"Twenty million dollars?"*

"Detective," Grady said evenly, "she already told you she didn't know Mr. Biscardi had a will."

My head was spinning. The amount was so huge it made me sick for the position I was in. It was almost impossible *not* to believe I killed Mark for that much money. I gave in to a panicky urge to explain. "I knew Mark's family had money, but not *that* much. They weren't showy about it. They had a split-level, a station wagon—"

"Bennie, please," Grady said, his fingers clutching like talons.

Azzic's gaze was point-blank. "So you're saying you had no idea Mr. Biscardi had inherited most of this money from his parents?"

My mouth must have dropped open, because Grady answered, "That's what she's saying, Detective."

"Didn't you attend their funeral with Mr. Biscardi?"

"Uh, yes." The service had been tense, with very few mourners, since the family was so small. Mark had almost no grief reaction, even at the cemetery. His parents had died together in a car accident, but Mark had grown up in Catholic boarding schools, estranged from them for a long time. "They weren't a close family."

"Didn't Mr. Biscardi mention anything about an inheritance?"

"No." I glanced at the two-way mirror and saw with dismay that I looked nervous. Who was on the other side of the mirror? Meehan? "Nothing."

"And you didn't ask?"

"No, it never came up." It did seem odd, in retrospect. But it was Mark's business and I always respected his privacy on family issues. God knows, I needed my own.

"One thing I don't get, Ms. Rosato. I understand Mr. Biscardi told you during your discussion he wanted to make more money. Why did he want more money when he had so much already? Can you help me out with that?"

"Detective," Grady said, "you're asking her to speculate about Mr. Biscardi's state of mind."

"She was his girlfriend, wasn't she? Maybe they talked about it."

"Bennie, I'm instructing you not to answer."

"Well, Ms. Rosato?" Azzic's eyes bored into me again.

"I refuse to answer on the grounds that it may incriminate me," I said, the words sour in my mouth, like any lie. Mark had always competed with his father, a self-made businessman, and he'd wanted to be as successful as his father had been. Still, I had no idea he aimed to be *that* successful.

Detective Azzic fiddled with his Merit, tamping it end over end. "So you didn't know about the will, even though it was prepared by a very close friend of yours?"

"Who prepared it?" I asked.

"Bennie!" Grady snapped, but I couldn't help myself.

"Who was it, Detective?"

"Sam Freminet," Azzic said.

Sam? It shocked me. Sam hadn't said anything, ever.

"You're friends with Mr. Freminet, aren't you, Ms. Rosato? Good friends?"

Grady stepped forward into my field of vision. "I'm instructing my client not to answer." He put his hands on his hips, pushing his jacket aside in a gesture that was as menacing as they got south of the Mason-Dixon line. And not to the cops, to me.

"I refuse to answer on the grounds it may incriminate me," I said obediently. But I was still thinking, *Sam?* He was a bankruptcy lawyer, not an estates lawyer.

Azzic shook his head. "Isn't Sam Freminet an attorney at Grun & Chase, where you and Mr. Biscardi used to work?"

"I refuse to answer on the grounds it may incriminate me."

"When was the last time you spoke with Mr. Freminet?"

I'd called Sam from the Roundhouse before this interview, but hadn't reached him. Even that would make me look bad, now. "I refuse to answer on the grounds—"

"Ms. Rosato," Azzic said, his voice growing loud, "weren't you jealous of Eve Eberlein?"

I said my line. I refuse to answer on the grounds it may make me look like a smacked ass.

"Didn't you throw a pitcher of ice water at Mr. Biscardi in open court? Just yesterday morning, the day he was murdered? Because you were so jealous of Ms. Eberlein?"

Oh, damn. "I refu—"

"Detective Azzic, this interview is over," Grady said abruptly. "I won't let you harass my client." He took my arm and I stood up, surprised to find my knees wobbly.

Azzic stood up, too. "You're gonna hide behind the Fifth Amendment, Ms. Rosato? Like the scum you represent?"

"That's it!" Grady announced. He started to hustle me out, but I wouldn't budge, infuriated.

"You don't have any evidence against me, Detective, because I didn't kill my partner. It's simple logic, but maybe not simple enough for you."

Detective Azzic met my eye. "I'll be working this case myself, and as soon as I have the evidence, you'll see me again."

"I hope that's not a threat, Detective," Grady said, but I opted for a less mannerly response and delivered it with my usual aplomb.

TEN

The press mobbed the sidewalk in a dense pack, overrunning the curb and spilling onto the Roundhouse's parking lot. Grady and I pressed forward as they scurried around us on all sides. I'd run this gauntlet with clients a zillion times, there was nothing to do but bear down and go forward. Cameras with rubber filters popped into my face, video cameras whirred beside me in stereo, and TV newspeople pressed microphone bubbles at my lips. Each reporter shouted his own version of my name. "Bernadette, look this way!" they called. "Belladonna, just one picture! Benefaci, over here!"

I stared straight ahead, my mind clicking away with the cameras. I knew how this would play out. I'd be the lead story on the local noon news, CNN, and Court-TV. The cops would leak the details about me and Mark, including the will, and by nightfall, I'd be labeled a murderer. My media clients would drop me quick as you can say "film at eleven." My police abuse clients would find a lawyer who wasn't under investigation. My career was crashing and burning around me. And Mark's killer was free.

Suddenly I recognized a couple at the curb on the other side of the crowd. The woman had her arm in a sling and the man was a strawberry blond. It was Bill Kleeb and Eileen Jennings, together. They stood with a heavyset man with slicked-back hair and a shiny Haliburton briefcase, hailing a cab.

"Miss Rosato, did you do it? Miss Rosato, just one question! Please! Over here!"

How had Eileen gotten out? What was she doing with Bill? Then I remembered the death threat to the CEO. "Bill!" I shouted over the sea of cameras, since I had the height advantage. "Bill Kleeb! Over here!"

Bill turned vaguely in my direction just as a Yellow cab pulled up behind him. The man with the Haliburton ushered Eileen into the cab and climbed into the darkness beside her.

"Bill!" I hollered, trying vainly to be heard over the reporters. I could see him scanning the crowd, but he didn't see me. I waved wildly while the cameras whirred, even though I knew it would end up as teaser footage. "Bill!"

"Are you nuts?" Grady asked, wild-eyed. "What are you doing?"

I was trying to save a life. *"BILL!"* I screamed, but Bill got into the cab, closed the door, and took off.

Outside my closed office door, uniformed police and crime technicians inspected, measured, and photographed every inch of R & B, trying to gather evidence against me. You would think I could have barred the front door, but they'd had another search warrant and presented it to me and Grady in front of the few associates still left. Wingate had looked down, shamefaced, and Renee Butler had run out the front door, disappearing into the crowd of reporters I couldn't seem to shake, like a low-grade infection.

"This is Bennie Rosato and I just spoke with him. Can you put me through?" I was standing, phone to my ear, in the middle of the disaster area that used to be my office. The cops had searched and confiscated most of my client files, and the few they left were dumped on the floor. The mess I could clean up, but there was nothing I could do about the breach of client confidentiality.

"You have to hold while I find him," said a rasp I recognized as Meehan's. I replaced a casebook that had been torn from the shelves. Papers were scattered over the floor and tables. A jade plant had been knocked over and its dirt spilled out. Fingerprint dust covered everything. What did they expect to find? My prints and Mark's? What would that prove?

"I don't know what you think you're doing," Grady said, from the wing chair in front of my desk. "We agreed I was running this case."

"You are. I told you, this is on another matter."

"A criminal matter?"

"Sort of." I righted the jade plant, cupped the loose soil in my hand, and dumped it back in the pot.

"You can't tell me more than that?"

"No." Before I made this call, I'd checked the ethical rules for lawyers, which is not an oxymoron. I could tell the cops what I knew, but I couldn't tell an associate, friend, or the intended victim. I didn't see what good it would do to tell Grady anyway. He'd just try and stop me. "Give me five minutes, okay?"

"You telling me I have to leave?"

"Sorry," I said, covering the receiver. "I have to make this call."

"To Azzic? Have you lost your mind?"

"Just trust me, okay? And go, please. I'll let you win the next power struggle, I promise." Grady frowned and left the room just as Azzic picked up. First things first. "Detective, this is Bennie Rosato. You boys did a nice job on my office. Why'd you take my client files?"

"They were covered in the first warrant."

"'All client files from 1980 to present'? It was overbroad. If you'd tried to serve it on me, I wouldn't have honored it."

"Oh really."

"My clients have nothing to do with this, and it's their confidential information you took. If I hear that they got a visit or a call from you or your men—"

"I don't have time for this, Rosato. I gotta go."

"Wait, I need to talk to you, it's important."

"Now you wanna talk? Twenty minutes ago you told me to screw myself."

"It's not about me." I shoved my law dictionary into place with a smooth *thunk*. "One of my clients, Bill Kleeb, was arrested yesterday for protesting animal rights at Furstmann Dunn. I have reason to believe his accomplice, Eileen Jennings, who was also arrested with him—"

"I don't know anything about it, Rosato. I do homicide, not animals. You want to talk to the animals, they're in the cells." He laughed, then exhaled audibly. I gathered he was smoking, and it had brought his warm good humor to the fore.

"This is about a homicide, Detective."

"Something you know about, Rosato?"

"The CEO of Furstmann Dunn may be in danger. Eileen Jennings threatened him yesterday with a taser."

He laughed. "That's rich. He might like it, who knows, them guys."

"I'm not kidding around. I wouldn't call unless I thought there was something to this, I'm breaching my client's confidence here. Get Jennings in for questioning and put somebody on the CEO, or at least alert him."

"Don't tell me what to do. I'm sick of you dictating to this department, Rosato. You think you know what we do, but you don't. You wanna tell us procedure, you don't know procedure. You think you can jerk us on a string, but this time you're jerkin' the wrong guy."

Another Great and Powerful. They abounded, and I handled them wrong every time. "You have a choice, Detective. Pick her up or explain later why you didn't, even after you were warned."

"Warned? She didn't do anything about this threat, did she?"

"She told her boyfriend she was going to kill the man, and the boyfriend thinks she'll do it. They got a new lawyer. I think he put up bail." I was talking about the man with the Haliburton.

Azzic was silent a minute, exhaling. "Rosato, what's your angle here? You trying to distract me? Jerk me around? What?"

"I'm talking about a murder! Why don't you try protecting and serving, for just one single minute? I won't tell the other boys, I swear."

"Don't tell me I don't do my job. I'm talkin' about a murder, too! I'm talkin' about a lady who would kill her boyfriend for twenty mil. That's what I'm talking about, so excuse me if I don't have time to take your crap."

"It's not crap. She could be a killer!" I shouted, but Azzic had already hung up.

ELEVEN

An army of reporters swelled behind the police barricades outside, laying techno-siege to the townhouse. Grady and I ignored them, or tried to, and cleaned up the second-floor offices, excluding Mark's, which had been taped closed. Not that I had the heart to go in there anyway. It was hard enough trying to function, but I had to see if I could salvage R & B.

None of the associates except Grady stuck around, and I didn't blame them. I wondered how many would stay on now, assuming there was a firm at all. I drafted a letter to our clients explaining that their matters would be handled through this tragedy, and called to reassure them. Only thirty would even take the call, and some had already been contacted by a detective they chose not to name. Most told me outright they were taking their legal business to a lawyer who wasn't a murder suspect, and I couldn't blame them, either. Between Detective Azzic and the press, I was becoming a pariah.

The calls I dreaded most were to the drug companies Mark represented. I'd called Kurt Williamson and Dr. Haupt at Wellroth Chemical all day, but didn't reach them. I dictated a request for a postponement of the Wellroth trial, then tried Haupt one last time at the end of the day after his secretary had gone.

"Ms. Rosato," Dr. Haupt said, in a tone as distant as I expected. "I'm surprised to be hearing from you."

"I left several messages."

"I saw them, but I didn't feel it was appropriate to return the calls. I understand that you have been charged with murder," he said, in his stilted accent.

"No, that's not true. I haven't been charged with murder, and I certainly didn't kill Mark. I want you to know that."

"I don't wish to discuss this with you, Ms. Rosato. I find this situation rather . . . horrifying. We saw Mark only yesterday. He was more than a lawyer to me, he was a friend."

"I realize that. The purpose of this call is to tell you I've prepared a request for an indefinite postponement of the Cetor patent trial. I'd like to file it, with your permission."

"We don't wish to postpone the trial indefinitely, Ms. Rosato."

"I'm afraid there's no other choice. I'm not in a position to try the case."

He cleared his throat. "Ms. Eberlein is fully prepared to go forward with the trial. We wish it to go forward, so that it concludes sooner. She has already asked the judge for a one-week postponement, and he agreed, in view of the circumstances."

"What? How do you know this?"

"I have spoken with Ms. Eberlein by telephone. She is at home. Very upset, understandably, but as soon as she is feeling better we'll go forward with her. Now I really must go. Please do not call me or Kurt again."

"But Dr. Haupt—" I said, then the line went dead. I hung up slowly. Eve, trying the case herself? I was trying to process the information when the door to my office burst open. It was Grady, his print tie flopped over the shoulder of a blue oxford shirt. His eyes were bright with excitement behind his wire rims and he carried law books, legal pads, and photocopies.

"Look at this," he said, shoveling papers over the desk at me. "It's the will, Mark's will."

"How'd you get it?"

"The police, along with a real thin file. That's all the information they would give us so far. But look at the will! Do you know who Mark named as his executor?"

"Who?" I thumbed through the pages, looking for the answer, and found it at the same time Grady said:

"Sam Freminet."

I skimmed the provision, which looked standard. "So?"

"So! As executor, Sam gets two percent of the estate as a fee. He also has the power to choose the lawyers for the estate, and he can choose himself. This way, he gets the lawyers' fees on top of the executor's fees, also two percent, which can start right away if he wants them to. The topper is that the will sets up a trust naming Sam as trustee, so he also takes a trustee's fee, one percent a year *for life*. It's like an annuity. He'll never have to work again."

"I'm confused." Half of me was still thinking about my conversation with Dr. Haupt.

Grady stood over me impatiently. "Considering the size of the estate, that means Sam makes a *million dollars* in fees, and the trustee's fee goes on and on. It's double, even triple-dipping, and he also gets the billings as the responsible attorney at Grun. You don't think he'll see some kind of bonus for bringing in an estate of this size?"

"And?"

"Bennie, aren't you following me?" Two lines furrowed Grady's usually mild brow. "Sam gets rich from Mark's death. Does that say something to you about motive?"

"That's absurd, Grady!" I felt angry, insulted for Sam. "That's just absurd."

"Is it? Please be objective. I don't know Sam Freminet, only met him the one time, but money is a very powerful incentive."

"Sam kill Mark?" I shook my head. "No way. Sam and Mark were friends. We all started at Grun together out of law school. Besides, Sam doesn't need the money or the billings. He's a partner at Grun, he probably makes over four hundred grand a year."

"Do you know that for a fact? How's his client list, do you know?"

"Sam's a bankruptcy lawyer and everybody's going bankrupt. I have to believe he gets his share of business."

"You believe, but do you know? What about his bank account? Rich people are greedy. It's the nature of the beast."

"Come on, Grady, Sam has all the toys he needs. Literally." I smiled, thinking of the stuffed Tasmanian Devil and Pepe Le Pew. Then I remembered Daffy Duck and his moneybags and stopped smiling.

"Bennie, think about it." Grady unloaded his books and leaned on my desk, bracing himself on his arms. "Sam knew about Mark's will, apparently he was the only person who did. You say you three were friends, but I get the impression

Sam had more of a business relationship with Mark, but more of a personal relationship with you. Is that right?"

"Yes, I guess, since the breakup."

"Could Sam have killed Mark to get back at him for leaving you? And make a bundle in the bargain?"

"It's unthinkable!" I leaned back in my chair. "Sam Freminet is the gentlest soul in the universe. You don't know him. Forget it. Nice try, lousy theory."

Grady cocked his head. "Did you tell Sam that Mark wanted to break up R & B?"

"You mean after Mark told me? I went right to the river."

"Do you know where Sam was that night?"

"I never know where he is at night. He goes out a lot."

Then I thought of my meeting with Sam that day, in his office. "But he told me he heard some of our associates were leaving. Did you know anything about that?"

"Just that Wingate's been grumbling, but you could see that. Do you think Mark told Sam he was going to break up R & B?"

"No. Sam would have told me."

"Would he? He didn't tell you about the will and he didn't tell you he was Mark's executor. Maybe you don't know as much as you think about him."

"I know enough to know that this is crazy, this whole discussion."

Grady sat down, undaunted. "I'd like to call Sam and find out where he was that night."

"You will not."

"Bennie, we're fighting the clock here, you heard Azzic. He'll charge you as soon as he has something that can conceivably support it. Then where will you be? Murder's not a bailable offense in Philly. You'll go right to jail."

I flashed on the women's prison at Muncy. I'd been there to see clients and was always relieved to hit the front gate on my way out. "Are you trying to scare me, Grady?"

"I surely am." He smiled, but I didn't.

"Okay. Fine. But if anybody talks to Sam, it should be me."

"I'd like to, as your lawyer."

"No. You don't know Sam. He's one of the dearest men in the world, he volunteers for Action AIDs. He was mad at me because I had a client opposed to AIDS research. He—" I stopped in midsentence. Bill Kleeb. Eileen's threat against the CEO. I had completely forgotten. I checked my watch. 7:00. I wondered where Eileen and Bill were now, whether they were back at their apartment. If I couldn't get to Detective Azzic, maybe I could get to them. I got up and hustled to my briefcase for their file.

"Bennie? What in God's name are you doing?" Grady asked, astonished as I ran back and forth.

"I have to make another call." I found the phone number Bill had given me and punched it in.

"Now? We're in the middle of a conversation."

I held up a hand when Bill Kleeb's voice came on the line. "Can you meet me at eight tonight? It's very important," I told him. Bill agreed only reluctantly, and I named a place to meet, then hung up, feeling uneasy.

"Who was that?" Grady asked.

"A client." I replaced the file and zipped my canvas briefcase closed. "I have to go. You want to walk me out?"

"Which client? Where are you going?" He stood up.

"To meet a client, the animal rights guy, okay? Maybe his girlfriend."

"Why?"

"I have to."

Grady put his hands on his hips. "Bennie, I'm your lawyer. I'd like to know as much as the police and the press do about you. Besides, you said you'd let me win the next one."

He had a point. I would have smacked a client who was behaving as badly as I was. "I just want to check in with him, see how he is. I can't tell you more than that, it's confidential and I don't want you involved in it."

"You're worried about a client when you're being investigated for murder?"

We met eye to eye, and I wasn't entirely comfortable in his gaze. "I'm worried about all my clients. You saw me, I made a zillion phone calls today."

"Why does this client merit a personal visit?"

Because I wanted to see if he and Eileen were picking out china patterns or explosives, but I couldn't tell Grady that. "He's young, a kid. He needs some help. Extra help."

"Good. I'm extra helpful, I'll go with you." He retrieved his suit jacket from the chair and tossed it over his shoulder, hooking it with a finger.

"You can't come. You have to hold the fort." I opened my office door, but Grady halted the door's progress with a hand.

"I don't get it," he said, gray eyes frank behind his glasses. "I know how much you care about finding Mark's killer, but you spent the day doing everything else but. Now you're running off. Aren't you avoiding it?"

"I have some things to get in order," I said, though I sensed he was right. Somehow, the threat to the Furstmann CEO was urgent to me. Maybe it was a murder I could prevent, as opposed to one I couldn't. Or maybe it was just too hard to deal with Mark's death.

"Hello?"

"Grady, if all goes well tonight, we'll solve this thing together. You need my help, I can tell."

He laughed. "Oh yes, I need your help. Don't know how I got along without you before. Now will you call Sam Freminet or should I?"

"I will."

"Will you also think about who else had a motive to kill Mark? Was anyone angry with him? Any clients in the past, anyone like that?"

"Yes, sir."

He grinned. "I like the sound of that."

"Don't get too used to it."

"Don't worry. Call me here or at home if you need anything, after your meeting or anytime. I'll be doing my alibi research. I'd like to know where the other associates were last night about the time Mark was killed."

It caught me up short. "Our associates?"

Suddenly my office windows filled with a harsh white light. The TV klieg lights, fishing for file footage. Grady turned toward the windows, now bright as midday despite the growing darkness. "Wonder if they got the telephoto on us."

"Probably. Let's go say hi." I walked to the window, and Grady came after.

"Don't give them the finger this time," he said.

"You're no fun." I looked out the window, shielding my eyes from the searing light. Reporters thronged on the street below, silhouetted in front of the round lamps like shadows on the moon.

Grady scanned the crowd. "The First Amendment at work."

"Right. Half of them are my clients in the libel cases. I defend their right to hound people."

"Be careful what you wish for, right?"

I gazed into the hot white brightness, wondering whether the next scene caught in the spotlight would be my arrest for murder.

TWELVE

They sat before paper cups of tap water, looking hungry. If you're going to meet vegetarians for dinner, don't do it at McDonald's. I don't know what I was thinking when I picked this place. Maybe about Mark's death, Detective Azzic, and Muncy Prison. "I could get you some fries," I said lamely.

"Thas' all right," Bill said, sitting slightly apart from Eileen. If they'd made up, it was an uneasy truce. He wore a plain white T-shirt and jeans, and his injuries were healing only slowly. The swelling on his forehead had gone down but the gash remained, and the white of his left eye was still bloodred.

"How about a Filet-o-Fish? That's not meat."

Eileen wrinkled her upturned nose. She was all nervous energy, eyes roving the restaurant, foot wiggling in white Candies sandals. "No fish. It has a face."

"Not anymore," I said, and nobody laughed. I was losing it. I sipped my coffee. At least it was hot, but even that would change, now that they'd been sued. "I don't eat veal," I offered, but Eileen was looking away again. She hadn't met my eye once, undoubtedly blaming me for convincing Bill to plead out.

"You should read about factory farming," she said idly. "Cows, pigs, it's no different than veal. They grow them in pens and feed them antibiotics and steroids."

"Steroids?" I pushed away my half-eaten Big Mac. If I got any bigger, I'd be Alice in Wonderland.

"It's poison, and then there's the bacteria. Things grow in meat. Things you can't see." She flicked crayon-black bangs off a face that would be pretty but for its hardness. Her eye makeup was heavy and her spandex dress eye-catching. Her arm was still in a sling, but that was the only souvenir of her fracas with the police.

I wanted to swing the conversation around to her death threat without betraying Bill's confidence. "Bill told me all about the lab, Eileen. You must've seen some terrible stuff."

"I did."

"Are Furstmann's labs worse than others?"

She scratched under her cast. "What do you care? You're not even our lawyer."

Ouch. "That guy with the ridiculous briefcase my replacement?"

"What'd you expect?" she said, with a savvy laugh. Her gaze wandered around the restaurant, so I surveyed the place. It was empty except for an old man chain-smoking in the far corner. The dinner rush was over, nobody was coming in. What was Eileen looking at? Then I realized she didn't want to see, she wanted to be seen.

"How'd you find this lawyer, Eileen?"

"Celeste? He found me. He saw me on the news. I was on all the channels, even cable."

"Is he the one who bailed you out?"

"He wants to sue the police and the city. He says we can

get five hundred thou, maybe more, and that's only from the lawsuit."

Bill shifted in his slippery seat. "He said he'll help us stop the experiments, too. That's what we want to do."

Eileen nodded. "Stop them dead."

I felt a chill and leaned forward. "Eileen, nothing you can do will stop the experiments. The pressure for an AIDS cure is too great. I told Bill you ought to go after the fur companies instead of the drug companies. Remember, Bill?"

"Yuh," Bill nodded.

"I worked at Furstmann Dunn. I saw what they did," Eileen said.

"But people aren't ready to deal with animal experimentation yet, Eileen. Go after fur. The celebrities are all against it."

"Celebrities? Like who?" She inched forward on her chair, and for the first time interest glimmered in her eyes.

"Uh, Elle MacPherson."

"I like Elle. She's in the movies, like Rene Russo. Did you know Rene Russo was a model before she did that movie with John Travolta? She gets a lot of movie work."

"Really. You have momentum, since you had all the TV cameras and everything. Why don't you keep it alive by going after the fur companies? I don't know if Bill told you, but I represent a lot of radicals, a lot of protesters."

"Any celebrities?"

"No. No celebrities. And they, my clients, always use the press when they have it. It helps them win people over, get a lot of followers."

"Followers?"

"Sure."

She paused. "I gotta ask you something though."

"What?"

"Did you really kill your boyfriend?"

I felt a pang, deep inside my chest. "No."

"Oh," she said.

Her foot wagging.

"You, a murderer? How could they think such a thing?" Hattie said. She'd been waiting up, wrapped like a Havana cigar in her bathrobe, with her hair in pink foam curlers. She looked exhausted, her skin greasy and her eyes dark and sunken. "How could they even think it?"

"They're cops. They can think anything." I scratched Bear, asleep under the table, and stirred my umpteenth cup of coffee. I was fatigued, too, but satisfied that Eileen had forgotten about the CEO.

"The cops were upstairs, you know. They turned your apartment upside down. They woulda broke down the door if I hadn't stopped 'em."

"Sorry. I should've warned you when I called."

"They left your place a damn mess! I tried to put it together, but your mother was gettin' upset."

My heart sank. "Did they bother her? Did she see them?"

"I calmed her down." Hattie passed some papers across the table to me. "Here's a list of the things they took. The detective told me to give it to you."

I pushed the papers away. "Which detective?"

"I don't know. Mean-lookin', funny name."

"Azzic?"

She nodded.

"Tell me how Mom is."

"In bed, from ten o'clock. She hadn't slep' a wink. Don't they know what they're doin' to you?"

"They don't care. Did she eat?"

"They should care! It was a crazy house here today! That detective, askin' questions. They even went lookin' for your car, to search that, too. The dog was barkin', your phone was ringin' all day. One of the girls came with a box of stuff from your office and took it upstairs. Black girl."

"Renee Butler?"

She nodded again and rubbed her forehead irritably. "What a day. Reporters, buzzin' at the door through dinnertime. I went out there and ran them off! They called you a murderer!"

"That's what they'll keep calling me, until I can prove I'm not."

"You, with that rowing! It's what got you into this mess!"

"Not exactly—"

"I told you you should stop. You don't listen to me, you don't listen to nobody. Damn fool thing to be doing, rowin' a damn boat!"

I could almost see Hattie's blood pressure rising. "What are you so upset about? My mother? You don't have to be, I set up a trust for her. If anything happened to me, there's enough in there to keep her, and you—"

"Me?" Suddenly Hattie slapped me, right across the face.

"Hattie, Jeez! What'd you do that for?" I jumped to my feet, more shocked than hurt, but Hattie's features were contorted with a pain of her own.

"Fool! How can such a smart girl be so damn stupid?! I'm worried about *you*! Not me! Not your momma! You're the one!"

"Benedetta?" came a voice, agitated, from my mother's bedroom. "Benedetta!"

"Ma?" I walked past Hattie to my mother's room, responding on autopilot. I opened the door and the cloying rosewater filled my nose. It was stifling, assaultive. I felt suddenly anxious. Panicky. I hurried to the window and flung it open. The cool night air billowed in the light curtains.

"Close the window!" my mother said. "Close the window!"

"Shhh, it's staying open. Nobody's out there. Settle down." I breathed easier in the fresh air. "Stop worrying. Everything's okay."

"Did you do the dishes? Do the dishes, Bennie."

"The dishes are done."

"Do the dishes. Do the dishes."

"They're all done, Ma. Hattie did them." I went to her bed and took her hand, which felt weak and warm in mine. I brushed a damp curl from her brow.

"Do the dishes. The dishes are in the sink."

"Hattie did the dishes. They're put away. They're all done. How are you feeling? "

"It's dark." She tried to sit up, then flopped back on her pillow. "It's late. You should go home. Go home. Go home."

"I am home. Hattie told me you had some soup today. That was good."

"It's dark. It's dark. Do the dishes. Do the dishes. Get me a Kleenex."

"How are you?" I sat on the ancient bed, which creaked loudly. Another thing she wouldn't let me replace.

"Get me a Kleenex. I need a Kleenex."

"You don't need a Kleenex, forget about the Kleenex. Did you really eat lunch today? Some soup?"

"I need it, I need it. It's dark." Her voice rose, thinning out with anxiety. "I need it. I need it. I need it."

"All right, relax." I pulled a Kleenex out of the box on her nightstand, and she grabbed it from me, balling it up and squeezing it like a pulsing heart. In a minute she'd be tearing it apart and fingering the pieces, then stuffing the shreds in the pockets of her nightgown. The rest she would hide under the chenille coverlet and in her pillowcase. "Is that better, Ma? You happy, you got your Kleenex?" I couldn't keep the irritation from my voice. She went through a box of Kleenex a day, even though Hattie bought Family Size. We needed Crazy Family Size.

"Read to me. Read to me. Read to me. It's dark."

"Okay, fine." I dragged a wooden chair over to the bed, kicked off my pumps in the dark, and put my feet into the well of the nightstand.

"Read to me. Read to me. Read to me."

"Relax. Everything's okay, Ma. Settle down, and I will." I didn't turn on the light or bother with a book, there was no point to that. I simply told her about my day, from top to bottom, every night. I have no idea why I did this, nor did I kid myself I was getting through. I just told it to her as if it were a novel, and she would quiet in time, then doze off. I'd done this every night since she'd gone completely bonkers, which was almost as long as I could remember. Enough Kleenexes ago to reforest the Pacific Northwest.

"Read to me. Read to me. Read to me." She began to tear at the Kleenex. "Now. Now. Now."

"Well, today she found out that the man she loved was murdered," I said, and told the whole story. She muttered throughout, not listening to anything I said, and if the truth be told, I didn't listen to her either.

It was Hattie I was thinking of.

* * *

Later, I stood in the middle of my living room with Bear, listening to Sam's worried voice on my answering machine. He'd called five times to see how I was, his messages interspersed with the reporters', but I couldn't return his calls just yet. I was assessing the damage wrought by Hurricane Azzic.

The apartment was messier than even I liked it. Books had been torn from the shelves and spilled onto the rug. The contents of a drawer had been dumped on the coffee table in front of the TV and the stack of CDs had been rifled. The couch pillows, upended, lay on the floor next to the remote control. At least the cops had managed to find the remote. It must've been in the couch. It's always in the couch.

I stepped through the rubble into the kitchen with Bear at my side. Pots and pans littered the counters. An open box of Müeslix lay on its side and the kitchen drawers hung open. Fingerprint dust covered the counters and cabinet doors. Bear sniffed around, much as the cops had before her. What were they looking for? Mark had never even lived here, he'd always kept his own place. Why did they do this? Because they could.

The worst was the bedroom. I stood in the portal, taking it in. My bedclothes had been stripped and the mattress showed an old menstrual stain the size of a calf's liver. I imagined the cops joking over that.

I went to my bureau. My underwear drawer was in total disarray, invaded by unseen hands. The other drawers had been searched, too. Sweaters tumbled with T-shirts; pantyhose and socks were intertwined, half on the floor. Rowing gear had been jettisoned. My photos of Mark were gone, as were his early love notes and Valentine's Day cards. Even my diaphragm was missing. Terrific. Exhibit A.

I crossed over the debris to the closet, where it was more of the same. Suits had been trashed, even my silk dresses ended up on the floor. My shoes were piled in a mound. It was a nightmare, even for a slob.

I sighed, kicked off my pumps, and padded into the bathroom. A jar of Lancôme moisturizer was open, the costly creme churned up by a grubby finger, and the toothpaste was squeezed out into a turquoise squiggle. The door to the medicine cabinet was ajar; the aspirin and other pills had been uncapped and presumably gone through. I plopped onto the closed toilet seat and slipped the papers out of my jacket pocket; a search warrant, a list of what had been seized, and an affidavit of probable cause. I remembered affidavits as long as these from the old days. Now my name was on the caption.

Bear settled onto the cool tile floor and looked up questioningly, so I read aloud: "'Letters and correspondence, personal computer and diskettes, office supplies, files of household bills and the like, articles of clothing.'" I assumed this referred to the outfit I was wearing the day Mark was murdered, for fiber samples. Also all the clothes in the hamper, since police like that for evidentiary as well as shock value. Going through your dirty laundry, literally.

The list continued. "'Shoes and sneakers, overcoats and topcoats, and certain jewelry items as follows,'" and they catalogued every piece of jewelry I had, most of which was my mother's. They even took her engagement ring, a diamond chip from a man who didn't stick around for the wedding.

"Damn it," I said, and threw the paper on the bathroom floor, where it landed next to a large black smudge.

More fingerprint soot. I followed the smudge trail to the bathtub, where the cops had taken more fingerprints and probably samples of my head and pubic hair. Wonderful. At this point the police knew more about my reproductive system than I did. I rested my chin on my hand. The Thinker, on the potty.

Bear meandered over, turned around, and plopped her heavy tush onto my toe. Then she threw her head backwards and smiled at me, almost upside down. Someday she would figure out it was easier to see someone if you faced them. I scratched the spray of butterscotch fur behind her ears, and she eased sleepily back to the floor, nestling her head between her paws and flattening her body like a bathmat. Only her eyes stayed on me, brown marbles asking, "So, you gonna clean up or you gonna feel sorry for yourself?"

"I'm gonna clean up, okay?"

Satisfied, Bear closed her eyes.

I got off the seat, found the CD player, cranked up Bruce Springsteen's greatest hits, and went to work. In no time I was caterwauling along with Bruce, lost in my task, but then I reached a song that made me stop singing. A song that forced me down on the floor, to deal with what was going on.

"Murder, Incorporated."

Mark was dead. Someone had killed him. Deep inside was anguish, but out there was his murderer. Someone who drew breath while Mark didn't. It was unjust. Obscene. I knew what I had to do.

I had to find Mark's killer.

THIRTEEN

I stopped by my mother's apartment early the next morning and stood at the door, briefcase in hand, as if it were a typical day and I still had a law firm to run. Hattie was rinsing the coffeepot at the sink, dressed but still in her rollers. Later she would press her hair with an old curling iron, and the acrid smell would fill the apartment, upsetting my mother and costing me two boxes of Kleenex. I always teased her about it, but I wouldn't this morning.

"Hattie, I've been thinking about what you said. I decided you're right about Mom. You want me to call the doctor?"

"No, I'll call him." She was rinsing out the pot again and again, her back to me. Her shirt said I'M A WINNER! and red dice were sequined on her scapula. "I got the time."

"No, that's all right."

"You're the one who's busy. You got your apartment to fix up."

"I cleaned up last night."

"All of it? I heard the music, but I fell asleep."

"It's all taken care of."

"I'll call about your momma. I want to do it."

"You sure now?"

"I'm sure."

We weren't talking about the call, we were making up. Or at least trying to, as easy as that was without saying the words or even meeting each other's eye. "If the appointments are early morning, how will you do it? You'll have to get up early."

"I'm up anyway. Makes no never mind."

"I'll help you get her up."

"I can do that, too. I did it for the hospital, I can do it for the electroshock," she said, finally twisting off the water and placing the glass pot in the coffeemaker. Her back was still to me, and I wanted to go before she turned around. I didn't want to face her, because I was choking now, finding I couldn't say what needed to be said. But she turned suddenly, her eyes dark and sorrowful, and said to me, "You have a good day, now."

Thank you for smacking me last night, Hattie. I've never been smacked before. No one noticed how stupid I can be, or how careless my words.

"You too, Hattie," I said, and left.

I started the day at Groan & Waste, so early that the receptionist on Sam's floor wasn't in yet. I powered past the secretaries' empty workstations, ignoring the associates who were in at daybreak and walking around conspicuously enough to get credit for it. I never would've made it at Grun. When I get in early, I like to work. So does Sam, who was going full steam ahead when I walked into his office, his custom English suit bent over financial printouts.

"*Bennie!* Where have you been? How are you?" He leapt up when he saw me and came around to give me a hug.

"Sam," I said, embracing him. His hug was a comfort, even though he was so fashionably thin.

"I didn't sleep all night," he said softly, giving me a final squeeze. Close up, his eyes were red-rimmed and his skin pale. He looked distraught, unhealthy. "Can you believe that Mark is dead?"

"Not really."

"Why didn't you call me back? I was so worried. I stayed in, waiting."

"I'm sorry, I had to clean."

"What? You? Siddown and tell me what's going on." He pressed me into the sling chair across from his desk, taking the one next to it himself. "You want me to get you some coffee?" He waved at a Sylvester the Cat mug.

"No, thanks." Grun coffee was even worse than mine.

"I can't believe it." Sam kept shaking his neat head. "Mark murdered, and you a suspect. But don't worry, I have it all planned. I'm going to stop work at noon today, then take off for a few days. I canceled all my appointments, everything. I want to help."

"Thanks." Sam would be there for me, he always had been. Sometimes I thought we were all we had, a friendship of outsiders.

"Don't thank me. Now, listen, I already talked to somebody about representing you."

"I have a lawyer, Sam. I'm gonna use Grady Wells."

He blinked. "Do I know that name?"

"He's one of our associates. The Supreme Court clerk."

"The blonde on TV with you? He's cute, but is he a good criminal lawyer?"

"Yes, and forget about how cute he is. He has a girlfriend, at least he used to."

"Figures. All the good ones are either married or straight."

"Behave yourself." I smiled despite my mood, and he smiled, too.

"What can I do? Can I help with your caseload? I can still write a brief, I think." He raked his feathery haircut with a small hand, but there wasn't enough hair to mess up.

"There is no caseload. My clients don't want a murderer for a lawyer, they're so conventional. I'm out of business."

"What?" Sam looked appalled. "No R & B?"

"You got it."

He shook his head, disbelieving. "And what about Mark's funeral? What's happening with it?"

"I don't think I can do much, given my position. You may have to plan it, if Eve hasn't already. I thought about it last night."

"I'll do it, don't worry. A nice memorial service. Believe me, I can plan a memorial service." He smiled sadly, his shoulders slumping. "Have you thought about who . . . did it?"

"I'm starting to." I remembered my purpose in coming here. "The cops think it's me because of Mark's will. Why didn't you tell me he had a will, Sam?"

"I'm sorry, I couldn't. It was privileged." He swallowed hard, his Adam's apple moving visibly in a slender neck. "Besides, I thought Mark would tell you. It was his place."

"Why did you draft Mark's will?"

"He asked me to." Sam edged back onto his chair. "When

R & B grew, Mark started to think ahead. Right after his parents died, he said he needed a will. He told me the size of the estate and asked me if I knew any good estates lawyers at Grun. I told him I could do it for him."

"I didn't know you did estates work, especially for such big estates."

"Sure I do. Estates, some tax, even some corporate. I like to keep my billings up, and estates that big don't come along everyday. I wasn't about to refer it. What am I, stupid?"

I remembered Grady's suspicions. "But did you really need the business, Sam? I thought you had plenty of clients."

"I do, but I could always use more. I've developed my own practice group. A firm-within-the-firm, a small business practice. Take them from incorporation to bankruptcy—cradle to grave—and do estates work for the principals."

"Is it profitable?"

"Sure as shootin'. 'I'm the roughest, toughest, he-manest hombre as ever crossed the Rio Grande—and I ain't no namby pamby.' 'Bugs Bunny Rides Again,' 1948."

"Did you know Mark would make you executor?"

His smile faded. "Tarnation, Bennie. We're friends, so I'm going to keep my temper and ask you what you're suggesting. Are we hunting wabbits or what?"

"I'm not suggesting anything. I'm just asking."

"Are you accusing me of murder, despite the fact that we've been buds for God knows how long?"

I felt a stab of guilt. "Of course I'm not accusing you, Sam. But I have to talk to you about it."

"Me? Why?"

"Grady suspects you. He was going to call, but I wanted to be the one to do it."

Sam's face reddened and his mouth twisted bitterly. "Grady thinks I killed one of my dearest, oldest friends? What, are they taking anybody on that Court now? Who the hell did he clerk for? Clarence Thomas?"

"He's smart, Sam, and he's trying to help."

"He's not that smart. Why would I kill Mark, for God's sake?"

"For the executor's fee? The billings?" I felt like a jerk for even explaining, Sam looked so nonplussed.

"Come on, girlfriend! I need billings as much as the next lawyer, but I wouldn't *kill* Mark for them. I wouldn't kill *anybody* for them."

"Grady says there's a trustee's fee, too. It adds up to a million dollars."

"So what? Are you asking me for real?" His eyes narrowed, but I told myself to stay the course.

"Let's just get it over with, Sam. If we're friends, we can talk about anything."

"We're friends, so you can insult me? Bennie, listen, I don't need the money, I have plenty of money. 'I'm rich! I'm wealthy! I'm comfortably well off,' as Daffy would say. I don't need to kill my friend for a fee."

"I thought so," I said, backing off, but he leaned toward me, angered.

"You want details, I'll give you details. I own my condo at the Manchester. My firstborn, the Porsche Carrera, is one year old next week and I bought him with cash. I take only one vacation a year, to South Beach, and I don't have any dependents except for that Cuban waiter at The Harvest. I was with him on the night in question, by the way. If you want to check it, I'll give you his number."

"No, I don't mean to get personal—"

"As for my assets, which Ramon tells me is my best feature, I'm taking almost four hundred thousand this year, not including the bonus from the First Federal bankruptcy. It's in eleven mutual funds and some very frisky tech stocks."

"Okay, Sam. I get the picture."

"However, I do have a confession to make." He held up a palm. "I confess, I'm too heavily into Microsoft, but I want Bill Gates so much I can taste him. Can you blame me?"

"Sam—"

"Except for that hair. If he washed it from time to time, I'd be in Redmond in a heartbeat."

"Look, I'm sorry. I really am. Enough already. Sue me. Shoot me."

"Apology accepted," he said curtly. He slouched back into his chair, but he didn't look like himself. Or maybe he wasn't looking at me the way he always did.

I wondered if he ever would again.

FOURTEEN

Grady had me barricaded in my office with an amazingly good cup of coffee and the large wipe-off chart we use for jury exhibits. The chart rested on an easel and contained the names of all of R & B's associates, with a grease-pencil grid to the left. I took one look at it and saw what Grady had learned, but he wanted to explain it to me anyway.

"Are you listening, Bennie?" he asked. Wielding a long, rubber-tipped pointer, in his violet-covered necktie and fresh white shirt, Grady looked more kindergarten teacher than lawyer.

"Of course I'm listening," I said, but I wasn't, because I already had a chart of my own in my head. I needed him for the legal end, not for this. I was the one who had to find Mark's killer.

"You don't look like you're listening."

"No, I am. I'll be a good defendant, I promise." I smiled in a way I hoped was convincing and took another sip of coffee. I felt stronger since I had eliminated Sam as a murder suspect, and the coffee was tasting better and better. "Who made this? It's good."

"I did, I cross-examined each of them on the phone. I finished the last phone call, with Renee Butler, at one thirty. Except for Wingate, I went over and talked to him. He's real upset."

"Why? He didn't even like Mark. I meant the coffee, though. Who made it?"

"I did. Look at this." He pointed to Jennifer Rowland's name. "Jenny says she was working at home the night Mark was killed, editing a section of the brief in the Latorno matter. She said it was for you and it was due next week. Is it?"

"Yes. Did you use the Maxwell House?"

"Whatever was there." He made a neat check with a grease marker in the blank marked ALIBI. "I want to see Jenny's time records, though she could have lied on them, too."

"She wouldn't be the first lawyer to write fiction." I wanted to ask him how much water he put in, but it would be futile. The coffeemaker at work was a Bunn, the one at home was a Krups; it would never translate, English to German. At least not when I spoke the language.

"Amy here," he said, pointing to the line that said AMY FLETCHER, "was with Jeff Jacobs that night. It checks out from both sides. They're seeing each other, did you know that?"

"Yes."

He made purposeful checks by FLETCHER and JACOBS. "They could both be lying to me, but I don't think so. Wingate says he was online in the Grateful Dead chat room. Do you know he goes in the teen rooms and tells them he's Jon Bon Jovi?"

"Perfect. And I pay this kid?"

"He said he logged off at two in the morning the night Mark was killed. I'd like to check the AOL records, but Wingate has two housemates and they could have logged off for him." He made a question mark in the WINGATE box, next to a "WW" in Renee Butler's box.

"What's WW mean, in Renee's?"

"Weight Watchers. She didn't want to tell me at first. She took Eve with her, to get her out of the house. Eve's taking Mark's death pretty hard, you know. She's convinced you did it."

I ignored the twinge and gulped my brew. "What kind of filters do you use, Grady?"

He sighed, his gaze running up and down the chart. "That's everybody. They all have some sort of alibi, but I have to double-check Wingate's."

"Except for the secretaries and Marshall. Did you call Marshall?"

"Marshall? You suspect Marshall?" He looked surprised behind his glasses.

"No, I don't suspect any of them yet. I go slow before I point a finger, especially now. Tell me which filters. I bet you used the brown ones."

His eyes widened in frustration. "Lord, you are the strangest woman! I couldn't find the filters, so I used a paper towel, all right?"

"A *paper towel*? Is that even possible?"

He dropped his pointer, so I shut up about the coffee and let him go on, repeating everything and pointing with his pointer. When he ran out of lecture, he went to see if Marshall was in yet. And I went to the heart of the matter.

The computer.

Sitting right in front of me, next to my traumatized jade plant. The police would probably take the computers when they came back today, if last night's seizure at my apartment told me anything. I didn't have much time.

I stopped, fingers poised over the whitish keyboard. As I saw it, I had to know what Mark had been doing lately to understand why anybody would want to kill him. I thought I knew, but evidently I didn't, since I was completely blindsided by his desire to break up R & B. But the computer knew.

I hit LIST FILES. R & B's files—time records, correspondence, memos, briefs, client information, and our personal files—popped onto the screen. The police had taken hard copies of R & B's client and time records, and I could reprint them if I needed to, but I didn't need to. Mark kept his own cyberdaybook in a hidden file and generated a cleaned-up version of his time records from that. It was secreted under his password: Mook. What his father always called him. Thank God for pillow talk.

I typed it in and revealed the hidden files: CALENDAR, DAYBOOK, CHECKBOOK. The same directories as always, he hadn't changed them yet. I had Mark's most intimate information at my fingertips and I didn't have to leave my coffee. Our old firm investigator used to say anybody who thinks sleuthing starts with a magnifying glass is behind the times. It happens in front of microscopes and computers, in labs and test tubes. You could get cellulite from detective work nowadays.

I highlighted CALENDAR and hit ENTER. A grid appeared on the screen, this month's calendar with the appointments typed in. Mark used our old Grun code; CO stood for conference out of the office; CI for conference in the office; CD for client development; and TC for telephone call. Entries with notations filled the days, ending abruptly the day Mark was killed. I tried not to think about it and looked at the first week of the month.

Wellroth Chemical Trial.

I went backwards a week. Wellroth Chemical Trial.

A month earlier, and the picture changed. I scanned the screen. Lots of COs at Wellroth, lots of CIs with Dr. Haupt and E. Eberlein. Then a flock of CD, client development, with E. Eberlein and an array of area drug companies. SmithKline, Wyeth, Rohrer, McNeil Labs, and Merck. They were all there, in meetings that usually lasted an hour. Apparently, Mark had been pitching them during the day and courting them over dinner at night. It would be worth plenty of business, but it wasn't planned to enrich R & B's coffers. It was planned for Mark's new firm.

I sat back and tried not to feel entirely betrayed. He hadn't breathed a word, nor had he put it on his official time sheets where I would have seen it. I bit my lip and punched the page up key, scrolling backward in anger.

I stopped at another surprise entry. CO G. Wells. Mark had a conference out of the office with Grady? It was listed on last month's schedule. I searched the other calendar pages under Grady's name. Another CO popped up the week before Mark was killed, but there were no explanatory notes with it. I couldn't imagine why Mark would be meeting with Grady. They never worked together. Grady worked for me and the high-tech clients he was developing himself. He had a growing corporate practice with the new software companies out by Route 202, in the suburbs.

My coffee sat untouched, growing cold. Why was Grady meeting with Mark? For an hour at a stretch, at the end of the day, out of the office? I squinted at Grady's grease-pencil chart. There was no Wells listed on it. Where was he the night Mark was killed? I trusted Grady, but it nagged at me.

I didn't have time to puzzle it out. I got out of the CALEN-

DAR file and printed it, then hit PRINT for each of the other hidden files. I hated to make a hard copy of something only I knew existed, but I couldn't count on having the computers a minute longer.

Then it occurred to me. How was Mark funding all this client development? It had to cost thousands, yet I hadn't noticed any irregularities in the books or in any memos from Marshall, who managed them.

I highlighted Mark's CHECKBOOK file and a new menu materialized; R & B ACCOUNT and PERSONAL ACCOUNT. I hit R & B first. A check register appeared on the screen, its entries machine-neat. I skimmed this month's withdrawals. Nothing unusual; DHL, FedEx, Staples, Bell Tel, Biscardi Enterprises, the holding company that owned the building. Everything was in order, strictly kosher. I remembered Mark's will with a pang. It wasn't my money he wanted. I pushed my emotions aside and got out of the R & B file, then hit PERSONAL ACCOUNT.

The entries were to Acme Markets, Bell Mobile, and the like. Small amounts, frugal amounts. Mark never spent money on anything, which is why I never knew he had any. Then I saw them. Payments to American Express and Visa in three and four thousand dollar amounts, starting about the time the client development had. So it was true, and he'd funded it himself. Next to the credit card payments were bills posted to a local printer and graphic designer, undoubtedly for new business cards and a hipper logo. I spotted a payment to Philoffice Realty, in the amount of twenty thousand dollars. Earnest money for my sunny new office space.

Then another entry caught my eye. Cash. The withdrawal

was for two thousand dollars, last week. The memo line read SAM FREMINET, for legal fees.

What? Sam? In cash?

I scrolled backwards to last month. A list of routine entries, and another one to Sam. Cash, two thousand dollars. Three weeks before Mark was killed. Again, LEGAL FEES on the memo line.

I sat back in the chair, a hard knot forming in my chest. Why was Mark paying Sam? What legal fees and why in cash? It made no sense. I printed the checkbook files, then hit another key.

ARE YOU SURE YOU WANT TO DELETE THESE FILES? Y OR N? the computer asked.

I hit Y. I would've hit DAMN STRAIGHT if I could. The files held the solution to this puzzle, and I wanted it to myself. In twenty-four hours the system would delete them automatically from backup. I'd have the only copies.

Copies? Damn! I'd forgotten. The copies printed. They'd be spitting out of the laser printer in the secretaries' area, in full view of any cop who happened to be standing around. I leapt from my chair, tore open the door, and scrambled out of the office.

"My brief!" I yelped for show, but it was already too late.

FIFTEEN

A criminalist in a navy Mobile Crime jumpsuit crouched on the rug beside the laser printer, picking up the last page from the floor. She held a thick packet of already-printed pages to her chest, and I had no doubt she'd read them as she gathered them. Damn it.

"Excuse me, that's my brief," I said.

She straightened up. "I saw the pages falling out and thought I'd help." Her face bore little makeup and she had a cropped, no-nonsense haircut.

"Thanks. For the help." I eyed the papers in her arms and felt myself break into a sweat. I would've demanded them, but if she didn't understand their significance I didn't want to tip my hand and trigger another search warrant.

"You forgot you started printing, didn't you? That happens to me all the time. You start working on something else and you forget you started printing."

"Very good. You must be a detective," I said, and we shared a fake laugh.

"Nope, but I want to be some day. I'm just a crime tech, second year, but you gotta start somewhere." She hugged my

papers to a black nameplate that said PATCHETT and nodded in the direction of the empty paper tray. "It looks like the
printer ran out of paper."

"Naturally. Just my luck. Whenever you need something
fast, you run out of paper." I didn't want to print with her
watching, so I made no move to replenish the supply. We stood
on either side of the laser printer, implausibly ignoring the
flashing green lights. Playing chicken with the office supplies.

"Don't you hate that?" she asked. "When people see the
paper is low and don't do anything about it."

"It's like running out of toilet paper. Nobody wants to be
the last one. I hate that."

"Same. Aren't you going to add the paper now?"

"You know, I'm embarrassed to admit it, but I have no idea
how to add paper." It was a lie, of course. I could repair the
machine if I had to. "The secretaries do it for me."

"I don't think any secretaries are in yet, but I'll help.
I know how." She looked around for the paper supply, but I
edged to the left, hiding the ream that sat on the table.

"I can wait to print the rest," I said, when I heard footsteps
behind me. It was Grady, who was looking at me with a mysti-
fied smile.

"I'm surprised at you, Bennie. It's easier than it looks,
changing paper. You just watch me."

"No, it's all right—"

"Please, it's no trouble at all." Grady reached behind me
for the paper, reloaded the tray, and slid it back into place with
a metallic click. "Press RESET if it gives you a hard time."

I could have killed him. "It's so nice to have a sexist around
the house."

"I'm not a sexist, I'm a gentleman." Grady smiled politely

at the criminalist. "I shouldn't be telling you this, but she can't make coffee either."

Ha ha. "That's enough, Rhett. Ms. Patchett, I'll take those papers now." I yanked my papers from the criminalist's grip as the printer spat out another month of Mark's calendar. She eyed it as I snatched it up. "Thanks a lot for your help."

"No problem," she said, pursing her lips. "So that's what a lawyer's brief looks like? Like a calendar?"

"Yes, it's the appendix."

"Brief?" Grady said, then his face changed as he wised up. "Are you finishing that Third Circuit brief, Bennie?"

"All done. This is the appendix, with the calendars." The printer spewed more pages, which I gathered instantly. "I hope you didn't read any of my brief, Ms. Patchett. It contains a client's confidential information and is also subject to attorney-client privilege."

"Of course not." She smiled falsely.

"Good." I smiled back, just as falsely. I was gauging how long it would take her to get a warrant.

And wondering if it could happen before Mark's hidden files were deleted for good.

"Just who *did* you clerk for anyway?" I asked Grady, when we were safely inside my office. "Tell me it wasn't Thomas."

"Kennedy, and don't you say anything bad about him. What was that all about? You're not writing a brief. What were you printing?"

"Notes," I said, making a snap decision. I'd remembered the CO Wells on Mark's calendar and decided not to confide in Grady, at least not until I understood his secret meetings with Mark. "And next time, try to think before you help a criminalist in distress."

"Notes about what?"

"Just some cases." I picked up a red accordion file and slipped the copies inside, then threw the file into my briefcase behind the desk.

"What cases?"

"Those animal rights guys, their case." I was making it up as I went along, and from the expression on Grady's face, not doing a very good job.

"Thirty pages on an animal activist? What is it, a manifesto?" He folded his arms. "I'll ask again. What was it you printed, Bennie?"

"Tell me something first."

"Does everything have to be a negotiation?"

"Absolutely." I decided to cross-examine him, then watch his reaction. "Grady, where were you the night Mark was killed?"

His mouth opened slightly, then closed into a pat smile that masked something. Hurt. "You're serious."

"I'm sorry, I have to be. It wasn't on the chart you made."

"I had a date," he said evenly.

"Who with?"

"My old girlfriend. We see each other from time to time."

"What time did the date start?"

"At ten. I picked her up at her condo. She lives in Hopkinson House."

"What time did you leave work?"

"After we all met in the library. I packed and left." His answers were smooth and sure and he seemed poised, if piqued. It looked and sounded like the truth, so maybe it was. Still.

"When did you leave her apartment?"

"I'm not sure that's your business."

"I think it is, if you want to keep a client."

His mouth tensed. "About seven in the morning, then I went back to my apartment."

"In Old City?"

He nodded. "I got to work early to do some cleanup on <u>MicroMAXel,</u> and the police were already here. When I got the distinct impression it was you they were after, I tried to reach you. Because I knew you were innocent."

I ignored the accusation in his tone. "Grady, what were you working on for Mark?"

"Nothing. I haven't worked with Mark for the past two years. Not after my first year here."

Hmmm. "Why not? Didn't you like working for Mark?"

Grady's expression changed slightly, his forehead creasing with discomfort. "What's the difference? The man has passed, Bennie. I like working my own cases, that's all."

"That's not all. Why?"

"All right, all right. You're relentless." He eased into a chair like a benched basketball player. "I found Mark to be selfish. Unkind. He didn't like me developing my own practice, especially with the software companies. It threatened him."

"How do you know? Did he tell you?"

"No, but I got the message. Mark was more comfortable working with someone subordinate, like Eve. He wanted a permanent second chair, not a first chair. He didn't want an equal at all."

I still needed an answer for the CO Wells. "Did you meet with him and discuss it? You two have it out?"

"Fight? Lord, no. I haven't talked to Mark, alone, for ages. So, now will you tell me what you were printing? We have a deal."

"Oh, a personal file," I said, fumbling for an explanation. Grady was lying. The calendar proved otherwise. I couldn't tell him the truth, not now. I couldn't trust him anymore. And he was my lawyer.

"A personal file?"

"Love letters, to Mark. Seven years' worth, in a hidden file. I didn't want them on the computer anymore," I told him, in a nervous tone it wasn't hard to fake. Had Grady really killed Mark? Was he representing me to frame me? Outside in the hall there were voices, and bustling sounds. My house, full of my enemies. Now Grady. I felt paranoid, uneasy.

"The criminalist said it was a calendar."

"She saw my diary. I printed that, too, because I make notes on it. I wanted to keep it private, since the police took my computer at home."

His brow relaxed, and he seemed satisfied. "Did you delete the files from the hard disk?"

"Yes." I remembered Grady was a computer whiz. Did he know how to find hidden files, even in backup? "Could the police retrieve deleted files, if they got to the computers in time?"

"If they had a hacker on staff."

"How good a hacker? Good as you?"

"Good as Marshall." He frowned. "She's gone, you know."

"Gone?"

"That's what I was coming to tell you. I went to ask her about her alibi, but she wasn't in. I called her house and one of her housemates said she didn't come home last night. She's disappeared."

SIXTEEN

By midmorning I ventured out of my office to see if Marshall had materialized. I'd been calling her and leaving messages, but no one picked up. I was conflicted about her disappearance so soon after Mark's murder. Either she was in trouble or it was a vanishing act. A lose-lose proposition. Could she be connected to Mark's murder? Did the cops know she was gone? It seemed inconceivable she was the killer, and I wasn't about to put her on the hook to get myself off.

I was hoping one of the associates knew where she was. I walked down the second floor hallway, avoiding the stare of another criminalist, and knocked on Renee Butler's door. "Renee? You in? It's Bennie."

The door opened after a moment, and Renee, in baggy jeans and a gray sweatshirt, stood there, appraising me with a cold eye. "What?"

"Do you know where Marshall is? I've been calling her, but there's no answer."

"No," she said. She turned without another word, went back to her desk, and sat down. I saw with dismay that the office had been almost completely emptied. Cardboard boxes were stacked on the floor and files and books were packed in shopping bags.

"I think we need to talk, don't you?" I gestured at the chair across from her desk, but she shook her head.

"No, I don't have anything to talk to you about. <u>Latorno</u> is almost done, I'm double-checking the cites. It'll be on your desk in an hour. My resignation will be with it. Today is my last day."

"Today?" I sat down anyway, in what was left of her office furniture. Only her altar to Denzel Washington was still standing, in the corner; a poster of the star in a muscle shirt, sloe-eyed, with fan magazine cutouts beside it. I'd initially been opposed to the display, but Renee's domestic abuse clients were tickled by it and they needed the levity. So did I, right now. "You sure you want to go, Renee?"

"Yes."

"What will you do?"

"Go solo. I'll work out of my house, starting in a week or two. There's room enough, it's right in town, and Eve doesn't mind." She smoothed back her hair, which was pressed into a stiff French twist and emphasized the heart shape of her face. Renee had pretty features, her skin as rich a brown as her eyes, and I never minded her extra weight.

"Why not stay? I'm working on keeping the firm. We could use you. *I* could use you." It was true. She was one of the smartest lawyers at R & B, her raw intelligence emerging despite a childhood in the projects and an education in the city schools.

"I don't care if there's a firm or not, I won't work with you. I know you killed Mark."

It fell like a blow. "No I didn't. Why do you think I'm the killer?"

She leaned forward. "You saw Mark leaving you and taking R & B with him. You loved him and the firm, and you saw them both slipping away. You had to stop it. And you're big enough and strong enough to do it, and you have no decent explanation for where you were at the time."

"That's all circumstantial. None of it proves anything. The cops haven't even charged me."

"Whether they ever do or not doesn't matter to me. I know you did it. I know how angry you are inside."

"What's that supposed to mean?"

She eased back into her chair. "What's the point? I told myself I wasn't going to talk about this with you, and I'm not. Our association is over. I dropped off those books you lent me. I told the cops what I knew."

"Told the cops what? What do you know? There's nothing to know!"

"I told them about that day we ran the steps at Franklin Field," she said, the conviction in her tone infuriating.

"What day? What did I do?"

"It's what you said."

"What I *said*? You trying to hang me for something I *said*? I hired you, brought you along, and now you're trying to hang me? Don't you know you're playing with my life?" I stood up and Renee stood up, too.

"I don't have to lie for you, just because you gave me a job!"

"What lie? What are you talking about?"

"Get out of my office! I don't need you in here, shouting at me."

I almost laughed, but it hurt too much. "No, Renee. I still

own this place. *You* get out. Put your papers on my desk. Be gone in an hour."

I walked out of her office, stalked down the hall, and went into my office and slammed the door. I stood there for a moment, shaken. What did Renee tell the cops? What was she talking about? All I remembered was I took her running once. She had started another diet and asked me for help. What happened at Franklin Field? I had to know.

I took a deep breath. There was one way to find out. Retrace my steps. Go for a run. I needed to manage my stress anyway. My head felt like it was going to burst, and I hadn't exercised since everything hit the fan. I changed quickly into the running shorts and top I kept in the office, shoved a ten-dollar bill and my keys into the little pocket in my pants, and left the townhouse by the back entrance, ignoring the reporters who'd discovered the back door.

"Any comment, Ms. Rosato?" "Did you do it?" "What about the will?" "Going for a run?" "Ms. Rosato, Ms. Rosato, please!" I sprinted off, leaving the reporters behind, and it wasn't until I'd turned the corner of the backstreet that I saw him.

Detective Azzic. He sat, smoking, in a dark blue car parked on Twenty-Second Street. He was barely hidden, so he must have wanted me to know he was watching. He expected me to run scared. On the contrary. I sprinted down the row of parked cars until I reached the unmarked Crown Vic.

"Hey, good lookin'," I said, popping into his open window. "What's your sign?"

"Leo the Lion." He stubbed his Merit out in an overflowing ashtray, his mouth a twisted line. "Once I dig in I don't let go."

"Sounds sexy. So, what time you get off?"

His eyes remained flinty through leftover smoke. "You think it's funny, Rosato?"

"No, I think it's harassment, Azzic. Don't you have anything better to do? Suspects to beat up? Bribes to take?"

"I'm just doin' some routine surveillance. Anytime you wanna come down to the division and talk, you can."

"Is this an invite? Will there be a cheese-ball? And are you gonna wear that weird tie?" I waved at his paisley Countess Mara.

"If you talk, I'll listen. Leave the Boy Wonder at home. I think you can handle it on your own. I was surprised to see you takin' orders, big-time lawyer like yourself."

I smiled. "You're trying to get my Irish up, Detective, but I'm not Irish. I think."

His broad shoulder dipped as he started the car's huge V-8. "You know, I used to wonder why lawyers like you do what you do. Now I just don't care."

"It's cops like you that keep me in business."

"Oh, we do it, that's it?" He snorted. "Not the murderers, the rapists, the critters whose money you take."

"You mean my clients? They have rights, the same as you. The right to an honest police force. The right to a fair trial. I never understood it better than I do now."

He gunned the breathy engine. "You know what your problem is, Rosato? There's no right or wrong for you. We can't get a confession because of you, we can't get a conviction because of you. You're on the TV, in the papers, explaining everything away. Me, I was a priest before I was a cop."

"I was a waitress before I was a lawyer. So what?"

"I know right from wrong."

"I see, this is God's law you're enforcing now. You got a

personal relationship with the Chief Justice in the sky. He picked you, out of all the weird ties."

Azzic shook his head. "You don't believe in God, do you, Rosato?"

"That's kind of personal," I said, to jerk his chain, but the answer was no. I stopped believing when I realized my mother lived a nightmare, every day of her life. Haunted, terrified, every single second.

"All right, don't answer, I don't give a damn. Here's how it is. I have twenty other cases on my desk, but this is the most important."

"Is it my perfume?"

"Let me tell you something, funny girl. National clearance rate for homicides is about sixty-five percent. My squad, we run at about seventy-seven. Me personally, I'm doing even better than that. You know what that means?"

"You got a C average? You'll never get into law school with that, pal."

"It means I'm on your ass, wherever you go, 'til the day I put you behind bars."

"Oh yeah? Then catch me if you can, Detective." I ducked out of the car and took off.

The engine roared as Azzic pulled away from the curb, but I darted across the street and bolted the wrong way up the block. In two one-way streets, up Spruce Street and Pine, I had lost the local constabulary and was running free.

One, two, three, breathe. One, two, three, breathe.

Franklin Field is a football stadium and running track at the eastern edge of Penn's campus, ringed by bleachers and a high, redbrick wall. I'd been running its steps once a week since college, to increase my wind and build strength for rowing. The electronic scoreboard was dark this time of year and the bristly Astroturf empty, but the steps were open for anyone crazy enough to run them.

One, two, three, breathe. I pounded from bleacher to bleacher, bench to bench. Straight up, at a fifty-degree grade. We called it running the steps, but running the steps would have been easy compared with running the benches, which were farther apart. I broke a sweat in the humidity of the hazy afternoon. Keep your knees high. One, two, three, breathe.

At the top were old wooden benches that had weathered to gray and splintered. Here and there a new plywood board had been installed, and heavy bolts, black with age and tarnish, stuck incongruously through the new wood. I played a game as I ran up the middle of the benches, sidestepping the bolts and letting my mind wander. It was the only way to remember. And I needed to remember.

One, two, three, breathe. Land on the balls of the feet. I raced up, my footsteps thundering as I reached the vertiginous heights of the stadium. I darted out of the sun and toward the airy top deck, under the painted iron rafters that supported the upper level of the stadium. It was breezy here, dark and cool. Still, up, up, up. Sweat poured down my forehead. My heart pumped like a piston. I'd run hard like this with Renee, that day. I tried to reconstruct it in my mind.

The sun is unseasonably hot. Renee is wearing a pair of navy gym shorts and a T-shirt that's too thick. She's sweating, her chest heavy, and a silver chain with a key bounces around her neck as she runs.

I landed on the top bench and stopped a minute, panting, then turned around and ran down again. One, two, three, down. Harder than it looked, going down, trying not to lose your balance a hundred feet from the ground, with your head dizzy from exertion. The bumpy tread on my sneakers gripped the wood of the bench and I bounded down, down, down, leaping from one bench to the next.

One, two, three, breathe. The lowest fifteen benches were of gaudy red and blue plastic, and I aimed for them headlong, past the wooden benches, down through to the plastic. When I reached the bottom I huffed just long enough to turn around again and start back up, an Ivy League Sisyphus.

One, two. I was breathing hard. Trying to maintain my rhythm. Trying to remember. Renee, at about thirty pounds overweight, isn't able to keep up. She stops and rests, huffing and puffing under the rafters at the top of the stadium. It's chilly there, cool as under the boardwalk. It feels private, too, almost secretive. She stops to catch her breath and I keep her company. We start talking.

I dashed up the red and blue benches and reached the wooden ones. There were numbers painted on them, white-stenciled; 2, 4, 6, 8. They were a blur then and they were becoming a blur now.

Renee's conversation turns from work to clothes to men. I *used to have a boyfriend,* she says. *But he threw me over.*

I charged up the steps, past the white smear of numbers, the sun prickly on my back and shoulders. One, two, three. Breathe, girl. There were thirty-one benches in all. Or thirty. I tried to count them but each time it came out different. My conversation with Renee came back to me in bits and pieces, like a radio signal piercing static.

Sounds familiar, I tell her. Our eyes meet and we both know I'm talking about Mark.

Told me to get out, just like that, in the middle of a snowstorm. And we were gonna buy a house together. We're sitting in the breezy shade under the rafters, our backs resting against the crumbly brick wall. *I wasn't so hurt, really. What I was most was angry. Damn, was I angry.*

Me, too, I say, thinking of Mark.

Remember. Think. I reached the top of the steps and stood in the shade, chest heaving, heart thumping. The wind swirled around me. My muscles tingled, my veins swelled with blood. I felt strong, good. I wanted to remember, I had to. I threw my arms out, stretching my fingers to the sky. Willing the memory to me, pulling it out of the blue.

I used to hope he'd die, like in a car accident, she tells me, with a naughty giggle. *Every day I'd read the obituaries and pray he'd be there.*

Really?

And every time I'd see that somebody younger than him died, I'd think, Damn. That was my chance. She snaps her fingers.

You should've just killed him, I say. *That's what I'd do. Why leave it to chance?* We both laugh out loud because we both know I'm kidding.

But it won't sound that way in the telling. To Azzic.

Or to the jury.

SEVENTEEN

Marshall's rowhouse was in a gentrified part of West Philly, not far from Franklin Field, with a gingerbread porch in three different Cape May colors. I knocked at the green-painted front door in my damp tank top and shorts, and the door finally opened. Tiny bells attached to the inside knob made a tinkling sound.

"What do you want?" said the woman who answered. She was a long-haired waif in a long, filmy skirt, who evidently shared Marshall's politics but not her sweetness.

"You must be one of Marshall's housemates. I'm—"

"I saw you on the news. You're Marshall's boss."

"Yes. She didn't come in to work today."

"I know that."

"I'd like to speak with her."

"She's not here."

"Where is she?"

Her only reply was a shrug, her shoulder bones protruding in the tie-dyed T-shirt.

"What's that mean? You don't know or you're not telling?"

"Look, what do you want?"

"I want you to give Marshall a message for me, it's important. Tell her I didn't do it. And tell her I hope she didn't either."

She slammed the door in my face, and the bells jingled madly.

I jogged back toward the office over the South Street bridge, running into the city at a time when everybody was leaving. Traffic snaked toward the Schuylkill Expressway. The sun hung low, burning orange behind my left shoulder. Drivers flipped down their visors as they reached the crest of the bridge.

I was breathing smoothly, thinking about Renee and Marshall. There was nothing I could do about Renee, and unfortunately, the same was true of Marshall. Apparently, she wasn't in danger, from her housemate's reaction. That left one possibility. Did Marshall have something to do with Mark's murder? She was the only one in the office who could navigate the depths of the computer system. Maybe she'd discovered Mark's hidden files. Or were there other cybersecrets, ones I didn't know about?

I loped up Lombard, going against the traffic, and turned down Twenty-Second Street, pounding past the Greek pizza place, a video store, and the fancier townhouses. I slowed to a walk when I neared the office, because of the commotion.

Squad cars lined the cross street, their red, white, and blue lights flashing a silent warning. Police sawhorses blocked off traffic, and cops blew whistles to keep the drivers moving. I felt wary, edgy. A crowd was gathering, and I strayed to its fringe, next to an old woman who stood squinting at the scene, her meaty arms folded over a sagging chest.

"What's going on?" I asked. "An accident?"

"Don't know 'xactly," she answered, peering at me through thick Woolworth's glasses. Her eyes, supermagnified, looked deranged. At her side stood a matted white mutt on a rope leash, with bluish cataracts over his eyes.

"Nice dog," I said. I like all dogs, even ugly ones.

"Name's Buster. He's blind."

"Blind? Does he bite?"

"No."

I bent over to scratch the dog's head, but he lunged at me with the two teeth he had left. "Hey! I thought you said he didn't bite."

"He nips, but he doesn't bite."

Sometimes I hate the city.

"The cops are lookin' for somebody," she said.

"Who?"

"Don't know. Just heard it myself. It was drugs. That's what caused the bombing."

"What bombing?"

"That man, that drug man. They done got him." She pushed up her glasses. "Put a bomb in his car, on account of the AIDS."

"*What?*"

"The AIDS. It was on the news."

"When?" Was it the CEO of Furstmann? Was it possible? "How?"

"They're looking for the lady who done it. That's what I heard."

"What lady?" Eileen? The cops already had her address.

"A terrorist done it. Works right down here, right here in Center City. A lady lawyer. They're gonna arrest her."

My throat caught. Lady lawyer. Lives and works in Philly.

It had to be me. What was going on? I felt stricken. I turned and hustled away from the police cars, my feet carrying me forward almost automatically. Where was I going? I didn't even know. Away. Out of the city, far from the cops.

I picked up the pace to a jog then accelerated to a nervous sprint. My heart thudded, my pulse raced. It wasn't exercise anymore, it was flight. I fled the city, away from the business district. Twilight descended as I ran, but I didn't stop until there were no more police cruisers and I was out of breath. I lurched into a graffitied phone booth with a busted light, panting hard. I slammed the door closed and punched in my credit card number with clumsy fingers.

"Wells," he said when he picked up.

"Grady, what is going on?" It would have been good to hear his voice, if I trusted him at all.

"Bennie! Bennie, where are you?" His tone was urgent. "The police are looking for you. They found a pair of scissors in your apartment, with blood on it. They tested it and it's Mark's. They say it's the murder weapon, Bennie. I have the arrest warrant in front of me."

"What?"

"Wait, it gets worse. They want to question you about another murder, the president of Furstmann Dunn."

"Oh, God. He was really killed?"

"A car bomb, in the driveway of his house. The cops know you met with the animal activists the other night. How do they know that?"

My mind clicked away. Azzic must've been following me, unless Grady was lying and he'd told them.

"Bennie, are you there? Are you all right? They think you're involved with his murder, too. Azzic picked up Eileen on your tip and she turned state's evidence. She told the cops you masterminded the bombing, then set her up to take the fall."

"That's ridiculous!"

"They have her confession, implicating you. Her boyfriend, Kleeb, is on the run. Azzic is downstairs right now. They want you to turn yourself in."

"But I didn't do it. I didn't do any of it!" It was crazy, and getting crazier.

"Then don't come in and don't say anything more. They're probably tracing the incoming calls, maybe even tapping the phones."

I thought fast. "Go to my office and get my briefcase. Meet me at midnight at my favorite place in the world. Make sure you're not followed. Got it?"

"Got it."

I hung up the phone, debating the wisdom of what I'd just done. I'd delivered myself to someone I had every reason to distrust, but I had no choice. Would Grady even be able to figure out what I meant? Could the cops trace the call? What was going on? Where was I, anyway? The streetlights were broken, it was dark on the street corner. Outside the phone booth was an abandoned store, with particle-board nailed over its windows and graffiti on top of that. I tried to find a street sign but they'd been harvested for scrap metal.

I had no idea what to do. I slumped against the wall of the dark booth, next to a jagged crack that ran the length of the plastic pane. I felt heartsick, drained. The CEO was dead because I'd let Eileen con me. Now she was setting me up, and so was someone else. I wondered if the cops had enough to charge me with a double murder. I had no alibi for the

CEO, I was running at the time. They'd ask for the death penalty, for sure.

I sank to the gritty floor of the booth and pulled my knees to my chest. I was half naked and chilled. I was the prime suspect in two murders I didn't commit, and somebody had planted a murder weapon in my apartment. My lawyer, my only link to the outside world, was a man I hardly trusted. Everything was falling apart, and I wasn't strong enough to keep it together. For the first time in my life, I felt helpless.

Stone, cold helpless.

EIGHTEEN

I kept an anxious eye out for squad cars, but there were none except the one that ordinarily cruised Kelly Drive, the winding road along the east bank of the Schuylkill River. Maybe the cops hadn't gotten the phone tap, not enough evidence or time, or maybe they were too dumb to figure out my favorite place in the world. Or maybe they were waiting, watching me, hidden. I scanned the riverbank, a bad feeling in the pit of my stomach.

It was a breezy night by the river and the wind off the water carried a misty chill. I shivered under a bush in the Azalea Garden, where I was masquerading as a runner at rest. It wasn't far from the truth and it was the perfect camouflage, since the asphalt paths on the river drives attracted in-line skaters and runners even at night.

I checked my watch: 11:30. Time to go. I picked up my small paper bag and rose slowly, my knees weak and stiff. I looked around for the cruiser, but the coast was clear.

I jogged lightly over crushed paper cups littering the path along Boathouse Row, the messy aftermath of a three-mile race. Brightly colored boathouses lined the row, and Penn's was in the middle. I reached its red door, made sure no one was watching, and punched in the combination that opened the door. I slipped in and shut the door behind me.

The entrance hall of the boathouse was roomy, unlit, and empty. There were two large windows to the street, so I didn't risk turning on a light. I didn't need to anyway, I knew the place by heart. Rowing photos covered the walls and an old green leather couch sat next to the door. To the left of the entrance hall was the huge room where the men's boats were housed; to the right was the women's annex, built later.

I plopped onto the couch and breathed in the familiar odors of axle grease, polished wood, and human sweat. I was safe, temporarily. It was my favorite place in the world. I rested my head back. On the wall behind me was a picture of myself in college in one of the first womens' crews; a young, strong, sunny blonde, standing next to an oar with a red-and-blue painted paddle. I knew without looking at the photo that I looked a lot better then than I did now. My eyes scanned the other photos in the faint light from the windows. Faded pictures of the men's and women's eights at various regattas, the crew holding trophies aloft or throwing their pint-sized coxswains into the water. It was a rowing tradition, like losing your T-shirt to the winners, a graphic lesson in public humiliation. Having lost not only my shirt but everything else by now, I was feeling it rather acutely.

I was wanted for two counts of murder. It would be all over the news. What would Hattie be thinking, and what about my mother? What would happen to them if I went to prison, or worse? I allowed myself ten more seconds of self-pity, then went upstairs with my paper bag to save my life.

* * *

"Bennie, is that you?" Grady whispered.

I grabbed him by the jacketsleeve and yanked him into the boathouse, closing the door behind him. "Of course it's me."

"But your hair, it's short."

"It's chin-length." I'd hacked it off with a scissors from the workshop in the boathouse.

"What happened to the color? I can't see, it's so dark in here. Is it black?"

"No, red. Bright Coppery Disguise Red." I ran a hand through my damp, newly colored locks. Between my dye job, hot shower, and clean clothes, I felt better, more in control. "It's L'Oréal, eight bucks at your local drugstore. Because I'm worth it."

"Isn't red kind of obvious for a disguise?"

"I'm six feet tall, Grady. I was born obvious. Besides, it would've taken two boxes to go from blond to black, and I'm not worth it. Now, did you bring the briefcase?"

"Here." He handed it to me. "Where'd you get the suit? Is it yellow? Isn't that kind of bright?"

"What are you, the fashion police? It's the only one I had in my locker." I unzipped my briefcase and squinted inside. Mark's computer calendars, Bill Kleeb's file, and a cell phone. I zipped it shut, too wary to feel grateful. Someone was framing me for Mark's murder, maybe it was him. "You should go now, counselor. Thanks for your help."

"What? I just got here. What are you going to do?"

"Don't know yet, I'll think of something." The way I figured it, I had to get out of town and find Bill Kleeb, but I wasn't going to tell Grady more than I had to. "You have to go, please."

"I want to help."

"I don't need help."

"Why are you acting so strange? Did you know about that CEO's death?"

I stepped back at the accusation. "Of course not. Did you tell the cops I met with my clients that night?"

"No. Azzic questioned me, but I claimed attorney-client privilege and they let me go."

Hmmm. "I don't like it. I would think they'd hold your feet to the fire."

"Me, too. I thought they let me go to see if I would lead them to you."

I froze. "And did you?"

"No, no. If they were following me, I lost them. I worked out a plan with my cousin. He came over, picked up my bike, and rode it to New Jersey. You can't tell us apart with a motorcycle helmet on. If they followed him, they're in Marlton by now."

Smart, if it was true. "Good. Thanks. Now would you go?"

"Why are you trying to get rid of me? I'm your lawyer. Let me lawyer."

"This isn't lawyering, this is aiding and abetting. You shouldn't be any more involved than you are."

He looked over my shoulder. "What's in here, anyway?"

"Boats, Harvard."

He walked past me and disappeared into the men's half of the boathouse. It was a huge room, long enough to accommodate two lengths of eights, on racks. Moonlight shone pale through the windows in the garage doors and glistened on the shellacked finish of the fiberglass sculls. Grady's white shirt picked up the light as he moved, but I couldn't make out what he was doing.

I stood rooted to the threshold, too nervous to follow. No

one knew we were here. He could kill me and no one would know. I'd slipped a screwdriver from the shop into my waist-band in the back, but didn't relish having to protect myself with it. "I want you to go, Grady," I called out, hoping my voice didn't betray how jittery I felt. "You're an accomplice after the fact."

"This is amazing," he said, his voice coming from the shad-ows. "The boats have names." My eyes adjusted to the gloom and I made out his tall outline next to the eights. He was run-ning his fingertips on the stenciling on one of the sleek boats.

"Yes, this is America. Now, show's over. Time to go."

"Stop being so jumpy, will you? There's no cops outside, I checked. Look at this. This one says, *Paul Madeira,*' and here's another, *Ernest Bollard IV.*' Who are they?"

"Rich white guys. Shouldn't you be leaving?"

"I've never been in a boathouse before. Why don't you show me around? Rowing is a big part of your life. I'd like to know more about it."

"There's nothing to see but boats, Grady. They're brown, they float in water. Boats galore. Nothing to see. Time to go."

"Show me or I won't tell you the surprise I brought you." He walked toward me, but I edged back into the entrance hall, keeping my distance.

"Surprise? I don't want any more surprises. I hate sur-prises."

"Then I'll show myself around. Lord." He brushed by me and crossed the entrance hall into the women's annex on the other side. "What's in here?" he called out. "More boats?"

"Girl boats."

"They pink?"

"They're lighter. Bye, now."

"You can be so rude. Do girl boats go as fast as boy boats?"

"If the right girl's rowing."

"Are you the right girl?"

"Aren't you leaving?" I felt for the screwdriver, but he turned quickly and almost caught me.

"Guess your surprise, then I'll leave. Here's a clue." He was grinning with an anticipation that looked genuine, at least in the dark.

"Grady, I don't feel like playing games. It's that murder suspect thing. No fun at all."

"Come on, take one guess. It's bigger than a bread box."

"Your ego?"

"Hardly. It's parked down the street, full of high octane."

"A car? You brought me a car?" My heart leapt up, then I doubted him again. "How did you know I'd need a car?"

"I knew you had to get out of town." He produced a silver key from his pocket and dangled it in the moonlight. "It's a brand new car."

"How'd you manage that?"

"It's my cousin's. I swapped it for the motorcycle. He's wanted to borrow it for a long time."

"Way to go." Despite my wariness, I snatched the key from his hand. "Now out with you." I pushed him toward the door, but he wouldn't budge.

"I want to go with you, Bennie."

"Out of the question."

"Why? Why should you go alone?"

"I like being alone."

"That's not it," he said firmly. "Something's bothering you. You're cold to me now, it's obvious. You don't trust me, do you?"

"What makes you say that?"

"It's because I lied to you about meeting Mark, isn't it? You don't have to say so, I know that's what it is. You found out I met with Mark from his calendar. I looked in the briefcase, Bennie, I know. I can tell you why I lied. Let me explain."

"I want you to go, Grady. I can't be any clearer about it." I stepped around him and headed for the door, but he caught my arm, startling me.

"I did meet with Mark. Two times. The first time he told me he was leaving the firm and he wanted me to go with him. He said I was the only associate he wanted to take besides Eve."

"What did you say?"

"I told him no. The second time I called him and we met at The Rittenhouse. I was trying to talk him out of it."

"Why?"

"Why do you think?"

"I have no idea," I said, though I had an inkling. I could sense it. Feel it coming in the increasing huskiness of Grady's voice and the way he was leaning toward me in the darkness.

"Because of you. I didn't want him to hurt you. I know how much the firm means to you."

I didn't say anything. I didn't know what to say. My throat was tight.

"Bennie, you can trust me. I'll never keep anything from you again, I swear it. I'd never hurt you, not for all the money in the world." In that second he reached into his jacket, and when his hand came out I saw the steely glint of a gun.

I gasped. My heart stopped. Grady was the killer. He was going to kill me. I reached for my screwdriver, but Grady grabbed my hand and slapped the gun into it.

"Here. It's yours. Keep it."

"What? How?" I looked down at the gun. It was a pistol with a cross-hatched handle, cold and heavy in my palm.

"It's for protection. The safety's on, but it's loaded. It's my gun from home. Shoot anything or anybody that tries to hurt you. If you won't let me protect you, then let it."

I couldn't process it all fast enough. A screwdriver was one thing, a gun quite another. I'd never held one that wasn't tagged as evidence, and even with an orange exhibit number they struck a dissonant note in me. I'd seen the damage guns did, how they tore at faces, heads, hearts. I handed the weapon back. "No, Grady. You keep it."

"Why?" He slipped the weapon into his jacket. "You're being silly."

"No I'm not. Besides, I have my trusty screwdriver." I drew it from the waistband of my shorts and held it up.

Grady laughed. "Aren't we the well-armed couple? But the screwdriver's not exactly effective at fifty yards." He took the tool and tossed it over his shoulder.

"Hey, yo! That's my protection."

"You don't need protection from me. If I were going to hurt you, would I have given you a gun?" he asked, stepping closer.

My mouth went dry. I felt exposed and vulnerable, and it had nothing to do with who had the loaded gun.

"Mark wasn't good enough for you, Bennie." Bitterness tainted his soft drawl. "He couldn't give, he could only take."

"I don't want to talk about Mark."

"I do, I want you to understand. You were too much in love to see him clearly. I always used to think, I wonder what it would be like to have that woman so in love with me. I wonder what that woman would be like." He leaned over and kissed me gently.

"Grady," I said. I pressed him back, but he didn't move.

"'Grady,' what? Why can't it be, because of Mark? Ask yourself, would he have come here? Would he have helped you?"

"Stop that."

"No. You ask yourself," he said urgently. "Did he ever, once, do a damn thing for you? Did he ever, once, do a thing to deserve your love?"

"We built the firm."

"That helped *him*, Bennie, and when he started to make money he cut you loose. He was your lover, but was he your friend? Did he help you with your mother?"

I felt a hot flush of shame, unreasoning. "How do you know about my mother?"

"I made it my business to know. I saw you come in late some mornings, I heard you on the phone with the doctors. I know she was in the hospital awhile back. But all through it, Mark stayed at the office. He never went with you. I would have been there. Why wasn't Mark? Why didn't he help?"

"I didn't need him to."

"Sure you did. All of us could see you looked tired. Stressed. Marshall and I picked it up right away."

"I never asked him to help."

"Why did he need to be asked? The need was obvious. He could have just done it. Showed up. Been there."

"It's not that easy," I started to say, but he interrupted, touching my shoulder.

"You know what I think about love, Bennie? I think it's more than a state of being. Not just a feeling, or something you say. It's what you do. If you love a woman, you love her every day, and you *do*. You do, for her. I love you, Bennie. I *do*. I swear."

I started to speak, but he took me in his arms and kissed me again, longer this time. His jacket was smooth under my fingers, his arms bulky in the light wool. His mouth felt warm and open, and I let his kiss wash over me, trying to feel it, test it. I couldn't remember being kissed or being held this way. It was an offer, not a demand, which made it suddenly compelling.

He slipped out of his jacket, and his body felt fully as strong as mine, stronger, because he was in love. He was telling me so by his kiss, by his embrace, by his hips pressing into mine, backing me onto the couch. I felt myself responding to him, because it felt as if he were giving me something, not taking. Giving me himself.

He lay me back against the couch, his mouth and body hard on mine, and I felt myself arch up to him. Giving back. I couldn't see him, but my other senses felt heightened. I ran my hand over the scratchiness of his chin, sensed his muscles straining under his shirt. I breathed in a trace of aftershave at his jaw, mingled with the musky sweatiness of his neck.

There was a metallic jingling of his belt, then a whispered curse as he fumbled with his zipper. My own breathing, low and excited. The sounds of my own need and his, there in the darkness.

In the middle of the night.

NINETEEN

I hit the road in the brightness just before dawn, streaking down the expressway in a brand-new Juicyfruit-yellow Chevy Camaro. Not exactly inconspicuous, but between my red hair and gold suit, we weren't into subtlety on the lam. The car's vanity license plate read JAMIE-16, the front seat was littered with grunge rock CDs, and a banana-shaped deodorizer swung like a pendulum from the rearview mirror. BANAN-AROMA, it said, and smelled it.

I was running from the cops and heading to western Pennsylvania to find Bill Kleeb. I'd reread his file while Grady slept, then showered and tried to call Bill on my cell phone. No one had answered, and I'd given up. The police would subpoena my cell phone records, and I didn't want them to know who I was trying to reach. They'd be looking for Bill, too, and at the same time I was.

I glanced anxiously in the rearview. No cops in sight and not much traffic. It was too early for commuters, who would be heading into the city anyway, not out of it. I switched lanes under a cloudy sky, going as fast as I dared. The car rumbled smoothly as the virgin tires met the expressway.

In the back of my mind were my mother and Hattie. When could I call them? Had Hattie set up the electroshock? How could I help her now? I was leaving them, maybe for a long time. I checked the rearview again. The city was far behind, the skyline shrouded in gray clouds.

I thought about Grady, asleep with my note on his chest. *I'll call when I can. Take care.* Not very romantic, but I didn't know how I felt about him and I didn't want to say more. It was no time to start a meaningful relationship. Meetings between bulletproof glass didn't appeal to me, no matter how heart-wringing in miniseries prison.

I put Grady out of my mind, brushed back my carroty bangs, and trounced on the gas. I drove for two hours, sped past Harrisburg, then headed west through the fields through to Altoona in the mountainous middle of the state, and jumped off the main road. There were a few roadside bars, truck stops, and produce stands that reminded me of how hungry I was, but I didn't want to waste time eating. I passed a series of Toro dealers, then a shack selling cement lawn statuary with a hand-lettered sign: GIVE CONCRETE—THE GIFT THAT LASTS A LIFETIME. Whoa.

I drove for hours on two- and one-lane roads, then end-lessly around loops and detours until I found the bumpy route I hoped led to Bill's hometown. I got lost twice in a maze of dusty backroads that crisscrossed fields of corn and spinach. I couldn't orient myself in the fresh air and vegetables, I needed smog and Dumpsters.

I hung a left at the apples, a right at the blueberries, and finally reached the dirt road to the Kleeb farm. It said THE ZOELLERS on the mailbox, but the address was the one in

Bill's file. I pulled over next to a cornfield and cut the ignition.

I opened the window and waited for half an hour, watching tensely for any activity. Cops, press, anybody. There seemed to be none but I waited longer. The sky grew opaque with clouds, the air thickened with humidity. It soured the fresh smells of the farmland and brought up the stink of the assorted manures. Still I kept the window open, preferring it to the fruity stench of the bananamobile. I wished I had a hot coffee. It sucked, being a fugitive.

The farmhouse was a clapboard ranch, freshly painted white, and prosperous looking. Behind it to the left were two late-model pickups, a stone and clapboard barn, and a silo. Horses grazed freely on a large, grassy hill, their long necks dipping gracefully. It looked idyllic to a city girl raised by a crazy mother. The only hills I saw growing up were made of Kleenex.

I checked my watch. 12:15. If the press were coming, they would've been here already. I got out and stretched with my briefcase in hand, leaving the car hidden in the cornrows. I wanted to look more lawyer than lawbreaker, and the bananamobile wasn't exactly standard-issue with a J.D.

I had to get Bill's parents to trust me. All I would need was a little luck.

And a lot of coffee.

"God, this is good," I slurped. It was my second cup.

"Thank you," said Mrs. Kleeb—Mrs. Zoeller since her remarriage. Her face was round and soft, floating like a motherly balloon over her pink sweatsuit outfit. She had wavy hair that matched Bill's reddish shade, but it had thinned and gone gray at the roots.

"I mean it, this is one terrific cup of coffee." I caught Mr. Zoeller looking strangely at me over his white Nittany Lions mug.

"So you really are Bill's attorney," Mrs. Zoeller said. She sounded like she believed it, now that I'd told them the whole story. Mr. Zoeller, who sat next to her at the dining room table, hadn't said anything during my pitch, except for asking to see my credentials and my file on Bill. He glanced at the mug shot of Bill's injured face coldly, and I got the impression he wouldn't mind if his young stepson went to prison for life.

I set my cup down. "Yes, I really am Bill's lawyer, despite my new hair color."

"You did a nice job," Mrs. Zoeller said, nodding.

"Thank you. Who says I can't cook?"

She smiled. "You really don't act like an attorney, or at least the attorneys I've seen. On the TV, I mean."

"Ellie, honestly," Mr. Zoeller said, and a flustered Mrs. Zoeller placed her hand over mine.

"Oh, I mean that as a compliment of course. Of course."

"My wife's always runnin' off at the mouth like that," Mr. Zoeller said with a frown. He was a large man, so beefy his striped polo shirt rode up his arm past his sunburn. "She doesn't mean anything by it."

"I took it as a compliment. Forget it."

Mrs. Zoeller blushed slightly. "It's just that I don't like that other lawyer Bill got, the new one. Celeste. He keeps calling us on the phone, wantin' us to sign something for some book or something."

"A release," Mr. Zoeller said. "He wants us to sign a release."

Mrs. Zoeller shook her head. "I don't think he has Bill's interests at heart. He's seeing dollar signs. Now, Bill did tell me about you. He said there was no way you could have murdered anybody."

"It's true."

"He told me he trusted you. I think he really likes you."

I felt touched. "I like him, too. He's a nice kid, but he's in way over his head."

"I know, I know." Mrs. Zoeller ran her fingernails across her forehead, leaving a tiny red wake. "It's all because of Eileen. I warned him about her. First time I met that girl, I said to Gus, 'She's half crazy, I swear.' Didn't I say that, Gus?"

Mr. Zoeller didn't reply, but continued staring at my attorney's card for the Pennsylvania bar. What could be so interesting? Supreme Court ID No. 35417?

Mrs. Zoeller kept shaking her head. "I tried to tell him, but he fell so in love with her you couldn't tell him anything. Thought she was so smart and exciting. Sophisticated, I guess. He couldn't see what was right in front of him. That's just the way he is. The way he's always been."

I nodded, identifying.

"And that girl has some history, I'll tell you. He knew all about it, but he ignored it."

"Mrs. Zoeller, I can help Bill if you let me. Tell me where he is. I know he's not responsible for the murder of that CEO."

She frowned. "Oh, I mean, I don't know. What do you think, Gus?"

He didn't answer, but switched the focus of his attention from my bar card to the white doily at the center of the table. Silence fell, and I became suddenly aware of a loud grandfather clock in the corner. *Tick, tick, tick.*

"Mrs. Zoeller," I said, "I know it's hard for you to trust me with Bill's life, but you have no choice. I'm the only one who can clear him."

"He's the only one who can clear you," Mr. Zoeller countered gruffly.

"Fair enough, I need Bill as much as he needs me. But that doesn't change the fact that he needs me. I'm the only one who can prove the murder of the CEO was Eileen's idea. If she did it without him, as I'm sure she did, I may be able to get his charges dropped or at least get him a plea bargain."

"How can you do that?" Mrs. Zoeller asked, arching a delicate eyebrow. "You're hiding."

"I know plenty of criminal lawyers. I'll get your son the best one I know and tell them he's telling the truth. I can help Bill without showing myself."

"What if they put him on trial for murder?" Her voice began to tremble slightly. "Won't you have to be there and testify?"

"By then I'll have this thing over with. I have a life to get back to, and a mother of my own." It was a corny touch, but I wasn't above it. Not with the stakes this high.

"Oh my. Your mother, too." Mrs. Zoeller's hand flew to her chest. "She must be so worried about you."

"Worried sick." Sick, sick, sick.

Tick, tick, tick.

"Mrs. Zoeller, you can trust me. I believe in what I do. I believe in the law, whether you're rich or poor or cop or bad guy. And that's enough with the speech."

She smiled cautiously, then looked at her taciturn husband. "Gus, what do you think? Do you think you should take Bennie to see Bill?"

Eeek. "No, wait, Mrs. Zoeller. Tell me where Bill is and I'll go alone." I didn't want Mr. Warmth anywhere near his stepson. Unless I missed my guess, he was half the reason for Bill's acting out.

"Why? It's far from here and hard to find. You said you got lost finding us."

Think fast. "The police might be surveilling you and Mr. Zoeller. They know your car, but they don't know mine. You don't want to lead them to Bill, do you? Tell me where he is. I'll go alone."

She looked at Mr. Zoeller, who looked at his fingernails. "Gus? Should I?"

He turned his fist over, making her wait.

Tick, tick, tick.

"Gus?" she asked again, and it occurred to me there are many forms of domestic abuse. "Honey?"

"Up to you. He's your son."

She turned back to me. "More coffee, dear?"

"I'd love some," I said.

And she smiled.

Tick.

TWENTY

I got back in the bananamobile with my written directions and Mrs. Zoeller's homemade map. Bill was holed up in a cabin his uncle owned and kept for hunting. The Zoellers thought it was untraceable to them and also that Bill hadn't told Eileen about it. I wasn't so sure. I had to believe Eileen knew about it, and had maybe even been there. A young man and a young girl, not shacking up in a shack? This was still America, wasn't it?

I studied the map. The cabin was at the godforsaken frontier of the state, probably seven hours north of here and as far west as Pittsburgh. I needed gas, food, and more coffee. I ended up getting it at a minimart far from the Zoellers' farm, in case there were any cops around.

"Nice car, Jamie," said the teenaged attendant, who also sold me two bloated hot dogs.

"Jamie?"

"Your license plate."

"Oh. Right." I kept my head down, hurried back to the car, and took off.

I drove through tunnels blasted out of stony mountains and around corkscrew highways carved into grassy hills. It began to rain, and I sped by strip mall after wet strip mall. By the time I had gulped down the hot dogs and terrible coffee it was the worst storm the radio disc jockey had ever seen. Thunder rumbled in the western sky and my stomach rumbled, too, but not from the provisions. Finally I couldn't stand it anymore and made a call on my cell phone.

"Is she okay?" I asked, when Hattie picked up.

"What? Bennie? Is that you?"

"Yes. Is she okay?" Gray rainwater pounded on the windshield. Between the storm and the static, we could barely hear each other.

"She's fine! Fine!"

"When does she have the ECT?" The signal broke completely, and I waited for the crackling to subside.

"—Saturday morning, eleven o'clock! Bennie? You there? You okay?"

More crackling. It was maddening. When it stopped I yelled, "Why so soon? Can't it wait until I'm there?"

"You worry about yourself! Your momma's fine!"

"Make them wait, Hattie! You can't do it alone!"

"She can't wait!" she shouted, before the signal broke for the last time.

It was inconceivable that cops had followed me here, I couldn't have followed myself here. I was utterly and completely lost. I sat in the bananamobile with the ignition off and the car light on. Rain pelted the roof, and I turned the homemade map this way and that. As best I could tell, I was in the middle of the woods, in the dark, in a thunderstorm.

There were no streetlights in the magic forest because

there were no streets, just skinny, unmarked roads that snaked through the woods. I'd passed a nature preserve an hour ago, but since then the roads meandered around forgotten ponds and alongside endless stretches of trees. Trees were even less help than corn, and they all looked the same. Brown with green at the top. I wished for a match.

I grabbed the Keystone AAA map I'd found in the glove box and held it next to Mrs. Zoeller's map. I would've called her if not for the cell phone records. I didn't want to leave a paper trail, especially one consistent with the cops' theory of me as Eileen and Bill's accomplice. Besides, I should be able to figure this out myself. I stared at one map, then the other. Damn. I should be close.

Screw it. I felt like I was close; I'd rather drive around and find it. I threw the maps on the mustardy hot dog wrappers, snapped off the light, and slammed the car into reverse. When I clicked on the high beams, they shone on a tiny sign through the trees. 149. What? I rubbed a hole in the foggy windshield with the side of my hand. 149 Cogan Road. That was it! The cabin!

I turned off the ignition and climbed out of the car, covering myself with an Eddie Vedder CD. Rain spattered through the tree branches and onto my suit. I tramped through the underbrush in leather pumps, finding my way in the darkness with an outstretched hand. If I planned ahead I would've kept the headlights on, but if I planned ahead I wouldn't be wanted for a double murder.

Light shone like a yellow square from the cabin through the trees, guiding me as I trudged on. Luckily there were no creepy animal noises. I like my wildlife on leashes, with faces you can kiss. I picked up the pace and bumped into a branch, pouring rainwater onto my padded shoulder.

Damn. I stepped over a fallen log, shoes soggy and shrinking at the toe. I was in sight of the cabin, but could make out only its outline. The block of light looked bigger, closer. I slogged through mud and wet leaves and in ten minutes arrived at a clearing. There it was. The cabin. It was made of wood, weathered and ramshackle, and stood one story tall and barely twenty-five feet wide.

My heart lifted. I would see Bill and get to the bottom of this. I went to the door, also of wood and bearing a Z brace it clearly needed. I stepped on the ratty doormat and knocked.

"Bill?" I called softly, too paranoid to shout even in Timbuktu. There was no answer.

"It's Bennie. Let me in." I knocked again, louder this time. Again, no answer.

"Your mom sent me. I want to help you." I reached for the doorknob, but there wasn't one, just a metal latch and hook that had rusted years ago. I gathered security wasn't an issue up here in the wholesomeness.

I pressed open the door. Suddenly, something clawed at my ankle. "Aaah!" I yelped. I flailed and shook it off. The CD clattered to the ground.

"Miaow!" came a thin, high screech, and I looked down. Cowering in the yellow slice of light from the room was a tan kitten with a spiny back. I swallowed hard, picked up the kitten, and told my heart to stop pounding. I went through the door and inside the cabin.

"Bill, look what the cat dragged in," I called out, but there wasn't a sound except for the rain's patter on the roof. I stood motionless in the living room, which was empty and still. It contained a tattered couch, a lamp with a dim bulb, and a spartan galley kitchen. Hunting fatigues hung on an industrial rack against the wall. There was no TV, phone, or radio. Bill was nowhere in sight. Nobody was. Nothing looked out of order, but I was getting the creeps.

"Miaow?" The kitten jumped from my arms, her tail curled like a question mark.

"Don't ask me, cat."

The kitten padded into a dark adjoining room I presumed was the bedroom. I followed, edgy, and groped on the bedroom wall for a light switch.

I flicked it on and gasped. The sight was horrifying. There, stretched out on the bed in shorts and a T-shirt, was Bill.

Dead.

TWENTY-ONE

Bill's eyes were wide open in a face that looked frozen, and his skin had the unmistakable gray-white of a corpse. Blood caked in a parched river from his nose and dried over his child's freckles, staining his shirt brown and soaking stiff a shabby plaid bedspread. I couldn't believe my eyes, even as they moved down his body.

A twisted pink balloon was wrapped around his upper arm like a tourniquet. It was jarringly out of place, cheery and bright, next to a lethal syringe still stuck in the crook of his arm. The balloon was still taut, so Bill's forearm was the only part of his body that had blood in it. It was red and grotesquely swollen to the size of a club, rendering his fingers shapeless and puffy. Lying beside him on the bed was a plastic Baggie.

I backed against the bedroom door. My eyes smarted but I couldn't look away. Bill, on drugs? An overdose? Was it possible?

"Miaow?" asked the kitten. It had jumped to the bed and was futilely rubbing against Bill's too-pale leg.

Bill hadn't been the type to do drugs. Had he just become

despondent, or made a mistake? Maybe whatever happened with Eileen and the CEO had set him off. I remembered Mrs. Zoeller. Bill was her only child. If only I'd gotten here sooner. If only I hadn't gotten lost.

Why had he died?

I forced my brain to function. I flashed on Bill at the stationhouse, his arms flabby and white in his jumpsuit. Weren't his arms clean when I saw them? I'd had a client, a former heroin addict, and he'd showed me his arms once. They were so bumpy with scar tissue they looked like Amtrak's eastern corridor.

"Miaow?" said the cat, pacing back and forth on the bed.

I fought back my emotions and leaned over Bill's body, catching a scent of blood and feces. His arms lay stiff at his sides, and I squinted at them. No needle tracks on either one. It didn't make sense. Was it the first time Bill had tried heroin? How likely was that? What about Eileen, did she have something to do with this? Who else did Bill know?

"Miaow!"

I looked around the bedroom. There was a bare night table and a cheap dresser with some paperbacks on top, next to an Ace comb. There was no sign to reveal what had happened. Beyond the dresser was the bathroom, and I crossed to it and peered inside. A tube of toothpaste and one of Clearasil sat on the tiny, dirty sink. There was no medicine chest, just a toilet and an old frameless mirror, its silvering wrinkled.

I faced the bedroom and poor Bill's body on the bed. My heart felt heavy, my chest tight. From all outward appearances, he had sat at the end of the bed, mixed himself his first hit of heroin, then flopped backwards, dead of an overdose.

"Miaow! Miaow!"

"Oh, shut up," I shouted at the animal, instantly regretting it. It was Bill's, after all. I picked it up from the bed. It felt frail and bony, but I found myself hugging it. It gave more comfort than I expected, or knew I needed. I took one last look at Bill and a fruitless look around the cabin, then retrieved the CD and left.

I struggled back through the woods with the kitten's flimsy claws stuck in my suit. Rain drenched us until I finally got a bead on the glow-in-the-dark Camaro. I headed toward it herky-jerky, confused and distracted, thinking about Bill. I'd have to call Mrs. Zoeller. To hell with my cell phone records, her son was dead. I dreaded how she'd take the news. I reached the car, pried the kitten off, and dialed the Zoellers.

"Murderer!" she screamed, as soon as I told her.

"What?" I asked, stunned.

"*Murderer!*" It came out like a scream of anguish.

"No—"

"You killed him! Bill? Bill? Oh God, Bill!"

"No, wait. I didn't kill him, nobody killed him. He overdosed, I saw the needle!"

"Overdosed? Bill never took drugs a day in his life! Never! You killed him and made it look like he did drugs!"

"No! He must have—"

"Never! With a needle? Never!" She burst into sobs. "Bill fainted . . . when he saw blood, all his life! They couldn't . . . put anything in his arm without him lying down first, even the school nurse!"

My heart stopped in the cold, dark car. She was confirming something I hadn't allowed myself to suspect. Mark murdered and now Bill? Where did the CEO fit in? I felt sick inside.

"His stepfather always called him a . . . sissy on account of it, but he wasn't! He wasn't! You killed him! You said you were going to help him but you went up there to . . . to . . . kill him!"

"Mrs. Zoeller, why would I do that? It makes no sense!"

"Bill knew you killed that company president! He was gonna tell the police . . . and you killed him! Gus? Gus, call the police! Call 911!"

I hung up the phone, my hand shaking. I slammed the car key into the ignition and roared out of there.

I had to get away. Fast. Faster. I careened through the woods, tearing up the road I hoped led out. My high beams swung in an arc on wet tree trunks as I took the curves. In time the dirt and rocks under my tires turned to asphalt and I was rolling. Out of the woods. Gone. The rearview was clear and the hammer to the floor.

The next few hours were a dark blur of rain and fear as I sped down the slick highway. I watched the rearview for cops, trying to wrap my mind around what I'd seen and heard. Bill fainted at the sight of blood and there were no needle tracks in his arms. It was a murder set up to look like an overdose. Who had done it? Was it connected to Mark? I sensed it was, but didn't know how. It made me more determined than ever to find out what was going on.

I clicked on the car radio for the news. Would they announce the murder? They didn't have enough to charge me with, did they? I accelerated despite the yellow caution signs. I knew where I was going, I had decided almost as soon as I started the car. I'd felt out of place the whole time I'd been out west. The country, the woods, inland. I got lost out here. I didn't fit in, with my tailored suit and pumps. I was out of my element, a rower out of water.

I needed to get back to Philly. It was the most risky place

for me, but it was also the only place I had any leverage. I'd lived there all my life. Knew its neighborhoods, its ways, its accents. I could disappear there, I knew how. What place is more anonymous than a city? What person more forgettable than a lawyer in a suit?

Going where the weather suits my clothes. I drove into the night and the storm and the fear, Midnight Cowboy with an attitude.

TWENTY-TWO

It was 6:15, Friday morning. I had driven all night.

I took inventory in the underground parking garage of the Silver Bullet building. My hair, suit, and shoes were dry. I had a briefcase, a cell phone, and a kitten. Also a master plan.

I fingercombed my new hair, threw on some eye makeup, and grabbed my phone and briefcase. "Wish me luck," I said to the kitten, who didn't. I shut and locked the car door.

6:20. I knew the rhythms of the Silver Bullet from my days at Groan & Waste. The security guard would be at the desk upstairs, his shift started at six o'clock. I reached the elevator bank and punched the up button. I'd have to stop at the lobby floor and sign in, since the elevators didn't go all the way up. The guard would be the first test of my redheaded persona.

I stepped into the elevator and when it let me out I took a deep breath and entered the lobby like I was sleepwalking, which wasn't much of a stretch.

"Miss!" called the guard. A young black man with handsome features, he was sitting behind the front desk.

"Yes?" I turned in character, looking confused, exhausted, and beleaguered. In other words, the typical oppressed associate in a major law firm.

"You have to sign the book." He waved at a notebook on the desk.

"Oh, sorry." I walked over and dragged my heels loudly on the white marble floor. The desk was also of white marble and surrounded the guard like a corporate cavern. On the cave walls were the scratchings of modern man: flickering security screens and a computer directory for the building. I wouldn't be on it; I'd have to fix that when I got upstairs. "I'm not awake yet," I said sleepily. "Got a pen?"

"Sure." He handed me a ballpoint, smiling easily. "I'm with you on that. TGIF." His red uniform looked boxy on his shoulders and his hat was too big for his head.

"I'm working way too hard lately," I said, stalling with the pen in hand. I needed a name. Damn.

"Where you work? Grun?" His nametag said Will Clermont, and next to him on the desk was a folded *Daily News* and a covered cup of coffee. It smelled like hazelnut. Ah, civilization.

"Yeah, I work at Grun. How'd you know?"

"Everybody there works too hard." He laughed again, and I sensed he was lonely on this gray morning, happy to have even a lawyer to talk to. It served my purpose just fine. I needed information.

"How come I never saw you before, Mr. Clermont? You must work the early shift."

"Yeah. Call me Will."

"So you're out by three, huh, Will? Banker's hours."

"You got that right. Gets me home in time to see my girl,

my Oprah. She's too skinny now, but I like that lady, I sure do."

I shook my head. "Three o'clock, you're lucky. I leave late, so I know the night guys. The nice one, what's his name again?"

"You mean Dave?"

"Dave, right. I forget his last name."

"Ricklin."

"He's comes on at three, right? He's nice."

Will's dark eyes lit up. "You just like Dave 'cause he's tall, like you."

I made a mental note. "Hah, I could kick his butt, no matter how tall he is. Him and the other one, you know him?"

"Jimmy? Black guy, kinda heavy?"

"Right. Heavy."

"Not too heavy."

Whoops. "Not to you. You think Oprah's too thin."

"She is! She looked better before. I would tell Stedman, marry that girl, she's lookin' good!" He pushed the notebook toward me. "Say now, don't forget to sign in."

"Sure." As soon as I think of a name. I took a closer look at the tabloid. LAWYER ON THE LOOSE! screamed the headline. My throat caught. Underneath it said, EXCLUSIVE INTERVIEWS INSIDE, BY LARRY FROST. I lowered my head and scribbled into the book, then stepped away from the desk to the elevator bank. "Well, I'd better get going. See you."

"Stay 'wake now," he said. He was trying to read my entry when the elevator arrived.

I scooted in and hit the button, but felt uneasy even after the doors closed. I was in the news, probably with a photo, but

I'd passed the first test despite it and collected the names of the security guards. Maybe my plan would work. I geared up for the next step as the elevator whisked me silently toward Grun.

The doors opened with a hydraulic *swoosh* onto 32, the Loser Floor. Every big firm has a Loser Floor. It's where you find the low-wattage lawyers who attract lint more easily than clients and spend way too much time with their families. At Grun, the losers lived on the same floor as the conference rooms and were viewed as equally productive.

I looked around the empty offices and for the first time the Loser Floor seemed like heaven to me, not corporate hell. It was deserted, with everything mine for the taking. None of the losers were in this early, being losers, so I borrowed an office, a computer, and an office directory, and went to work. Or rather, Linda Frost did.

She found Grun's New York office in the directory and picked out the people she needed. Then she wrote a memo to the personnel office in Philadelphia, informing them that a new associate, one Linda Frost, would be arriving from the New York office this Friday to prepare for trial in a very important securities matter, <u>RMC v. Consolidated Computers</u>. The memo requested Personnel to issue Ms. Frost a Grun ID card, a building pass, and a set of keys, and also to list her on the computer directory in the building's lobby. Given the traditional close communication between Grun's Philly headquarters and its branch offices, it would take Personnel two or three years to catch on.

For good measure, Ms. Frost backdated the memo to last week, printed it, and stuck it in a confidential interoffice envelope. Then she stomped on it, crumpled it up, and ripped off an edge to make it look lost in the interoffice mail before she set it in the nearest out-box. It would produce the desired effect as soon as it reached Personnel, which would hop to, since it'd apparently screwed up. Again.

Next, Ms. Frost typed a memo to the billing department, requesting a client code and matter number for <u>RMC v. Consolidated Computers</u>. She opened the matter as a "transfer" from the New York office so that it wouldn't be flagged by the New Client Committee, set up to screen out those wannabe clients who couldn't afford to be gouged by Grun. In addition, the industrious Ms. Frost wrote a memo to the facilities department, reserving Conference Room D on the 32nd floor for "the foreseeable future" for her exclusive use on the above-captioned confidential securities matter.

Finally, she fired off a note to the supplies department, ordering a computer and office supplies be sent to Conference Room D for use in trial preparation, and sent a separate note to the kitchen, requesting that a sandwich be sent up every day at noon, with a Diet Coke and a carton of whole milk, such meals to be billed to <u>RMC v. Consolidated Computers</u>.

I sent the last memos by e-mail, so that in a nanosecond, I would have a new identity, an office, and a job. An entirely new life and citizenship. True, it was temporary, valid only within the Silver Bullet, like a corporate green card. But for the time being, I was hiding in plain sight.

But wait, a loose end. I sat back in the Loser Chair and thought for a minute. Other lawyers might become curious about the redhead in the conference room. Maybe they'd inquire, even stop by. No lawyer is an island. Hmmm. I called up a blank screen and tapped out under today's date:

TO: All GRUN PARTNERS and ASSOCIATES
FROM: LINDA FROST
RE: HELP!

I am an associate from the New York office presently in Conference Room D on the 32nd floor, working on <u>RMC v. Consolidated Computers,</u> a massive securities matter with extensive document work. Although the case is dry and somewhat technical, I would appreciate some help, as trial is in two weeks in the Middle District of Pennsylvania. I cannot promise your time would be billable, since this client is extremely touchy about its bills. Anyone wishing to lend a hand in this difficult case should feel free to stop by at any time.

Perfect. It would send any lawyer worth his billings screaming in the opposite direction. I'd be dead and petrified before I'd see a partner or an associate from this firm. They'd slip the food under the damn door, like I carried Ebola. I hit the SEND button on the e-mail menu, feeling a swell of satisfaction.

I was back in business.

TWENTY-THREE

I spent the morning in Conference Room D, working and watching wage slaves bring me a computer, a phone, and office supplies. I thanked them enough to be polite but not memorable. Between their visits, I studied Mark's file, which was spread out at the far end of the conference table, shielded from view by a bunker of dead files from one of the other conference rooms. I kept the door closed, so the room was soundproofed against the losers trundling in at nine o'clock. Didn't they know the day was half over by then?

My best friend Sam Freminet would have arrived at work bright and early. He would already be at his glass runway, billing time in his office just floors above me, on the polar opposite of the Loser Floor, the Gold Coast. The Gold Coast was home to Grun's heavy hitters, rainmakers, movers and megashakers: the offices of high-density department heads and Executive Committee members, not to mention the throneroom of The Great and Powerful. Pay no attention to that man behind the client.

I scanned the computer printouts of Mark's checkbook

and found two additional cash payments to Sam Freminet, for one thousand each, in the months before Mark was killed. The midday sun edged onto the papers, but I wasn't distracted. I was wondering why Sam, he of Gold Coast and gold card, had taken cash payments from Mark. *Sam?*

I powered up my new computer and fiddled around until I remembered how to find the New Matter Reports, the listing of the new cases opened each month. The New Matter Reports were supposedly put on the computer to alert the partners to possible conflicts of interest, but the real reason was so they could say, LOOK AT THE BUSINESS I'M BRINGING IN! I'M PAYING FOR YOU, CHUMP! And of course, the time-honored, MINE REALLY IS BIGGER THAN YOURS. YOU'RE GONNA NEED A CRANE FOR THIS MOTHER.

I selected number 4 from the menu.

SEARCH WHICH ATTORNEY? said the computer.

I tapped out Sam Freminet.

SEARCHING FOR NEW MATTERS OPENED BY MR. FREMINET, said the computer. PLEASE WAIT.

"Sure," I replied, just to have someone to talk to. I thought of Grady, but pushed that thought away, and fast. There was no contacting him. The cops had to be watching, maybe tapping his phone. Then I thought of my mother. Dare I call?

THE INFORMATION YOU REQUESTED IS ALMOST READY. PLEASE WAIT.

I half expected to hear a little *ca-ching.* Maybe the screen would turn green.

HERE IS THE INFORMATION YOU REQUESTED. IT IS CON-FIDENTIAL AND SHOULD NOT BE RELEASED TO THIRD PAR-

TIES WITHOUT THE EXPRESS WRITTEN APPROVAL OF THE
EXECUTIVE COMMITTEE.

"Kiss my ass," I said, skimming the long roster of Sam's
new matters. Twenty-one corporate bankruptcies: Rugel In-
dustries, Lafayette Snacks, Inc., Zaldicor Medical, Quaker
Realty Trust, Genezone, Ltd., Atlantic Partners. Apparently
solid, certifiable, and marked Approved, meaning they had
passed the New Matter Committee. New business, each one
a transfusion of fresh whole blood, keeping alive the body
corporate. Sam was doing great. Why did he need cash from
Mark? By the same token, why would he care about the executor's fee?

Maybe the clients weren't paying, or couldn't. They were
bankrupts, after all. Or maybe Sam's receivables were low,
and The Great and Powerful was withholding his distribution
check. I needed more information, namely Sam's monthly billings and his partnership distribution record.

I clicked around the computer menus, looking for the billing information, but no soap. It was computerized, but I'd
never seen it because it was hidden. Associates couldn't ac-
cess those menus, Grun being as free with information as the
Kremlin. So my first task was to convince the computer I was
a partner, preferably Sam, since it was his information I was
after. To do it I'd have to guess his password. I thought a minute and typed in:

DAFFY DUCK.

WRONG PASSWORD, said the computer.

I tried: FOGHORN LEGHORN.

WRONG PASSWORD.

SYLVESTER THE CAT.

WRONG PASSWORD.

"Sufferin' succotash," I said, and got busier.

Half an hour later, I still hadn't hit the password. Luckily there was no limit on attempts, because I'd gone through every Looney Tune I could dredge up, then tried TV characters I knew Sam loved: Gilligan, Little Buddy, Maynard G. Krebs. Jeannie, Master, Major Nelson. Lucy, Ethel, Little Ricky. Still, no show.

A woman from Grun's kitchen brought me a tuna fish sandwich when I was in my rock 'n' roll phase. Jerry Garcia, Bootsie, RuPaul. John Tesh, for a wild card. I gobbled half of the sandwich as I segued into show tunes. Rodgers, Hammerstein, Andrew Lloyd Webber. I had high hopes for Stephen Sondheim, but washed out.

If I saw *wrong password* one more time I'd scream. I felt rammy, cooped up. It was the golden retriever in me, I needed exercise. I stretched and walked around the conference table, then lapped it. I jogged to the window. I raised the Levelors and lowered them again. I was running in place when there was a sudden knock at the door, which gave me enough time to scramble back to my chair. "Come in!"

"Ms. Frost?" said a young messenger. "This is from Personnel." He handed me the envelope, sniffing the air. "What's that smell?"

"What smell?"

"Kinda like a gym?"

"Tuna fish," I said, waving him gently out of my lair. I opened the envelope and spilled its contents onto the conference table, where they slid out like precious emeralds and rubies. A Grun ID, a building pass, and a set of keys to the firm. Beautiful. Plus a LEXIS/NEXIS card. Good, it would get me online. I could read the newspapers on the computer and see how close the cops were to nailing me. It had been at the back of my mind all through the musicals.

I plopped down in my chair and typed in my new LEXIS number. Then I went into NEXIS, popped in Rosato, and limited the search to the past week, which is when I got really famous.

YOUR REQUEST HAS FOUND 345 STORIES, said the computer.

"Terrific," I mumbled, and punched up the first one, which would be the most recent. The headline told it all: FUGITIVE LAWYER SUSPECTED IN THIRD DEATH.

I read it, then the stories that followed. RADICAL LAWYER ON KILLING SPREE. WOMAN ON THE RUN. There were interviews with "highly placed sources in the police department," but they didn't tell me more than I already knew about the cops' efforts to find me. No mention of sightings, no quotes attributed to Azzic. The party line was the same: she can run, but she can't hide. Oh yeah?

I hit a key for the next story.

AND THEY ALL CAME TUMBLING DOWN, read the headline. The byline was Larry Frost, my long-lost cousin, and his story was a collection of interviews with R & B associates. A quote from "Rosato associate" Renee Butler, who said she felt "betrayed" by me. Bob Wingate "just wanted to forget about it" and was conducting an unsuccessful job search. Eve Eberlein was unavailable for comment but was reportedly preparing the defense of the Wellroth trial. Jennifer Rowlands had landed a job with another Philly firm. In a sidebar, SILVER LINING IN CLOUD OVER LAW FIRM, Jeff Jacobs and Amy Fletcher announced their engagement.

I hit the button and the next story appeared. Its headline caught me up short.

MEMORIAL SERVICE
TODAY FOR ATTORNEY

A memorial service was held at the Ethical So-
ciety today for Mark Biscardi, Esq., Center City
resident and named partner in the law firm of
Rosato & Biscardi. The service and the following
interment were attended by many of the attorney's clients and friends, and was organized by
Eve Eberlein, Esq., an associate in the firm. A eu-
logy was given by Sam Freminet, Esq., of Grun &
Chase.

I leaned back as if a weight had pushed me there. Mark
was gone, really gone. I'd even missed his funeral. I fell into
a fugue state, thinking about him, then what Grady said that
night in the boathouse. Turning it over and over. Had Mark really loved me? Did Grady?

My heart ached. I sat staring at the story on the computer until the monitor was the brightest light in the room, a
modern-day beacon. I checked my watch. 7:45.

The floor sounded quiet, all the losers had gone home. The
cleaning ladies made their rounds about 8:00, but the sign I
put on the door would have warded them off. It would be safe
enough to go out at this hour, especially on a Friday night. I
had lots of questions I couldn't answer from a chair.

But first things first. I stood up, uncramped my legs, and
turned off the computer. Then grabbed what I needed and
ventured out of Conference Room D.

* * *

It turns out you can use an in-box for a litter box. Fill it with machine-shredded legal briefs, add one kitten, and there you have it. A Martha Stewart Moment. I sat contented in the front seat of the bananamobile as my little tan furball scratched through the spaghetti of citations. It was an improvement over her using the car for a litter box, or Grun lawyers using their briefs for anything else.

Afterwards, the kitten batted a morsel of tuna fish around the front seat, ignoring my attempts to get her to eat it or drink the milk I'd brought her. I petted her as she played, and she looked up at me with that delicate triangle of a face. China blue eyes, spongy pink nose. She was cute even though she wasn't a golden retriever, and she deserved a name.

"How about Sylvester the Cat?" I asked her.

She blinked. Wrong password.

"Gilligan? Little Buddy?"

She looked bored, then climbed onto my lap, curling into a clump.

"Samantha? Endora? Tabitha?" I didn't even know if the kitten was a boy or girl. I picked her up and was finding out when I heard a sharp rap on the car window, next to my ear.

I turned, startled, and found myself eye-level with a nightstick. A gun in a black holster. Round chrome handcuffs hanging from a thick belt. I felt a bolt of fear and looked up, into the shiny badge of a Philadelphia policeman.

TWENTY-FOUR

Out of the car, Miss," the cop said.

My heart stopped. I had no choice. I flashed on the women's prison. Then on my mother, lost. I held on to the cat and opened the car door.

"That's her! That's the one!" said an old woman behind him. She was strange-looking, with penciled-in eyebrows and lipstick crimson as Gloria Swanson's. She had an oddly receding hairline, with platinum-white hair covered by a white hairnet. She pointed at me with a bony finger that ended in a scarlet-lacquered nail. "She's the one, with the red hair!"

The cop waved her off with a large hand and focused on me with a grave expression. "I have a few questions for you, Miss."

"Yes, Officer." My heart began to pound. I scanned his ruddy face, but it wasn't one I'd sued. Stay calm, I told myself. Think Linda Frost.

"This your car?"

"Yes."

"I told you, she's the one!" said the old lady, louder.

"You have a registration card for it?"

"It's in my office upstairs."

"Your driver's license?"

"It's upstairs, too. I can get it if you want." If he let me go, I'd run for my life.

"That won't be necessary. What's your name?"

"Linda Frost." I tucked the kitten under my arm, dug into my blazer pocket for my ID, and handed it to him as casually as possible. "I work in this building, for Grun & Chase. I'm a lawyer."

The old lady clawed at the cop's uniform. "She did it, Officer! Arrest her before she gets away!"

My gut tensed as the cop studied my Grun ID. "Your name's Linda?"

"Yes."

"Then who's Jamie?"

"Jamie?"

"The license plate says Jamie 16, and you say it's your car. If your name is Linda, then who's Jamie?"

Oh-oh. "Uh, the cat?"

"You named the car after the cat?" he asked slowly.

"Sure. Yes. Why not?" Indeed.

"Arrest her! Arrest her!" squawked the old woman, shrill as a parrot.

The cop winced at the sound. "But it's a young cat, a kitten. How'd you get the license plate so fast?"

"All my cats are named Jamie. Jamie 16 died, so I got this little kitten, Jamie 17. I transferred the license plate to my new car."

He blinked in disbelief. "You have *seventeen* cats?"

"No, not at the same time. In a row. When one Jamie dies, I get another Jamie."

"You've had seventeen cats in your lifetime? How old are

you?" The cop looked honestly confused, and I didn't blame him. God, I was a bad liar. Most lawyers are much better liars than me.

"No, Officer. See, I started with Jamie 15, because fifteen is my lucky number. Isn't she cute? I love all my Jamies." I held up the squirming cat like a trophy.

"Stop that!" screeched the old woman. "That's not how you hold a kitten, for heaven's sake!" Suddenly she lunged forward and plucked the cat from my arms.

"Yo!" I blurted out. "What do you think you're doing?"

The woman stepped behind the cop, her spiky nails locked around the kitten like an iron maiden. "You kept her in the car all day! You didn't take proper care of her. If I hadn't called the police, she'd be dead!"

So that's where the cop came from. "No, the cat was fine. It's not hot down here. I left the window open a crack."

"You don't keep a baby like this in a car all day long!"

"It's not a baby, it's a cat."

"It's a *kitten*!"

"So what?" You could leave a golden retriever in a garage all day, no problem. Everything is okay with a golden. "It's none of your business anyway."

"It is too!"

"What are you, the pet police?" I was angry. Meddling bitch. "Now give me my cat."

"No." She stepped farther behind the cop, hugging the kitten. "It's mine now! I'm keeping it!"

"You are not!" I made a move for the cat, but the cop pressed us apart.

"Ladies, please," he said wearily. "Miss Frost, did you leave the cat in the car?"

"Yes, but—"

"That wasn't a good idea. There was another woman who complained about the mewing, besides Mrs. Harrogate here. The security guard was looking for you, because of it."

Terrific. KITTEN LEADS TO KILLER. FELINE FINDS FUGITIVE. "I'm sorry. I didn't think I'd be so long upstairs. I went to pick up a file from my office and got held up on the phone."

"That's a lie!" screeched the old woman. "This poor baby was crying all afternoon! I got here at three o'clock to see my lawyer. The kitten was crying when I went in and she was still crying when I came out. You're not fit to have this kitten!"

"I am too!"

"You are not! And it's stupid to name all your cats the same thing!"

"*Stop!*" thundered the cop, holding up both hands. "Enough!"

We were scared into silence, me more than she, since I had a little more to lose. That death penalty thing and all.

"Now, let's settle this," the cop said. "Miss Frost, there are laws on the books against cruelty to animals. Ordinances. You did leave the cat in the car all afternoon. Maybe if you let Mrs. Harrogate keep the cat like she says, we can all go home."

I felt a mixture of resentment and relief. I was almost off the hook. The cop was ready to leave. I would be safe again.

"She'd have a better home with me," clucked the woman. "I'd take good care of her."

The cop put his hands on his hips. "Come on, Miss Frost, I don't have all night here. Why don't you give Mrs. Harrogate the cat? She says she'll take good care of it. You, being a lawyer, you must work long hours. What do you say?"

"Let me think," I said, but I knew it made sense. I was on the run, I couldn't keep a cat. What kind of outlaw has a pet? I looked at the kitten in the woman's embrace. It wasn't mine anyway.

"Well, Miss Frost?" The cop checked his watch, and I made the only decision I could.

"Gimme back my cat," I said.

I stuck Jamie 17 under my blazer and smuggled her into the elevator. When the doors opened onto the lobby, I waved hello to the two night guards behind the desk. "Hey, Dave," I called out. "How's it goin', Jimmy?"

"Hey back at you!" said Dave, grinning, and Jimmy waved back vaguely as I strode to the other elevator bank. I was inside before they could figure out how they knew me.

I got off on the Loser Floor and dropped Jamie 17 at the conference room, where I made her a new litter box and poured some Diet Coke into a paperclip holder for her. Then I closed the door, straightened the Confidential sign, and left. I had some sleuthing to do.

I took the elevator to the Gold Coast and waited in the ritzy reception area as the doors *swooshed* closed behind me. It looked as empty as I'd expected, but I listened to make sure it was absolutely still. There was no sound in the hallway. Not a phone, not a fax, not even a *ca-ching*. All the heavy hitters were out at the restaurants, the orchestra, or a baseball game; anyplace you could conceivably take a General Counsel and bill his company for it. Not only would they expense the duck à l'orange, they'd charge for the time they took to eat it. Turn down that second cup of decaf, it'll cost you $350.

I took a left and snuck down the corridor, grabbing a legal

pad from one of the secretary's desks, the better to look official if caught. I slunk past the patchwork quilts and pastel landscapes, glancing in the offices to make sure they were vacant. The offices were massive because Gold Coast egos demanded lots of square footage, and each office was decorated with whatever fetish appealed to its resident ego. I skulked past a flock of duck decoys and a half-dozen fake Fabergé eggs, then tiptoed by a flotilla of model sailboats and a secret stash of Glenfiddich until I got to Wile E. Coyote and Tweety Bird.

The door was open and Sam's office was empty. I took a quick look behind me, then slipped inside and closed the door. I needed Sam's billing records, and if I couldn't get them from the computer, I'd get them this way. If there was ever an unreasonable search and seizure, this was it, but I had to find out who killed Mark.

I set the legal pad down and walked past Sam's desk to the sleek walnut credenza behind it. Plush versions of Daffy Duck, Porky Pig, and Elmer Fudd sat atop the credenza. Its polished surface reflected their fixed expressions.

"Don't look, guys, I'm hunting wabbits."

I opened the top drawer. Inside were case files in alphabetical order: Asbec Commercial Realty, Atlantic Partners, Inc., Aural Devices, Ltd. Most of them were bankruptcies, and only two estates matters. I looked under Biscardi, for Mark, but there was no file. Had Sam taken Mark's file home? Is that where Sam kept his billing files?

I closed the drawer and opened the one underneath it. More of same. Bankruptcies, a few estates. One tax matter. No billing information and no Biscardi file.

Damn. I straightened up, thinking. Outside the windows, long ribbons of mercury vapor streetlights led down Market

Street to the train station and the Schuylkill River beyond. I couldn't think about rowing now. I had to ransack my best friend's desk.

I turned around and went through the papers next to Daffy Duck on the glass desktop. There were message slips and correspondence, Daffy pens and carrot pencils, but no billing sheets. I turned and looked around the office.

There was one cabinet left, next to the black leather couch against the wall. It was walnut, too, a smaller version of the credenza. In front of it flopped a king-sized version of yet another cartoon character. I crossed the room, moved aside the toy, and dug into the top drawers. Correspondence files.

I closed it and opened the second drawer. Son of correspondence files.

I tried the third. Beyond correspondence files. This was in the nowhere fast category. I closed the drawer, sat cross-legged on the dense carpet, and thought a minute. Billable time records are a Grun attorney's most personal papers. Maybe Sam didn't keep them in hard copy at all, but had them shredded. Or maybe he had them at home. I tried to remember where Sam kept the files in his apartment, but I hadn't been there in over a year, lately we'd met at restaurants.

My gaze fell on the giant plush toy and I returned it to its home in front of the cabinet. Its huge eyes scowled at me from under the brim of an oversized Stetson, and I righted its redder-than-red handlebar mustache. Its cloth mitts held six-guns. I never liked Yosemite Sam.

What?

Of course! Yosemite Sam! I'd forgotten him. I ran to the computer on Sam's desk, called up the menu, and punched it in.

HERE IS THE BILLING INFORMATION YOU REQUESTED, said the computer.

"Dagnabbit!" I whispered, scrolling the first page, then the next and the one after that. Lists and lists of bills sent and payments received, lots of money flowing into Grun, all for Sam's account. He was squeezing the last dollar out of those bankrupts, to the tune of $50,000 a month in billings. Yosemite Sam was doing just fine. In fact, he had to be one of the most productive pardners in the firm. So why did he take money from Mark, and in cash?

I still had no answer. I got out of the computer file and sat back, which was when I spotted something on Sam's desk. I moved aside the papers and stared at the Steuben bowl. It was full of paperclips, Bugs Bunny thumbtacks, and rubber bands. But there was something else. Something I'd missed before. I dug in the bowl to the flash of color and fished it out. It wiggled between my thumb and forefinger like a pink worm.

A skinny pink balloon. The same kind and color I'd seen on Bill's arm in the cabin. I felt my mouth go dry. What did it mean?

I gaped at the bowl. A patch of green rubber stuck out, and I fished that balloon out, too. Then a yellow balloon and another pink, a red, and a bright blue, until they were scattered across the desk like so much lethal confetti. I stood shocked in the quiet of my friend's office. Trying to fathom how Sam could be connected to Bill's death. It didn't seem possible, but I was holding the link in my hand.

I thrust the pink balloon in my jacket pocket, replaced the others, then slipped out and broke for the Coast.

TWENTY-FIVE

I grabbed a late-night shower in the firm's locker room after my discovery. The pink balloon was uppermost in my mind, but I couldn't complete the connection between Bill and Sam, if there was one. My brain was too tired. The hot water made it worse, enervating me.

How much had I slept in the past few days? I gave up trying to count as I toweled off and dressed, then lay down on the single bed in the room's so-called rest area. I set my runner's watch for 5:00 A.M., but despite my fatigue I was barely dozing when the beep sounded. I was seeing pink balloons in a nightmare birthday party.

I let myself into the firm's kitchen for muddy coffee and an early morning bagel. Sam's connection to Bill's death nagged at me, though I had a more mundane problem. I had nothing to wear. I'd worn the yellow linen suit two days in a row and it was starting to look like an accordion, and smell worse. By Monday, even the losers would begin to wonder.

So at nine o'clock, coffee and half-eaten bagel before me, I was back in my conference room, on the phone to a personal shopper at a local department store, masquerading as busy lawyer Linda Frost. I ordered clothes and shoes to be delivered ASAP to Grun & Chase and even gave the shopper my proxy to pick what she called some "happening" suits.

After I hung up, I typed a memo to Accounting, instructing that a check be drafted payable to the store, the amount to be billed to <u>RMC v. Consolidated Computers</u> for "assorted business gifts." The clothes would be paid for as soon as they arrived, and I'd be happening. Then I grabbed Jamie 17 and left.

I was safe on the Loser Floor, since no losers worked on Saturdays, but once I left the floor it would be duck season. I stuffed Jamie 17 in my purse, scooted under the security gate that came down on the weekends, and punched the button for the elevator. I hopped in as soon as it opened, feeling nervous and exposed, even inside.

I could be recognized by the security guards downstairs or maybe a new guy on the weekend crew. I could be spotted by someone on the street who'd seen my picture in the paper. And what about the cops? Would any be in the vicinity, in the parking garage?

I was running a risk, but I had to. I fumbled in my purse for my sunglasses and slipped them on.

Nowhere to go but down.

I slunk low in the driver's seat of the bananamobile, waiting across the street from the city hospital. Gargoyles grimaced from its granite facade, but I gathered they didn't recognize me in my sunglasses. My mother's appointment wasn't for an hour or so, but I wanted to make sure she wasn't being surveilled.

"Right, Jamie 17?"

The kitten only purred in response, fast asleep in my lap. A miracle, considering she'd lapped up half a can of Diet Coke. Poor thing should have been flying on caffeine by now, or her tiny stalagmite-teeth should have dropped out. It was sad, I was turning out to be a bad mother. I stroked her and waited for my own.

They pulled up exactly on time in a Yellow cab. Hattie got out first; a bright spot of orange hair, then turquoise pants with a white scoop-neck shirt. She held out a palm, and my mother moved slowly into the light of day.

She looked up at the sky when she emerged, her mouth agape with wonder and confusion. She was so frail, a wraith in a housedress and sneakers. Hattie gathered her up in strong arms and practically lifted her up the gray steps into the hospital's entrance, where they disappeared from view.

I sat in a sort of shock. Hattie had been right. My mother had been dying right before my eyes, but I hadn't seen it. I fought the urge to follow them and forced myself to watch for the cops. I waited and waited. No squad cars, no unmarked Crown Vic.

Still I waited, stalled in a memory. It's Thanksgiving dinner at my uncle's, at a time when the family is still in touch. All of us are seated around the steaming turkey and lasagna, all except my mother. She's marching in the living room in a tight circle, banging a Kleenex box on her thigh, a madwoman in protest. *It's getting late, it's getting late,* she says over and over, but they all ignore it. All of them around the table, happily passing the Chianti and the broccoli rabe, a bustling Italian holiday over the heaping plates.

Except one of us is dancing with the Kleenex.

And the people around the table, they keep chattering and passing the food as if nothing is happening. Her voice grows louder, *it's getting late, it's getting late, it'sgettinglate,* but they just talk louder, shouting over the clamor she makes. Meantime, I'm gagging on this wonderful meal, so I put down my fork and go to her, bundle her in her wool muffler and coat, and call us a cab. I want her out of there. I'm not old enough to drive, but I'm old enough to know that these people, the ones pretending everything is fine, are even crazier than she is. They have a choice my mother doesn't, and they choose insanity.

I shook it off, got out of the bananamobile, and crossed the street to the hospital. Out in public, smack in the middle of the city. For the first time in days I wasn't worried about myself, I had someone else to worry about. It was a relief, in a funny way. I reached the hospital steps, stuck out my tongue at the gargoyle, and went in.

I found Hattie sitting in a chair in a waiting area which was otherwise empty, and took a seat two chairs over. "You like cats, lady?" I asked her, deepening my voice.

"Yes."

"You want one?" I opened my purse and showed her Jamie 17.

"Bennie, where'd you get that cat?" she said, eyes wide.

I laughed, even more surprised than she. "How'd you know who I was?"

"I'd know who you were no matter what kinda wig and glasses you got on. Now put that damn cat away. What are you doin', bringin' a cat in a hospital?"

"What do you think, I'd leave it in a car?" I took off my sunglasses and stuck them in my purse next to Jamie 17.

"How the hell you been?" Hattie said. She leaned over and gave me a hug redolent of talcum powder and singed hair. "I knew you'd come, you're so crazy." She released me, shaking her head.

"Don't worry, I'm fine. Where's Mom? Do they have her?" I craned my neck to see down the hall.

"She's in, the doctor just took her. Not her normal doctor, another one."

"Why not the normal one?"

"A different one does the treatments on the weekend. I didn't want to wait 'til Monday, when her doctor could do it." Hattie checked her watch, a thin, gold-toned Timex that choked her chubby wrist. "They had to give her a physical again, to check her out. It'll be a while before they start the treatment. The doctor will come out and tell us."

"Was she scared?"

"What do you think? She's scared of air."

I swallowed hard. "Did she fight you?"

"No. Good as gold, after I told her she had to go. That you said it was okay."

My heart sank. "Did she ask where I was?"

"I told her you were at work. So where you been stayin'?"

"If I tell you, I'll have to kill you," I said, but she didn't laugh.

"That detective, the big one, he's been over lookin' for you. Wantin' to know all about you. When you came, when you went."

"What'd you tell him?"

"What you think? Nuthin'. I didn't tell him nuthin'. Throwed that man right out."

"Good for you. You didn't tell him about Mom?"

"Said she was sick, from a flu. I didn't want him knowin' about her. But he's lookin' for you, all right."

"He has to catch me first, and I have this kitten for protection. He better watch out. We're bad."

"Well, I'm worried about you. I'm worried."

"Don't worry."

She frowned deeply. "It's my business if I want to worry. My business. Bennie, these cops, they ain't playin' no games."

"I know. They're no fun at all."

"What you gonna do? You can't keep hidin' forever."

I told her the short form of the story, and she listened the careful way she always did, which made me think more clearly. Something was telling me the link was Yosemite Sam. Suddenly a door opened down the hospital corridor and a short-haired woman in a dress-length white jacket came out and strode toward us.

"That's her. That's the doctor," Hattie said, and we both stood up. I tucked my purse behind me, with Jamie 17 in it.

"How is she?" I asked the doctor, as she approached. Stitched in red curlicues onto her coat was DR. TERESA HOGAN; her face was pinched and stern. I guess you toughen up when you electrocute people for a living.

"Who are you?" Dr. Hogan asked me.

Whoops. "Uh, me?"

"She's my daughter," Hattie blurted out, and I looked at her in astonishment. It was a good lie except for the obvious.

The doctor blinked. "I'm not sure I understand."

I cleared my throat. "My father was white, doctor. Not that it's any of your business."

"Excuse me." Barely flustered, she addressed Hattie. "We're ready to begin. The notes in Mrs. Rosato's file indicate you requested to be present during the procedure."

"No!" Hattie shook her head. "Not me! Nu-uh."

It had been my request, raised when the treatment was theoretical. Now that it was at hand, I wasn't sure I could go through with it.

Dr. Hogan nodded. "Good, because I would never have consented to this for one of my cases. It's unnecessary and there's no telling how a spectator might react."

I made up my mind. If I could sanction it, I could watch it. "I was the one who made the request, Doctor. I'd like to be there."

"You?" Her eyebrows arched. "You're not even immediate family."

"I'm very close to Mrs. Rosato. I'm her lawyer."

"I doubt she'll need her lawyer in a hospital."

"Come now, everybody in a hospital needs a lawyer."

She folded her arms. "I don't find that amusing."

"I wasn't kidding. I'll be right in."

Dr. Hogan whirled around on her heel, coat flying like a pinwheel, and I passed the purse with Jamie 17 to Hattie, smooth as a quarterback sneak. I caught up with the white coat midway down the hall and chased it through a door whose RECOVERY ROOM sign almost swung closed into my nose.

I entered a large room, lined with patients apparently resting after surgery. They lay in steel hospital beds in various stages of drugged sleep. Most of them were older, and I found myself wishing my mother were one of them. They had illnesses you could cure. Tumors you could excise, wounds you could suture. They didn't know how lucky they were.

"Step inside, please," Dr. Hogan said, as she pushed open a wide door off the recovery room.

I followed her into the room and stopped, riveted, on the

threshold. At its center was my mother, lying motionless on a gurney in a blue hospital gown. An oxygen mask covered her face, an IV flowed into her arm, and a blood pressure cuff was wrapped around her leg above the ankle. She was fastened by electrodes to a blue machine that spit out a thin strip of green graph paper, apparently monitoring her vital signs. I wanted to scoop her up and run like hell.

"Are you coming in?" Dr. Hogan said.

"Yes. Sorry." I stepped inside and shut the door.

"You can return to the waiting area if this is going to be too difficult for you. I assure you, we can continue without you."

"No, thanks." My stomach felt tight and my knees loose as I glanced around the small room. It felt cold, painted a chilly blue. The air smelled of chemicals and on the wall were wire racks of bottles and medicines. Two other doctors stood at my mother's head, men whose white coats said they were from the anesthesia department.

"Gentlemen," Dr. Hogan said, addressing them, "this is Mrs. Rosato's attorney, who feels the need to be here for the procedure."

"Hello," said one of the doctors, and I nodded back as he took the oxygen mask off my mother's face. It left a pinkish ring, limning her features like a death mask.

Dr. Hogan bent over and injected something into the IV line. "Let's get started, gentlemen."

"What are you giving her?" I asked.

"Atropine."

"What's that?"

"It dries up her secretions, keeping her airways clear. It also prevents the heart from slowing, the so-called vagal faint."

I tried not to faint myself, and watched Dr. Hogan check the monitor, then fix another syringe and inject that into the IV. "What's that?"

Dr. Hogan straightened up, her forehead wrinkled with annoyance. "Methohexital. A fast-acting anesthetic. It's standard procedure in every hospital."

"Why does she need it?"

"It will make her comfortable, obviously. Now, with your permission, may I continue?"

I didn't press it. Only doctors perceive a question as a challenge to authority, and obviously a woman doctor could be as arrogant as a man. It didn't matter anyway, only one thing mattered. I walked to the gurney and took my mother's hand, cool, blue-veined, and knobby.

Dr. Hogan touched my mother's eyelid, tickling it. "In case you're wondering, I'm doing this to confirm that the drug has taken effect. The eyelid is loose, so it has." She glanced at the monitors again, then prepared another syringe and injected it. "This is succinylcholine. It's a muscle relaxant, to prevent convulsions."

"But I thought we wanted convulsions." I squeezed my mother's hand, more for my comfort than hers.

"It's a paralyzing agent," offered the anesthesiologist who had greeted me. "It causes paralysis, so the body doesn't injure itself during the treatment."

Some things are better not to know. I looked at my mother, rapidly becoming paralyzed before my eyes. She lay very still, then suddenly a wave-like twitching spread throughout the muscles in her tiny body. "What's happening? What's the matter?" I said, panicky, hanging on to her hand.

"It's perfectly normal," Dr. Hogan said. "It will stop in a

minute. It shows the drug is working. Now please step away from the patient."

I gave my mother's hand a final squeeze and edged backward. What happened next was so quick and so awful I perceived it only as a horrible blur of motion and purpose.

The anesthesiologists strapped a rubber headband around my mother's forehead. Dr. Hogan plugged a heavy gray wire into the blue machine to her left. At the end of the gray wire was a black plastic handle. On the top of the handle was a bright red button. I knew what this had to be. I felt like my heart would seize.

An anesthesiologist wedged a brown rubber mouthguard between my mother's lips. Dr. Hogan squirted gel out of a white tube onto the crown of her head and called, "clear the table." She bent over my mother's head as one of the anesthesiologists touched a flashing button on the machine. It blinked green as a traffic light. Go. But I was thinking, Stop. Stop this. Stop right now. Don't you dare.

Dr. Hogan pressed the black thing onto my mother's head, then depressed the red button and held it there for a second.

Instantly my mother grimaced against the mouthguard, her features contorted. I felt my own face contort in unison. No, stop. You have no right. *I* have no right.

"The seizure will only last a minute," somebody said, sounding far away.

I couldn't help but watch. I couldn't help at all. The current ended and the seizure began. My mother's body lay rigid, but under the blood pressure cuff her foot jerked and twitched. It was sickening. It was appalling. It reminded me of the tourniquet balloon on Bill's arm. I blurted out, "Is that supposed to happen? Her foot, I mean?"

"Yes. It's a tonic clonic reaction," the anesthesiologist said. "The cuff prevents the muscle relaxant from reaching the foot, and we can watch the progress of the seizure. It'll only last a minute. She's fine."

But it was my mother, not his, and she was in the throes of a medical maelstrom. A tempest in her brain, in her body. I wanted to cry. I wanted to scream. I couldn't believe it was the right thing to do and it was too late to do anything about it.

"It'll be over before you know it," he was saying.

And it was, mercifully. Just when I thought I would rip off the electrodes, the twitching in her foot ceased. Her entire body lay still. The seizure was over. She seemed at rest.

I took what felt like my first breath. My stomach would not stay put. Call the cops, haul me off to jail, none of it could shake me the way this had.

"She'll sleep now," Dr. Hogan said. "She'll sleep for maybe half an hour. When she wakes up she may have a headache, like a hangover. Her jaw may hurt. She may be confused or disoriented."

I fumbled for words. "Can I do anything for her, to make her—"

"No. Just let her rest." Dr. Hogan squinted at the graph paper coming out of the machine. The black line spiked like the Rockies. "It was a good seizure."

A good seizure? My gorge rose and I fled the room.

TWENTY-SIX

I was still queasy and upset, but I had a job to do. I stuffed two pieces of Trident into my mouth to chase the bile from my teeth and tried to push the horror of what I'd done to my mother from my mind. I didn't care if it cured her, at this point I was just relieved it hadn't killed her.

I slipped on my sunglasses and drove down Pine Street in the bananamobile. Stately colonial rowhouses stood on either side, many of which bore the black cast-iron plaque of the National Register of Historic Places. But I wasn't sightseeing, I was trying to keep my eye on a license plate that said LOONEY1.

I wove through the city traffic, stalking my dearest friend. There was no justification for this second breach of Sam's civil liberties, except, like my mother, necessity. I had to find out about that pink balloon.

Sam steered his red Porsche Carrera left onto Sixteenth Street, without using his blinker. Men never use their blinkers, women do; that's all I'll say about it. I took a quick left, almost hitting a pedestrian foolhardy enough to walk her cockapoo through my surveillance, and slowed as we came to the light.

The Porsche turned the corner, then pulled up in front of The Harvest restaurant, letting out a passenger. A young man, dressed in a waiter's white shirt and black bow tie. Sam's Cuban alibi. The door closed with an over-priced *ta-chock* and the car pulled away.

I followed, expecting Sam to drive back to his apartment building, but the Porsche went right on Eighteenth, headed for the Vine Street Expressway, then took the highway to I-95. Odd. I punched up the bridge of my heavy sunglasses and tailed him, checking the rearview mirror to make sure no one was tailing me.

"Miaow," said Jamie 17. She looked up from her meal, a Snickers bar I'd found on the car floor and broken into pieces.

"What do you want?" I asked, but she paced back and forth in the front seat, jostling slightly as the car took the bumps in the road. I pressed her ridged back, but she refused to lie down. "Be good or Mommy won't take you on stakeout."

"Miaow," she insisted, and I was hoping it wasn't the bathroom again. Her last mission had stunk up the in-box, and I'd had to scoop the stuff into my makeup kit and throw it out the window so I wouldn't asphyxiate.

We drove up I-95 north, me and Jamie 17 behind Sam, through endless stretches of billboards into the ugly industrial sections of Philly. Huge, empty warehouses stood crumbling, their windows punched out. The highway signs were covered with graffiti. Hattie had lived here for a time, and it was hard to imagine her growing up on any mean streets, because she was so kind. She'd even volunteered to take Jamie 17, but I knew she'd have her hands full with my mother.

"Miaow!"

"Please." I picked her up and set her on my lap, almost

driving right past the Carrera in the process. Sam had turned off I-95 and was heading down the off-ramp from the highway, running parallel to me. I wrenched the car onto the shoulder and came to a full stop. The Carrera roared ahead, down the exit ramp, and I risked my life by backing up to the exit on the potholed shoulder. Jamie 17 fell asleep, oblivious.

I hit the gas and shot to the exit ramp. Where was Sam going? I'd never been here, and my practice took me to some of the seamiest precincts in the city. I sped to the end of the ramp and looked right, then left. I'd lost him.

I tore off my sunglasses and turned left, squinting through the growing darkness. The day was almost over, but it was still light enough to see that this was one of the worst neighborhoods ever. I hit the gas and drove by one deserted brick rowhouse after another, a painful contrast with the colonial homes lining Pine Street. These rowhouses wouldn't find their way onto any historic register, they were already history.

Most of the vacant houses were boarded up with tin or plywood. Some weren't, and their upper two windows were empty and black as the eye sockets of a skull. The porches that still existed sagged dangerously and every three blocks was a vacant lot strewn with rubble, broken bottles, and trash. Children played on one of the blocks, skipping double Dutch on the sidewalk, a feat as accomplished as any Olympic athlete's. But these kids would never make it to the Olympics. They'd be lucky to make it out of the neighborhood.

I turned the corner, looking for Sam, wondering when my hometown had turned into a war zone. Struck with the same insight I'd had at the Roundhouse, then again at the Homicide Division. Only now I knew which side I was on. I didn't look like them but felt just as alienated, or at least as alienated as a former blonde can be. I was wondering whose side Sam was on when the light changed.

I cruised forward and a squad car popped into my rear-view mirror. Oh, no. Stay calm. It joined the line of traffic behind me, swinging into place only one car away, behind a red TransAm with smoky windows. I couldn't take my eyes from the rearview mirror. My fingers tightened on the steering wheel. I slouched in the bucket seat, and Jamie 17 lifted her triangle head from her paws.

"It's the heat," I told her and she went back to sleep, apparently less anxious than I. I had no registration for the bananamobile, no driver's license, nothing in a Linda Frost name except the Grun ID.

The TransAm took a hard left down a side street, leaving no buffer between the cops and me. The police cruiser pulled up closer, bridging the gap. I felt my hackles rise, from fear. The squad car was on my bumper as I reached the next traffic light, which turned red. I didn't dare run it. I groaned to a stop, wishing I were blond again. Cops love blondes, especially young cops like these two, sitting side by side in the front seat like the Hardy Boys.

The light turned green and I hit the gas, trying not to speed in panic. I knew I was acting nervous, I was feeling nervous. The cops tailed me as the street widened to two lanes. I could see the cop in the passenger seat talking on the radio. Was he calling in the plate? My God.

The traffic light at the corner changed from yellow to red as I reached it. Damn it! I stayed in the left lane so if they ended up next to me, they'd be as far as possible from my face.

It was exactly what happened. I drove up to the light. They pulled up next to me, on my right. I kept my face straight ahead, but I could feel their eyes on me. Scrutinizing me, wondering. What's a dressed-up redhead doing here in a new banana?

I had to do something. Hide in plain sight. It had worked, so far. "Officer," I called loudly, leaning over to the cop in the driver's seat. "Thank God you're here! I wonder if you could help me. I think I'm really lost."

"I think you are, too," he said with a smile, and his partner laughed and hung up the radio. "What are you looking for?"

"I-95, going south. I took my cat to the vet, but I must've got off on the wrong exit on the way back." I held Jamie 17 up by the scruff of the neck and she mewed on cue. "Isn't she cute?"

He nodded without enthusiasm. "Go to the next light and take a left. Follow it out and take that all the way to 95."

"Thanks."

The light changed to green. The cops cruised ahead of me. I exhaled, resettled Jamie 17, and followed the cops, waving like a dork. We reached the light together, me and my police escort, and they went straight at the light. I took the left they'd prescribed and traveled down another street that seemed to get darker and more deserted the farther I went.

Then I spotted it. There, on the right. Parked at the curb after the line of lesser cars sat the gleaming red Porsche. The license plate said LOONEY1.

I lurched to a stop. The car was empty. I looked behind me. The cops were gone.

I parked in an empty space on the left side of the street, locked the doors and windows, and stroked Jamie 17 while I watched the Porsche. She purred softly, completely at peace in the middle of this hellish neighborhood.

I watched the Porsche from way down in my front seat, not knowing which building Sam had gone into. It was too dark to see much around the car, most of the streetlights were unlit. I slumped deeper in the seat. The cops had been too close a call. A wave of exhaustion washed over me. I tasted the bile still coating my teeth. Drained, I leaned back on the headrest.

No children were out at this hour, there were no games of jump rope. It was quiet and still. A hydrant leaked water into the street at the far end and it trickled down the filthy gutter under the Porsche. I wondered vaguely if I should've kept the gun Grady had offered me, but I was too tired to care. Where was Sam? I checked my watch. 9:15. I closed my eyes and waited, one hand resting on Jamie 17. I hadn't slept in days. I didn't know how much longer I could go on.

The next time I checked my watch it was 11:30. I'd fallen asleep. I woke up scared. I felt my body, my chest. I was safe. Jamie 17 was walking around, scratching in her box. The street was still dark, but the Porsche had vanished.

"Damn it!" I said, hitting the steering wheel. I started the car, flicked on the lights, and pulled out of the parking space. I drove to where Sam's car had been parked and squinted up at the deserted houses. Then I looked down on the sidewalk.

It was Sam. Huddled, fallen, the figure of a man lying at the curb. Even though I couldn't see him clearly, I knew who it was.

"Sam!" I called, panicked. I twisted the steering wheel to the curb, yanked up the brake, and jumped out of the car.

"Sam! Sam!" I knelt down when I reached him and touched his forehead. It was covered with sweat, blood, and pavement dirt. I threw myself on his chest, listening for a heartbeat.

His eyelids fluttered and he grinned crazily. "'Assault and Peppered.' 1965," he said, as his eyes closed again.

"I can't believe they took my car," Sam moaned, while I held an ice pack over his eye.

"You have bigger problems than your car."

"No, I don't. How can I be Porscheless?"

"Many of us manage to. You can too."

"No, I can't. They can take my money, they can take my watch, they can even take my bone marrow. But don't take my Porsche." Sam sighed as he slouched on the lid of the toilet seat in his tiny bathroom. Dirty clothes overflowed the wicker hamper and Tasmanian Devil towels lay heaped in a soiled bunch next to the toilet. The white tile walls were gray and dingy, the shower curtain was spotted with black mildew. Sam's neat haircut was stiff with blood, and his pink Polo shirt was torn and sullied. It was hard to tell which was in worse shape, Sam or his bathroom.

"What'd you expect, in that neighborhood?"

"I expected to say hello and leave."

"You went up there to say hello? Here, hold the ice pack," I said, taking his hand and putting it atop the plastic cap.

"You could ask nicer."

"I could, but I won't." I wrung a grimy washcloth into a sink covered with caked blobs of Colgate, and turned on the faucet for hot water. Jamie 17 watched every move, sitting neatly on the wet and cluttered counter. "So that's why you were up there, in Beirut? You were visiting a friend?"

"Yes."

"What's the friend's name?"

"Mike."

"Mike? How come I never heard of him?"

"He's a new friend."

"Mike the New Friend. Is this a cartoon character or a real person?"

"A real person."

I waited for the water to get hotter. "And this real person would leave you on a sidewalk, bleeding? After some other friends beat you up and stole your car?"

"He's not a good friend."

"No, not at all. 'Mike the Bad New Friend.' 1952." Steam came off the tap water so I ran the washcloth in it, then pressed it to Sam's raw forehead.

"Ouch!" He reared back, letting the ice pack fall to the floor.

"Ouch, what?" I yelled. "Ouch, how stupid do you think I am? Ouch, why are you lying to me? Ouch, what kind of friend are you supposed to be?"

"What? What?" He looked for the ice pack like a befuddled drunk, but I had no sympathy.

"You're lying, Sam. You're lying about why you were up there. You lied about money and about Mark. You lied about everything!" My voice echoed harshly in the tiled bathroom, and Sam covered his ears.

"'The Yolk's On You.' 1979, I think."

"It's not funny, Sam. I could've been caught, saving you. And downstairs, trying to explain to the doorman!" I threw the washcloth on the counter, and Jamie 17 jumped. "Level with me. What were you doing up there?"

"You got an Acme portable hole? An Acme time-space gun? An Acme deluxe high-bounce trampoline? Or how about spring boots, any make or model?"

My temper ticked like a cartoon time bomb. "I want the truth, Sam."

"Ooh. 'Nothing But the Tooth.' That was Porky."

Before I knew what I was doing I had exploded, grabbing Sam by both arms and pushing him easily against the wall. As surprised as I was at my own violence, I wasn't about to let him go. "This is not a cartoon, Sam. I want the truth."

"Bennie, please!" he croaked, blue eyes wild and unfocused without his glasses. He struggled but he was too weak to escape my grip.

"You're in real trouble, Sam. So am I. What were you doing in that neighborhood?"

"I don't want to tell you. I don't want you to know. I don't want anyone—"

"Is it drugs?" I tightened my grip until tears formed in Sam's eyes. It wasn't pain, it was something else. Humiliation. I wanted to stop, but I couldn't. I had to know. Not only for Sam's sake, but for Bill's.

"All right, all right." A tear formed in the corner of one eye and rolled down his mottled cheek. "Yes, drugs. Heroin."

Heroin. The word cut deep inside me. I flashed on Bill, dead with a syringe in his arm. The balloons on Sam's desk. Had Sam killed Bill? And Mark? I let go of his arm, stunned, and he fell onto the toilet seat.

"Bennie," he whispered hoarsely, beginning to sob. "I'm sorry. So sorry."

TWENTY-SEVEN

S am slumped in jeans and an undershirt on his brown leather couch, with Jamie 17 in his lap. The couch was the only piece of furniture left in the once-elegant living room. The state-of-the-art stereo system I remembered was gone, as were the VCR and large-screen TV. The funky Kosta Boda crystal had vanished with the wall of expensive Looney Tune production cels, including a tribute to Mel Blanc that had cost me $350. Anything of value had been sold for drug money. All that remained were a few droopy cartoon characters, including the bankruptcy lawyer.

"So how long have you been using?" I asked.

"Almost two years."

"Heroin?" I still couldn't believe it.

"A manly drug. Some coke, too, when I'm coming down."

I shook my head, amazed that this schizzy personality belonged to the same person I called my best friend. How could I not have known? And could Sam be a killer, too?

"Look at your face. You had no idea, did you?" he asked.

"None at all. I feel so dumb."

"Don't. I hid it like a champ. Long-sleeved shirts all the time. I keep my jacket on, even in summer."

"Here I thought you were just an uptight lawyer."

He half smiled. "Hides the tracks. And the blood, if there's spotting."

It made sense. As did his thin build and volatile temper of late. What I used to think was playfulness now looked like arrested development. "But it's crazy, it's self-destructive—"

"I agree. Don't start lecturing."

"How did you work? How could you concentrate?"

"I'm not gonzo all the time. Most of the time I'm up, so up I can do anything. Fool anybody."

"How much money have you blown?"

"A fortune."

"No, tell me exactly."

He cleared his throat. "Well, I sold the mutual funds I told you about and I can't afford South Beach. I stay home under the sunlamp, it's around here somewhere. There are no stocks anymore, I sold Microsoft right before it went through the roof. But I do have a crush on Bill Gates. Can you blame me?"

"So how much?"

"My whole draw, every month, and then some." He closed his eyes briefly. "I'm overdrawn on my checking and I owe my left nut to AmEx. Plus I have four credit cards with cash advances to the hilt. One card I even stole, from one of my partners, who left it on the table after lunch."

I bit my tongue. "Is heroin that expensive?"

"You get what you pay for. It's gotten purer, more bang for the buck. I support Ramon's habit, too, and some of his friends like to party."

I put two and two together. "Are you stealing from the clients?"

"No more than any other lawyer."

"Sam—"

"Okay, not so you'd notice. I overbill for reimbursements, a little here, a little there. Charges you don't need receipts for." He brightened. "Although your scam with Consolidated Computer is brilliant, Bennie. I never thought of inventing a client, then billing to it. That one's the big lie, all right."

My face felt hot, and I hadn't even told him about my wardrobe renaissance. "How'd you keep this up, Sam?"

"What?"

"The sham, the whole thing."

"I can't keep a secret? 'Deduce You Say!' 195—"

"Enough with the cartoons," I said, impatient with his rap. "No more Looney Tunes. I don't want to hear one more quotation out of that mouth. Got it?"

"What?" He blinked, incredulous. "You want me to quit, cold turkey?"

"You heard me."

"I can't do it, doc. I was born this way. It's genetic, not a choice."

"You were explaining how you could have a whole secret life."

"It's nothing new for me, Bennie, I get lots of practice. I'm gay, remember? How do you think I keep that afloat? I have my partners believing I screw anything with a pulse. I'm the envy of the Policy Committee."

"So it's brilliant lawyer by day, drug addict by night?"

He stroked Jamie 17. "That's a naive question. You don't

contain heroin that way. Only in the beginning, then it starts containing you. It sneaks up on you, especially stuff this good. No, I'm a junkie full time. It's a tough job, but somebody has to do it."

I was silent, waiting. He wanted to tell me something, unburden himself, I could feel it. Maybe his confession would be to murder.

"I've fixed in my office, in the parking garage, in the men's room, even in the bathroom at bankruptcy court. I've gotten out of more meetings to boot than I can count."

"'Boot'?"

"Shoot up."

"How could they not know?"

"I'd say I have to make a call. What lawyer doesn't have to make a call? When I was in the bathroom, I really would use the time, call either a connection or a client. I'd have a cell phone to my ear and a needle in my arm."

"It must be a nightmare, Sam," I said, hurt for him.

"It is. But you know what's funny? I need another hit, right now, and I'd do anything—*give*, *sell* anything—for it."

"Don't say that. Heroin kills." I was thinking of Bill.

"But it's true, Bennie. If I had my car back, I'd be up there in a minute. Let 'em beat the crap out of me, but after I fix. Only after."

"Is that why Mark gave you the money, the cash I saw in his checkbook?"

"Yes."

"Did you tell him why?"

"Of course not. I told him I was making investments for him. Some stock tips I got from a rich client. I told him I could double his money."

"You conned him out of it? One of your oldest friends?"

Sam looked away, and neither of us said anything for a moment. Neither had to.

"Sam," I asked, breaking the silence, "do you think Mark knew you were an addict, even though you didn't tell him?"

"I'm not an addict, I'm chemically challenged."

"Stop joking around. Mark made you his executor, so I would guess he didn't know. What do you think?"

Sam looked chastened. "He made the will about three years ago, and I was fairly clean at the time. He could have suspected, but he never said anything. I fooled you, didn't I, and you were always smarter than he was. Always."

I took a deep breath. "Sam, did you kill Bill Kleeb, that kid I represented? The animal activist?"

"*What?* No!"

"I found him dead of a heroin overdose. You didn't have anything to do with that?"

"No, of course not. What is this? I didn't kill anybody. I never would. The only violence I like is cartoon. Where you get blown up and show up in the next frame, with a Band-Aid, crisscrossed." He made a tiny x with his index fingers. "Like a patch on a flat tire."

"But the balloons on your desk, what are they for?"

"Honestly? I use them to tie off."

"You mean your arm?"

He rolled his eyes. "No, my dick. Of course I mean my arm. And don't look at me like that. I know somebody who shoots up there to hide his tracks. He's a doctor."

"Bill's arm was tied with a pink balloon when I found him."

"So?" Then it dawned on him. "*That's* why you think I did it?" He laughed, but it came out like a huff of stale air and disturbed Jamie 17. "I'm not the only junkie who uses balloons for other than their intended purpose."

"Is that common, to use a balloon?"

"Anything that works is common." He put a slim finger to his temple. "Let's see, I've used a belt, a rubber band, a leather shoelace. Even an Hermès tie. The one with the jugglers."

"But it was just like the balloons on your desk. The same color."

"You can buy them in Woolworth's! You should see the sleazoids buying those balloons. None of them are making giraffes with them, believe me. I had nothing to do with any death."

"But you were angry at Bill for protesting the AIDS vaccine."

"I didn't even know the kid! I wouldn't kill him for that! I'd have to kill every Republican in sight."

Still. My stomach was tense. "Where were you two nights ago?"

"Where I am every night. Getting high with Ramon, my little Speedy Gonzales."

"Really?"

"'Here Today, Gone Tamale.' 195—Oh, who cares?"

"Sam—"

"I mean it. I'm telling the truth."

I looked at him, near collapse in the saggy middle of the couch. "Sam, did you kill Mark? For the fees?"

"No, Bennie, I told you I didn't, that day in my office!"

"You also told me you didn't need the money, and you're a drug addict."

"That doesn't mean I'm guilty of every murder in the city!" He leaned forward urgently, seeming to summon all the strength in his body. "You don't get it, Bennie. If you're hooked, you need money now. This second, this instant. I don't need money a year from now or whenever Mark's will gets probated."

"What about the time you'd bill, the income from that?"

"Too late. I need cash, cash, cash, cash, all the time. You don't invoice for dope money, *chica*."

"With the trustee's fee, every year—"

"I'm in no shape to manage a trust! I can't even manage my own life!" His eyes glistened. "I didn't kill Mark. I swear to God."

I considered it. Was Sam lying or wasn't he? He looked like he was in pain. He'd been my friend as long as I could remember. I couldn't be sure, but I felt that I could trust him, for the moment. At least draw on his expertise to help figure out what had happened to Bill. So I told him the whole story, about how there were no tracks on Bill's arm, and what Mrs. Zoeller had said. When it was over, I asked him what he thought.

"It sounds like a setup to me," he said. "Though I'll tell you this—the last person to believe you're a junkie is your mother."

"Or your best friend."

He looked sad. "I really am sorry, Bennie. I never wanted to get you in trouble."

"Does your mother know?"

"You think I want to kill her? She knows I'm gay, that's enough."

I thought of Sam's lifestyle, a gay man, maybe even sharing needles, exchanging high-risk blood. "From the looks of it, I think it's yourself you want to kill."

Sam's anguished eyes found mine, and he didn't disagree.

* * *

Later, I bundled him into his bed, now a bare mattress with one of the most exclusive views in the city, overlooking Rittenhouse Square. Where the night table had been were pizza crusts, overflowing ashtrays, and other trash.

I set about cleaning the place while Sam fell into an exhausted sleep. Jamie 17 kept me company and I went from room to room sweeping and vacuuming, just as I had cleaned my own apartment after the cops searched it. I'd gone from relentless slob to white tornado in a matter of days and hated every minute of it.

As the night wore on and Sam woke up, the singing turned to persuading, then pleading, then yelling. I hugged him, ordered him food, and threw him into the mildewed shower as Jamie 17 scampered out of sight. Anything to get him through the night. I made him throw out all the drug paraphernalia from his hiding places; an array of bloody needles, spoons, and stuff he called his "works." I turned the place upside down, with him screaming at me, crying, begging me to stop. But I didn't listen and he finally gave in.

I lost track of time and at some point I called a drug hotline as Sam raved in the background. They walked me through it—sweats, shakes, and nausea—from wherever they were to wherever I was. At the other end of the phone line was a kind, knowing soul who stayed with me and Sam through the darkness, asking nothing but to help.

By the time dawn came around, Sam had slipped into the soundest sleep I'd ever seen, sounder than Jamie 17's at his feet, right through two calls from Ramon. The waiter's third call sounded panicky and it was clear it wasn't love he wanted. I hung up the phone.

When dawn finally broke, I rose from my spot on the hardwood floor and stretched, looking out the window over the Square. Every muscle in my body ached, but the scene was beautiful, Sunday morning quiet. The streetlights were still on around the Square, glowing dimly in the hazy gray morning. The green wooden benches were empty, even of the homeless. To my left twinkled downtown Philly, but the Silver Bullet seemed far away, draped in the mist. On the right were the classy rowhouses south of the Square and the backstreet that used to be ours, at R & B. I thought of Mark, then Grady.

Grady. I wondered how he was. I looked at the phone, off the hook on the floor beside Sam and Jamie 17. It was a chance, but I wanted to talk to him. A fugitive needs her lawyer, doesn't she? The dawn I left him was exactly like this one. How many days ago was that? The truth was, I missed him. I picked up the phone and dialed him at home.

"Wells residence," breathed a woman's voice, in a soft whisper.

It took me aback. I squeezed the receiver in my hand. His old girlfriend? Another woman?

"Hello?" said the woman. I could barely hear her.

Good-bye, I thought, and hung up.

TWENTY-EIGHT

Sunday morning dawned and I spent it taking care of Sam, who cried, slept, showered, and babbled a Foghorn Leghorn cartoon in a continuous loop. I'd wanted to read the newspapers to track what the cops were saying about me, but the news agency had long ago stopped delivering to Sam's condo, their bills unpaid. I tried not to think about Grady, which wasn't hard since my hands were full with Sam, who swore he wanted to get clean.

"For real?" I asked, making him a slice of toast, the only food I could find in the apartment.

"I'm ready to kick. This is it."

"You're halfway there, Sam."

"I'm no longer a duck amuck. That's 1953, by the way."

"Stop with the cartoons." I put the toast on a freshly washed plate and set it in front of him as he rested on his elbow at the counter. "I told you."

"Okay, okay." Sam waved me off with a trembling hand. His eyes were bloodshot behind his glasses, his skin a saffron hue, and his frame almost anorexic now that he was out of his tailored suits. "I thought you liked the 'toons, Ben. Why are you so cranky all of a sudden?"

"I decided you're using cartoons as a facade. You hide behind your humor, you don't want to face reality. I saw it on Sally Jessy."

He rolled his eyes. "Did Ramon call?"

"Forget about Ramon. He's a bad influence on you."

"Of course he is, that's what I like about him. So did he call?"

"It doesn't matter. I'm not letting you play with him anymore."

"You taking over my care and feeding?"

"Bingo."

"I hope you'll do better with me than with Jamie 17. She's too skinny." His eyes followed the cat as she walked back and forth on the floor, rubbing against his stool at the kitchen counter.

"I gave her a Snickers yesterday," I said defensively.

"She needs real food."

"When it gets dark I'll go out and get some food for both of you." I brushed the toast crumbs off my hands in the small, modern kitchen. It was spotless from my cleaning last night and so bare it looked like no one lived there.

"Thanks a lot for last night, for everything you've done."

"Forget it."

"No, I know you're in trouble. This must be the last thing you need."

"I don't mind helping you, but I'm no expert. The man on the hotline said you should check into a rehab center. He was telling me the Bar Association even has a service for lawyers with drug problems, there are so many."

"No. Never." Sam scowled. "I'm not doing it that way."

"He said Eagleville is good, not far from here."

"I don't need it. I can do it myself. I'm halfway there, you said so yourself."

"He said it's a pattern, though. A behavior."

Sam's face flushed. "I'm not going to any frigging rehab. I'm not losing everything I worked for at Grun, not for this. No. I appreciate everything you've done for me, I know it was a bitch, but don't push the rehab. That's all, folks."

"But you need therapy—"

"You want to shock me, too? Like your mother?"

It stung. I didn't know what to say. A lump formed in my throat.

"Damn." He rubbed his forehead irritably. "I'm sorry."

You want to shock me, too? I couldn't get past the phrase. It had a hangtime of its own and it lingered, suspended in the air between us. It was true. I had shocked my mother. Pushed a giant RESET button on her brain. Rebooted her. How was she? We lived not ten minutes from here. Did I dare go over in the daylight?

"Bennie, I didn't mean to say that. I was angry." Sam reached for my hand, but I was heading for the apartment door. I wanted to go. Maybe get some food, maybe stop by my mother's if it was safe.

"I'll be back," I told him.

"Bennie, I'm sorry. Don't go."

"You and the cat need food. Wait here and don't answer the phone."

"I didn't mean it." He got up unsteadily and almost stumbled following me to the door. "Bennie—"

"Take care of the cat," I said and closed the door behind me.

Outside the building, I fumbled for my sunglasses in the bright sun. I felt nervous, exposed. Too many people around Rittenhouse Square. A runner knocked into me, and I jumped.

"Watch it, buddy!" the doorman shouted. "You all right, Miss?" He rushed over, an older man in a maroon cap and a jacket with epaulets.

"I'm fine."

"You sure?" His watery eyes looked concerned. "I thought he bumped you. Did he bump you?"

"I'm fine."

"They're not allowed to do that, cut under the awning. This is Manchester property, not public property. It's private, not public, you know what I mean?"

"Yes. Thanks, but I have to go."

"They're runners, what do they want the shortcut for anyway? They're supposed to want the exercise, am I right?" he called, even as I walked away. "What are they doin, takin' the shortcut?"

But I was gone, eyes scanning the street behind my dark sunglasses. There was no police car, marked or unmarked, anywhere in sight, and the Square was crowded with Philadelphians enjoying the weather. Runners lapped the Square, lovers cuddled on the park benches over the newspaper. I walked quickly down the sidestreet next to Sam's apartment building, bypassing the gourmet grocery on the corner because I shopped there all the time.

I headed down a sunny Twenty-second Street, past the exclusive boutiques serving this upscale residential district. I kept my head down, hoping I wouldn't see anyone I knew, and barreled toward the supermarket on Spruce. It was huge, anonymous, and I never shopped there.

Only one block to go, but I was already warm in my wrinkly suit. My eyes shifted left and right behind my sunglasses, checking the parked cars on either side of the street. No Crown Vic, but when I turned the corner there was a squad car sitting there.

I sucked wind. A white police cruiser, with the turquoise and gold stripe of the Philadelphia police. The engine was running, but there was no cop inside. It was parked in front of a Chinese restaurant. Maybe he was grabbing coffee, maybe not. Were the cops looking for me around my mother's house, or Center City? The business district was small enough.

I hustled past the supermarket, skipping the errand. Instinct told me to run, to hide. I picked up the pace and rounded the corner, getting off Spruce Street and out of the cruiser's line of vision. I started a light run, fake-glancing at my watch. I was a woman, in a linen suit, in a hurry on a Sunday. Late for church? Late for brunch?

I jogged lightly, trying not to look too panic-stricken. I didn't know where to go. I couldn't return to Sam's, too risky. I was too far from my mother's house, even if I could go there. I had nowhere to go. I was running scared.

Ahead of me, a few blocks down the street stood the Silver Bullet. A gleaming spire. Grun. Why not? It was as good a place as any, and I was still Linda Frost. A New York lawyer working on a Sunday? It was a natural.

I kept the pace up, passed the shoppers and tourists, and

headed for the building. I was sweating, but not puffing too badly. Thank God for the stadium steps and the rowing. Thank God I was still free. Come to think of it, maybe I did believe in God. I slowed to a lawyerly cadence and pushed through the revolving door to the Grun building, where I suddenly lost my religion.

At the desk, talking to the security guard, were two uniformed cops.

TWENTY-NINE

I couldn't turn around and leave. I couldn't run. For a split second, I didn't know how to react. Then I did.

In character. I approached the front desk with an authoritative air. I was Linda Frost, New Yorker. A top-tier lawyer in a one-horse town. I hadn't had a decent tiramisu in weeks; I couldn't find an Ethiopian restaurant to save my life. I pushed my sunglasses up with a stiff index finger and reached for the sign-in notebook, ignoring everyone around me.

"His office is on the 35th floor?" one of the cops was saying to the security guard, Will, whom I'd met the first day.

"That's what it says on the directory," Will said, checking behind him. "Mr. Sam Freminet. He's at Grun, he's a partner there. I see him most mornings. He's always in early."

Sam. They were looking for Sam. My heart began to thud inside my chest, but I wrote my name in the book as coolly as possible.

"Maybe Miss Frost could take you up there," Will said to the cops. "You need a security card to get through the gate, but she's a lawyer at Grun, too."

What? I swallowed hard but kept writing, oblivious to all needs but my own. A bona fide New Yorker.

"Miss?" asked the cop. "Miss?"

I looked up. I had to. "Yes."

"Would you mind taking us upstairs, Miss?" The cop was about forty, with light blue eyes, furry blond eyebrows, and a brushy blond mustache. A certified hunk, but he wasn't my type. I sued his type.

"It's police business," added the other cop, tall, thin, and black. They both wore chrome badges and nametags, but I was too scared to read them.

"We'd appreciate it," said the blonde, expectantly.

Gulp. "I'll take you up." I turned on my heels like an automaton and led the police to the elevator bank. I fought to control my panic. My throat tightened. I wanted to run, but instead I pushed the elevator button and reminded myself I was not guilty of a triple murder, but was going to work to pad some pretrial time.

"Shame you have to work on such a nice Sunday," the blond cop said. He slipped his hat off with the cool of a major league pitcher.

"It can't be helped. I have a trial to prepare for."

I scanned his handsome features from behind my dark glasses and determined I didn't know him from my cases. He seemed to appreciate the appraisal, however, and if I didn't know better, I would have said he was taking a shine to me. COP FALLS FOR FUGITIVE.

I got in the elevator when it came, and they climbed in behind me, handcuffs jingling on their heavy leather belts. Each had a radio with a thick rubber antenna, and they carried service revolvers with worn wooden handles. I inched away from the guns as the elevator doors whisked closed and sealed us inside.

"We need to go to 35," said the blond cop.

"Oh, sure." I pressed the button, noticing with relief that my hand wasn't shaking.

"Do you know Sam Freminet, Miss Frost?"

"No, I'm not from the Philadelphia office." I kept my eyes glued to the glowing orange letters on the elevator cabin: *3rd Floor. 4th Floor.* It was sweltering in here, the air-conditioning must have been turned off for the weekend. "Is there some problem with Mr. Freminet, Officer?"

"Call me Bob. Bob Hall."

"You were saying. Bob."

"Right. We found his car, abandoned. Stripped clean as a wishbone."

8th Floor, 9th Floor. "Too bad."

"More than too bad. It was an eighty-thousand-dollar car."

"Jeez." No wonder Sam had cried.

"We found a briefcase in the trunk, with some of Mr. Freminet's papers in it. But his license plate was gone, and we couldn't find his registration or other ID. Do you have any idea where he lives? His number's unlisted and the DMV can't give us an answer until Monday."

"No. Haven't the foggiest." *13th Floor, 14th Floor.* Come on, faster. Damn elevators went too fast when I worked here.

"They have a directory in the office, don't they? We need to get in touch with him."

"I don't know, I'm from the New York office."

"New Yawk, you're kidding!" The blond cop's face lit up. "I grew up in the Big Apple!"

"Really." Terrific. *21st Floor, 22nd Floor.*

"Sure, I'm from Queens. Richmond Hill, but that was a long time ago." He was evaluating me more closely, as if he were wondering whether we'd been in French II together.

"Queens, really." I watched his eyes run down my body and up again, stopping and squinting at my sunglasses. I prayed he wouldn't recognize me, now that my 8 × 10 was undoubtedly hanging in the Wanted for Murder gallery. Women making progress on all fronts.

"I bet I can guess where you're from," he said. "Larchmont or Mamaroneck, am I right?"

Mama-what? "No." *23rd Floor, 24th Floor.*

"Where in New York, then?"

"Oh, I'm not from New York originally. I just work there."

His broad shoulders let down. "Where are you from originally?"

Here we go again. Worst liar in the bar association. I glanced at the black cop. Which state wasn't he from? "Iowa. Grinnell, Iowa," I said.

The black cop shrugged, and I flashed him a tight smile. *30th Floor.*

"Aren't you gonna take your sunglasses off?" the blond cop asked.

"I can't." *31st Floor, 32nd Floor.* I fought for air and a decent lie. "Hangover. Big, bad hangover. *Killer* hangover."

"I see." The cop's face relaxed into its confident grin. "Out partyin' last night, huh?"

"You got it," I said, with a matching grin.

"Even though you have to work the next day?"

33rd Floor, 34th Floor. Hurry, hurry, hurry! "You know how it is." What? Help!

He grinned slyly. "No, how is it?"

35th Floor. "Here we are!" The elevators slid aside with their characteristic *swoosh*, opening onto the snazzy reception area. I was so happy to see the Gold Coast I could have kissed the wafer-thin Persian. An air-conditioned blast hit me full in the face, carrying the twin aromas of power and money.

"Must be nice," said the black cop. He smelled it, too.

On both sides of the reception area were iron gates, blocking entrance to the floor on other side. I fumbled in my purse for my security card and inserted it in the metal box recessed next to the gate. There was a loud *click*, then the gate began to travel upwards. I almost applauded.

"There we go, gentlemen," I chirped. "You'll see the nameplates next to the office doors, everybody has a nameplate nowadays. I'll be in my office, drinking lousy coffee and working away." I heard myself babbling, so I clammed up.

The black cop nodded, and the blonde extended a large hand. "Orange juice," he said meaningfully.

"What?" My hand was still in a cold sweat, so I pulled it away.

"Orange juice. Lots of it. It's the best thing for one of those killer hangovers."

"That's just what my boyfriend says," I said, to discourage any ideas he might be having about our future together. After all, I was true to Grady, right? "Good-bye now," I called out, and returned to the elevator bank and punched the button. I watched the cops disappear down the hall and almost leapt into the elevator when it came.

It had been way too close a call. The cops were closing in because of Sam. They would find out where Sam lived, they would go there. They'd be one step behind me all the way, whether by accident or design. Chasing me. Until they caught up.

34th Floor.

My stomach tightened. Soon Azzic would catch wind of Sam's car and start asking more questions. I couldn't stay at Grun anymore. I had to go.

33rd Floor.

I took a tense inventory. I still had my cell phone but the bananamobile was stuck at Sam's with Jamie 17. She was better off there for now, I was back on the run. How could I get away without a car? It was a city. There were trains, buses, subways. Go!

32nd Floor.

The doors opened and I sprang out on the Loser Floor. The air-conditioning was feeble and the reception area smelled like a litter box. I carded my way past the security gate and slipped under it while it rattled upwards. I hurried to my conference room and opened the door.

My new wardrobe had arrived, all in plastic garment bags, complete with a shoe box. I grabbed my clothes, briefcase, and papers. I was about to run out again but suddenly there was a knock at the door. I held my breath. Was it the cops?

"Who's there?" I asked.

The knock came again, louder this time.

"Who is it?" I asked, louder.

Still, no answer. What was this? The Warrantless Entry Game, where the cops fool you into consenting? I put on my frosty Linda Frost face and opened the door.

I wouldn't have expected it, not in a million years.

THIRTY

He was shorter than I remembered, but his face was as pickled as always, puckering behind horn-rimmed glasses with transparent acetate frames. His bald head had grown elliptical as an egg and it was dappled with freckles from the sun. Even though it was Sunday, he was dressed in his standard white button-down shirt, rep tie, and Brooks khaki suit.

The Great and Powerful. Standing in the doorway to Conference Room D, listing gently to the right.

"Mr. Grun," I said, shocked.

"Wha?" he asked, touching his ear.

"Mr. Grun!"

He smiled, his lips an unexpectedly wet pink. "Yes. How do you know me?"

Eeek. "Uh, I've seen your picture. In the directory."

"Pleased to meet you." His voice wavered, but it was still strong. He extended a hand that felt dry and frail in mine. "You must be Miss Frost."

"Yes. Right."

He shuffled into the conference room, borne forward by

momentum and sheer will, then eased into a chair almost as soon as I yanked one under him. "Thank you," he said.

"You're welcome."

"So, you must be Miss Frost," he said again, squinting up at me. His smooth head moved like a turtle's in his stiff collar. "Why, you look very familiar to me."

My heart skipped a half-beat. "No. We've never met."

"Your father, do I know him?"

"No." I don't even know him.

"Was he at Piper, Marbury?"

"No, he wasn't a lawyer," I said, though I didn't know what he was. A sneak, according to my mother.

"But you look so familiar. His name, what was it?"

"Frost, the same as mine."

"What was his first name?"

Jack? No. David? Worse. "Grinnell. Grinnell Frost. Like the town, in Iowa." Please God, teach me to lie better than this.

"Grinnell Frost." He shook his head vaguely. "I guess not. So, you've come to us from the New York office. I like the New York office very much."

"So do I."

"We have some very smart lawyers there."

"Yes, we do."

"I do not like New York City, however."

"Neither do I." But I don't have time to chat about it.

"The people have no manners."

"No, they don't. They ignore everyone around them."

"They move," he waved a jittery hand in the air, "too fast."

"Much too fast."

"And the streets are dirty."

"Very."

"Filthy."

"Noisy." I never agreed with him so much. I never agreed with anybody so much, but I still felt like bolting for the door. Getting out of the building.

"You must be working hard, Miss Frost."

"I am."

"I read your memo, about the computer case you're preparing for."

"You did?" Oh, no.

"Yes. I'm sorry it took me so long to find you. I don't come in to work every day and I don't always keep up with my mail. As for my advance sheets, well, they're a dead letter, I'm afraid. Do you keep up with your advance sheets, Miss Frost?"

"I try to."

"You must, they're essential. You must to know what the courts are deciding, how the law is evolving. You know what Cardozo said."

Cheese it, the cops? "Of course."

"'The law changes in increments.'" He held up a finger that was very tan for this time of year, and I remembered he had a vacation home in Boca Raton. "You young people have the firm now. The firm, it runs without me now."

I couldn't ignore the regret in his voice. "But not as well, I'm sure."

"You're very kind, Miss Frost," he said, but stared past me. The bright windows reflected white off his bifocals, making him look sightless. "I built this firm, you know. With my friend. He's gone now."

"Mr. Chase?"

"He's gone."

"I didn't know," I said, but I had. I checked the open door behind him, and the coast was still clear.

"That was a long time ago."

"I see."

He sighed. "Anyway, you're on trial in a week."

I was on trial right now. "Yes."

"You said you needed help. In your memo."

"Help?" Stupid, stupid, stupid. Help!

"It was a silly memo, Miss Frost," he said, with a trace of the sternness I remembered. "You don't know us very well, in the main office. No one will help you here if they can't bill it."

"No?" Tell me about it.

"Not nowadays. In my day, we all helped each other. We wouldn't think of billing a client for helping a colleague. We ate lunch together then. Even had tea and a snack together. We were partners then. Truly. Partners."

"Snacks? At Grun?"

"Oh, yes." He smiled shakily at the memory. "Mr. Chase would make some tea and we'd all have tea and chocolate together. Just a piece, in the afternoon. Chase, myself, and McAlpine. Later, Steinman."

"Chocolate?" I forgot the cops for a moment, intrigued.

"Yes, chocolate. Now, Steinman, he loved chocolate more than all of us put together. Had to have some every day."

"What kind of chocolate, Mr. Grun?" Say *light chocolate.* Was that how it started?

"Always the same kind. We, all of us, liked the same kind."

Say *light.* So that was it. Not tyranny, comradeship. Collegiality. I felt terrible. I'd misjudged him, and for years.

"Do you like chocolate, Miss Frost?"

It didn't have to think about it this time. "I love chocolate, Mr. Grun."

"What kind of chocolate, light or dark?"

"Light, only." I felt a welling-up, unaccountably.

"Dark, it's too bitter."

"I agree."

He smiled shakily. "Light chocolate is a wonderful thing."

"It is."

"Some things in life cannot be improved upon."

"Like golden retrievers."

He smiled again. "Are you a dog lover, Miss Frost?"

"Yes."

"I like cats, myself."

I thought of Jamie 17, back with Sam. I actually missed her. "They're okay, too."

"I had a cat once, my Tiger. She was striped. She liked to eat cream cheese. Licked it right off my finger." He nodded. "We all helped each other, then. It didn't matter if it could be billed or not. Not in the least. Why bill it and make your friend look bad, eh?"

Why, indeed.

"That's how you build a law firm. Not with cases, not even with clients. With friendships. They grow from there, in reputation. In strength. They become . . . organic, that way."

I thought of R & B. Mark had been right. It was gone as soon as we were gone.

"The value is in the friendships, in the core." He breathed in deeply. "Well, here I am. I saw your memo, I knew you'd be working today. I thought I might be of some assistance. Could you possibly use my assistance, Miss Frost?"

Oh no. I didn't know what to say.

"I've worked on many securities cases. Argued twenty-five before the United States Supreme Court."

"Twenty-five?" I thought of my one dumb feather.

"I don't mind document work. I like to work hard."

But there were no documents, there wasn't even a case. I didn't know what to do. It reminded me of my mother, and that gave me a solution. It would slow me down, but I couldn't run off now and leave him feeling more useless than he already did. "I certainly could use your help, Mr. Grun. I'd be honored."

"Why, thank you." He nodded graciously.

"First, let me tell you the facts."

"No documents?"

"No. If I may, let me give you my opening argument."

"As you wish."

"It's a jury trial, so I want the opening to be just right."

"Good girl. Juries make their decisions after the opening. Be respectful. Don't talk down to them. Wear blue, I always did."

"I will," I told him, and began a story. A bedtime story in which an upstart computer company wanted to know the truth, but all the more powerful computer companies were lying to the little chip company and the government. I made up the story as I went along, taking half of it from my own predicament and the other half from what little securities law I knew.

He listened thoughtfully and in time grew very still, not flinching even when the afternoon sun edged in a brilliant square onto his face. He had fallen into that sound sleep known only to old men and golden retrievers. So I packed up my files, grabbed my clothes and briefcase, wrote him a little note, and left.

I dashed to the security gate and slipped under it, down the stifling elevator to the lobby. I'd be safe away from the Silver Bullet, out of sight somewhere. There were a million places I could go. The airport, the train station. I needed a place to collect my thoughts, stow my stuff.

29th Floor.

I had to figure out who killed Mark, and something Grun had said was sticking with me. In the back of my mind. I couldn't quite articulate it.

25th Floor.

About law firms. Collegiality. I thought of Mark, dead, and R & B, defunct. The associates. Who had put the bloody scissors in my apartment? I flipped backwards through time, in my mind.

15th Floor.

Hattie had said something. Who had brought some stuff to my apartment? Renee Butler. She said she'd brought books I'd lent her. Had she planted the scissors?

10th Floor.

Was Butler the one? If she were, she'd put on a good act for me. And she always seemed to like Mark, but maybe that was for Eve's benefit. But how had she found Bill? And why?

Lobby Floor. The elevator doors opened. I was about to step out but caught myself at the last minute.

Three cops were standing together in the middle of the lobby. Not the blonde or black cop, new ones. With them was a man in a dark suit whose rasp I'd recognize on a bet. Detective Meehan, from Homicide.

My heart stopped. I couldn't go into the lobby. I was too scared to fake Linda Frost anymore and it wouldn't work anyway, not with Meehan. It would be over.

I wanted out of the building. The freight elevator stood open across the hall. I'd used it once, moving my stuff the day I'd left Grun. It led to the basement and the parking garage.

I slipped out of the elevator, slid along the marble wall into the freight cab, and hit the first button I saw.

THIRTY-ONE

I got off the freight elevator on the lowest level of the parking garage, my mind racing. Had the cops found Sam? Was Meehan looking for me? Where was Azzic? I had to get away, but I didn't want to leave town. I had to follow up on Renee Butler.

I hoisted my stuff over my shoulder and hurried across the almost-empty garage, looking around for the exit stairs. Suddenly there was a blast of police sirens. I broke into a run and streaked across the garage. The only sounds were my heels, my panting, and the sirens.

I had to find a way out. I passed a metal MONTHLY PARKING sign on a stand and looked left. An exit ramp spiraled up like a corkscrew. I took it and ran up and up until I got dizzy and the hot yellow arrows led the way out in a blur.

EXIT, a red neon sign blinked from across the garage floor. I got a bead on it and had almost reached the cashier's booth when I froze on the spot.

There was a uniformed cop inside the booth, talking with the cashier and a red-jacketed security guard. I did an about-face and hustled back into the lot. I needed to get out of sight, but where? The sirens blared louder.

I dropped between a blue Taurus and a station wagon and scrambled away from the booth, using the parked cars as cover. I didn't know what to do when I reached the end of the line. I was trapped. I squatted low, panting, dipping a knee into spilled motor oil on the gritty cement floor. The sirens blared louder. More cops would be here any minute. I tried the handle of the Ford but it was locked. I looked wildly around, but there was no way out. Then I saw it.

Two parking spaces over, in the ceiling of the garage. A large, square-cut hole between the beams of the garage roof. A black oblong on the sooty concrete with its lumpy fireproofing. An Acme portable hole! I would have laughed if I weren't scared to death.

I had to get to the hole and the dark green car parked near it, but between here and there were no cars for cover. I would be exposed. The sirens screamed. My throat tightened. I had to go, they'd find me here. I inched to the edge of the row and peeked out. The cop and the guards were still in the booth. I waited until the cop's back was turned and sprinted for the green car.

I reached it, panting hard, more from fear than exertion. There were no shouts so I guessed I hadn't been seen. I leaned against the car, relieved. It was a Range Rover, and felt sturdy against my shoulder. It would need to be. The hole in the garage roof was catty-corner to it.

I inched up and peeked through the tinted car window at the booth. The cop was joking with the pretty cashier. *Go now.*

I reached up and threw my clothes and briefcase on the

roof of the car. Then I stuck my toe in the door handle and scaled the side of the tall car to its pebbled top and sunroof. As soon as I got there I flattened, breathing shallowly. So far, so good. No voices, no shouts. I looked up at the hole. Salvation. I eyeballed the distance from the hole to the roof. It was as far away as I was tall. I could do it, maybe.

I took an anxious peek sideways at the booth. The group was beginning to break up. I was out of time. I picked up my purse and pitched it into the blackness of the hole, like a bean bag into a clown's mouth. The purse landed inside and I pitched the canvas briefcase in after it. A soft thud. Neither rolled back out, so I figured there was room for me.

The sirens shrieked. They were right outside the building. I didn't dare look back at the booth. I hooked my clothes on the back of my neck, then scrambled to my feet and jumped into the dark hole, grabbing onto the jagged sides, hoisting myself mightily to get my chest in. I crawled forward on my elbows until my legs were inside. I lunged the final yard and was in all the way.

I had no idea why this hole was here, but it stunk. I wriggled forward, unable to see a thing in the pitch black, wishing I had a penlight or something more useful than a dog picture on my keychain. I dragged myself farther into the darkness. The stench got stronger. I reached my purse and my briefcase, realizing it was a tunnel of some kind. A very stinky tunnel. In three feet the odor grew unbearable and I was crawling in something cool. Crumbly. Revolting.

What was it? I scooped some up and held it under my nose, propping myself on my arms. I couldn't see a thing, but it smelled like poop. Then I sniffed again and realized that it was. Manure. I recoiled in disgust, but couldn't back out. Why would there be manure in a parking garage? Then I remembered the man-made forest in the atrium of the building. Their root system must have been between the ground floor and the garage, and was evidently serviced from this crawlspace. I was in deep doodoo, no joke.

Suddenly I heard men's voices. My heart pounded, I forgot about the smell. The voices moved closer, underneath the hole. I held my breath. Directly below me, a guard was telling a farmer's daughter joke. I didn't listen for the punchline. The voices receded, then disappeared. I exhaled with relief and spit the dirt out of my mouth.

It was all downhill from there. I spent the night in muck, watching the minutes tick by on the glowing green digits on my watch. By 5:30 A.M., I hadn't slept at all, I felt so raw and anxious. My knees were killing me, scraped up, and my back was crampy. My hair reeked of dung, and you could grow mushrooms in my mouth. But the sirens had subsided and I was safe. Quiet descended like a blessing. Still I had to get out of the tunnel before the business day started.

I looked over my shoulder toward the lighted square of the tunnel's entrance. I tried to turn around but it was too narrow, so I grabbed my stuff and crawled in reverse, toward the light. I reached the hole and straddled it, then did a push-up and looked down. The green Range Rover was still there. Were the cops? I squirmed backward and peered out.

No cops or guards were in sight, just an elderly cashier, evidently the morning shift, filing her nails in front of a portable TV flickering in the booth. Time to go.

I collected my stuff and lowered it onto the car's sunroof. No one came running, so I took a deep breath and dropped out of the hole. I hit the roof of the Rover with a decidedly uncatlike *thump* and flattened as soon as I made contact. I took one sideways look at the cashier, who was watching TV, then slid on my back down the far side of the Rover, grabbing my stuff at the last minute and landing in an aromatic heap on the garage floor.

I sat there a second, forcing myself to stay calm, squinting in the sudden brightness. I was a mess. Dirt and manure soiled my suit. My pantyhose were ripped and one knee was bloodied and filthy. I reeked of crap. I looked, and felt, homeless.

Then it hit me. The way out. The next step. I could be homeless, a smelly ruin of a woman with plastic bags and an oily canvas briefcase. I tore up the garment bags, then rubbed the manure into my hair and clothes, stifling my disgust. In two minutes, I was ready. I made sure no cops were in sight, then shuffled toward the exit. My heart was racing under my grimy blouse.

I staggered toward the exit. My heart beat louder with each step closer to the cashier, but I had no choice. I couldn't back down and I couldn't run or she'd call the cops for sure.

She turned from the TV and spotted me, her emery board poised in midair. Her hooded eyes narrowed instantly. She was no dummy and she didn't like what she saw.

Still I kept walking and when I got close enough I had a brainstorm.

THIRTY-TWO

Hide in plain sight. It was getting to be second nature.

I lurched directly for the booth, dragging my feet and shredded plastic bags. I stopped right in front of the window and pounded on the scratchy Plexiglas.

"Listen, listen, listen," I screeched at the cashier. I knew how to sound crazy, it was in my blood. "You got somethin' for me? You got somethin' for me? Yougotsomethin' forme?"

The cashier recoiled in alarm.

"I know you got money, honey! I know you got money, honey." I banged out on the windows, leaving an odiferous smudge. "Gimme, gimme, gimmegimmegimme!"

"Get away or I'll call the police!" she shouted from behind the thick glass.

Oops. I waved a loopy good-bye and staggered away from the booth, crossed the bumpy median at the exit to the underground garage, and walked the wrong way up the cement ramp out of the building. I breathed easier as I climbed, tingling with a heady adrenaline. I reached the top of the ramp to the pavement outside and smiled as I inhaled the night air blowing down the backstreet behind the building. I was on a roll. And I was free, even if I smelled like crap.

Then I saw that the stench wasn't coming only from me. Large rusty Dumpsters loomed in the dark, overflowing with garbage next to the black wells of the loading dock. The sidewalk was dirty and gum-spattered where the building faced the back end of the office building across the way. A homeless man slept like a crumpled puppet against the building, and I suppressed a twinge of guilt. I had to go. It was getting light, almost dawn. Like a vampire, I needed cover. I ran across the street to the back of another office building and slipped into the dusky shadows.

EEEEEEE! A squad car tore suddenly down the street, sirens screaming, red, white, and blue lights flashing on the top in an alternating pattern. I ducked against the wall in the darkness and almost fell backward. It was an open door, blistered and battleship gray. BUILDING PERSONNEL ONLY, it said, but it had been pried open, either broken into over the weekend or left unlocked carelessly. Another siren screamed at the other end of the street. I snuck inside the door before the cruiser passed and locked the door behind me.

I found myself in a hot, dirty hallway that smelled thickly of urine. The bathroom tour of Philly. It was dim inside with the door closed but I could follow a light at the other end of the corridor. A rumbling, mechanical sound emanated from it.

I lifted up my stuff, which was getting heavier and heavier, and trod cautiously down the corridor, running my fingers along the wall for guidance. The wall was painted cinderblock, cool and bumpy beneath my fingertips.

The hall ended in another door, defined only by the dim

light that outlined its perimeter, showing through the crack between door and jamb. I tried the knob and it moved freely. Unlocked. I paused a minute before opening it. There was no sound coming from behind it, but what would I do if there were people on the other side? Lie, badly. What could be worse than the cops? I held my breath and opened the door.

An empty staircase, lighted. No exit doors. There was no-where else to go, so I went down, first to one landing, then the next, ten concrete steps at a time. Descending toward the rumbling, which was getting louder, and the increasing heat. At each landing was a dim lightbulb covered by a wire cage. The sirens grew fainter as I traveled down, but I was still jit-tery. Maybe I shouldn't have left Grun. Maybe I shouldn't have given Grady back the gun. Jerk took my screwdriver.

The stairway bottomed on a gray door, less weathered than the exterior door and partly ajar. A yellow sliver of light streamed from the crack. I stood still and listened. There was no human sound; no radio, footsteps, or dirty jokes. Just the incessant thundering of whatever machinery was down here, in what I imagined was the subbasement to the building. My blouse was damp, my nerves were on edge. The heat intensi-fied. I pushed the door open a crack.

Nothing. Just another corridor, better lit than the one I was in. On the wall hung a tattered sign: RESULTS COUNT! DO THE JOB RIGHT! I peeked around the door but the hall was empty. The air was warmer here, more dense. Beads of sweat broke on my forehead. I felt creepy, as if something were right behind me. I peered over my shoulder. Nothing.

Nobody but me and the machine noise. If there were any maintenance types on duty, they weren't around. I had to be-lieve they'd come soon. I willed myself to step forward and sneak down the hall. The air grew hotter and hotter. It was hard to breathe.

I heard a scuffling noise and stiffened. I looked behind me just in time to see a small gray shadow scamper along the wall. Wildlife, without a leash. I scurried in the opposite direction until I reached an open door where the machine noise came from. A plaque on the door said TRANSFORMER ROOM. I stepped inside.

Instantly I felt my gut seem to vibrate and a tingling sensation like static pierced through me. It wasn't fear, it was something else. A low-frequency hum filled the air. I looked for the source, but it was all around. Huge gray metal boxes surrounded the room on all sides, floor to ceiling. HAZARDOUS VOLTAGE, said one of the boxes, with a red bolt of lightning. WILL CAUSE SEVERE INJURY OF DEATH. I'd had enough of severe injury and death. I got out of there in a hurry.

I hustled through the room to the adjoining one, where the machine noise was the loudest. The open door between the two said CHILLER ROOM, but the room was steaming hot for a chiller room. There was no place to hide in here, everything was too exposed. Sweat soaked through my suit, bringing up my awful smell. I wiped my cheeks on my skirt to avoid the inevitable poop-drip into my eyes. When I stopped, I was standing in front of a tall brown machine.

It looked like a tin cabinet and read DUNHAM-BUSH. Its round thermometers had stick-needles that hovered at 42 degrees. I guessed it chilled water, maybe for air-conditioning. Pipes and ducts of various colors spanned the ceiling and I realized they were color-coded. Red meant fire, blue meant water, and a yellow pipe read REFRIGERANT DISCHARGE VENT. Suddenly I heard a clanging sound and scooted in fear behind the big Dunham-Bush box. Behind it was a room, a tiny, empty room, with its dented metal door hanging open.

A saggy cot was pressed against the wall of the room and on the floor next to it were newspapers. A wrinkled poster on the wall displayed most of a brunette's anatomy, next to a dirty gray rag mop. I heard another sudden *clang*, so I ducked in and hid behind the door. I waited for the sound of footsteps but there were none. Maybe the clang was mechanical, part of the ongoing cacophony. As soon as I got the nerve, I ventured out from behind the door and set my stuff on the cot.

The place smelled faintly of marijuana. Two empty Coke cans sat on an orange crate at the head of the cot, and I picked up the newspaper from the floor. It was from so long ago I wasn't in it, so I guessed the room wasn't frequently cleaned. I could use this as a home base, at least temporarily. I imagined the police cruisers tearing around above me, hunting me. I'd gone underground. For real.

I plopped onto the skinny cot next to my stuff and forced my brain to come up with a next step. I was almost safe, and exhaustion sneaked up on me as my tension ebbed. I slumped over, resting my eyes. I felt myself drifting and almost began to doze. I checked my watch: 6:15. Whatever morning shift there was would be in any minute. I couldn't sleep now, I had to move on.

I imagined I was on the river, rowing. A sleek tan scull slicing a streak through a smooth blue river, running through the bright sunshine. I was exhausted, but pumping away still. Power-stroking toward the finish line. Rowing had taught me that when you thought your last reserve was depleted, you had another ten strokes left. Energy to spare. All you had to do was summon it up. Insist.

I stood up and stretched. I was groggy, disoriented, and exhausted. I figured that my mother's next treatment would be today, but it was too risky to show up at the hospital. I'd have to leave her in Hattie's hands.

I crossed to the scuzzy sink and washed my face with a desiccated bar of Lava soap. I shampooed my hair and dried it with paper towels. Then I redid my makeup, hid my clothes in a filthy corner under the cot, and did what everybody else does on Monday morning in America.

I got dressed for work.

THIRTY-THREE

The office building was on the other side of town from the Silver Bullet, but it might as well have been on the other side of the world. Its tiny lobby smelled of stale cigar smoke and the pitted floor felt gritty under my new spike heels. A cheap white-letters-on-black office directory revealed only three tenants in the low-rise: LAW OFFICES OF VICTOR CELESTE, ESQUIRE; CELESTE LAND HOLDINGS AND CELESTIAL ENTERPRISES, INC.

There was nothing else in the lobby except a grayish standard-issue desk, located in front of the elevator bank. An aged security guard hunched over the desk, studying the sports page as he fingered his ear, which barely held an oversized plastic hearing aid. A cigarette hung between his lips. It almost dropped out of his mouth when he saw me.

"Good mornin', Miss," he said, blinking as he took in my white silk tank top and black leather suit, whose skirt I'd rolled to an obscene length and paired with seamed black stockings. The personal shopper had promised "happening," which I now understood to mean tarty. So I'd completed the ensemble with my black sunglasses, a helmet of newly red hair, and a slash of the reddest lipstick sample at the drugstore counter. I was hoping I looked like a professional call girl and not an amateur secret agent.

"Good morning to you, too, sir," I purred, sashaying past him as if he had no right to stop me.

"Eh, Miss, wait. Wait. Please."

"Did you want me, sir?" I pivoted on my spikes and smiled suggestively. Or what I hoped was suggestive and not merely dyspeptic. I tried to recall the serial screen hookers I'd seen in movies, Hollywood having presented so many positive images of successful businesswomen.

"Miss . . . do you have an appointment or somethin'? I have to know before I let you through."

"My name is Linda. I'm a friend of Mister Celeste's. A personal friend, if you understand my meaning." I struck a Julia Roberts pose, hand on hip.

"Just Linda?" he asked, leaning forward in his creaky chair. I couldn't tell if he was becoming aroused or just couldn't hear.

"Linda, that's all. That's all Mister Celeste calls me, and that's all I am. Linda."

The old man stubbed out his cigarette. "Eh, Mr. Celeste isn't in yet. Nobody's in yet."

"I know. I'm supposed to get here before Mister Celeste does. He wanted me to get everything ready for him, the way he likes it." I waved my new black handbag in the air, as if no further explanation were required. Meanwhile, it contained a cell phone and three crumpled Tampax. Party time.

"Oh. Oh, I see," he said, and coughed nervously. "How are you gonna get in his office? I don't have a key."

"Mister Celeste gave me one, of course." I held up my

Grun key. "His law office is on the first floor, is it not?" A touch of Judy Holliday, for nostalgia.

"Yeh, but how do I know you're not gonna rob him?" the guard asked, only half joking.

"Do I look like a thief?" I pouted. All Marilyn. If she were tall as a house.

"Eh, no, not at all. But, I mean, I never seen you—"

"That's because Mister Celeste always comes to *me*." I swiveled around and punched the greasy button for the up elevator, street-smart as Jane Fonda in *Klute*. Bree, that's me.

"I don't know about this," the old guard fretted, rising slowly from behind the desk. "Mr. Celeste didn't tell me you had an appointment with him this morning." He shuffled to the elevator bank and faced me.

"Well, if I don't get up there and get everything ready, you'll have to explain to Mister Celeste why I wasn't there like he said." The elevator arrived with a tubercular *ding* and the doors rattled open. I scurried inside and hit the button.

"Wait a minute, Miss. Linda. I can't leave my post." The doors began to slide closed, but the guard stuck his veined hands between them and struggled to push them apart. I gasped, alarmed. This was more vigilance than I bargained for. I didn't want to see his hands crushed.

"Let me go, please! Mister Celeste will be real mad if I don't show! He's countin' on me. He told me, it was *real* important!"

"Press the OPEN button!" he shouted, pulling the doors apart like Spartacus in retirement. The gap between them began to widen, and I punched the CLOSE button frantically. Suddenly the elevator started to sound a deafening, continuous beep.

BBBBBEEEEEEEPPPP!

"When Mister Celeste gets disappointed, boy, does he have a temper! He's got a big gun, too! Did you know that?"

BBBBBEEEEEEEEPPPPPPPPP!

"A what?" the guard yelled.

BBBBBBBBEEEEEEEEEEEEEEEPPPP!

The decibel level apparently wreaked havoc with his hearing aid, because the guard took one of his hands off the door and covered his bad ear. The elevator doors struggled to close. The gap narrowed. The guard's fingertips turned white.

"Mister Celeste has a gun!"

BEEP!

I stood before an old-fashioned office door, a wooden frame with starry frosted glass, figuring out how to get inside. I was a worse sleuth than I was a hooker. A graduate of the crossing-that-bridge-when-we-come-to-it school of detection. What could I pick the lock with? I didn't have a bobby pin, they went out with pincurls. I jiggled the lock with the junk on my keychain; first my apartment key, then with my plastic-encased doggie picture. Both were spectacularly unsuccessful.

I checked the hall again, took off my spike heel, and broke the glass window with it. The patent pump as burglar's tool. I slipped my shoe back on and was inside in a flash.

The door opened onto a minuscule waiting room. A plastic rhododendron gathered dust in the corner. There was a worn cloth couch and a boxy old computer on the secretary's desk. Strictly low-tech, and I wasn't surprised. Lawyers like Celeste avoided writing anything, it took too much time. But their fee agreements they had printed by the ream and they took 40 percent. I crossed the waiting room to Celeste's office.

It was a piker's law office and they're all alike. A grandiose desk arranged against a cheap paneled wall and manila files scattered everywhere. Bookshelves that contained law text-books left over from law school, outdated and untouched be-cause the telephone was the only thing that mattered. Celeste's would be a high-volume practice built on slip-and-falls, ersatz workmen's comp injuries, and exploding Coke bottles. Turn-ing chronic sickness into a healthy living. Until Eileen Jennings came along, and Celeste figured he'd make a killing.

I had to find her case file. I'd taken my clues about Mark's killer as far as they could go, so I was working backward from Bill's murder, betting on a hunch it was connected to Mark's. And I needed to know more about Eileen to figure out Bill, so I started digging through the files on Celeste's desk.

Ten minutes later, I had the file stuffed with the Tampax in my purse, and jumped into the elevator. It wasn't until the steel doors slid open on the lobby floor that I realized I had no story to tell our septuagenarian Schwarzenegger. Why would I be leaving the party before Mister Celeste arrived?

"Linda," he said, surprised, from behind the desk. "You leaving?"

"I have to go." I walked quickly to the exit.

"But Mr. Celeste should be in any minute," he said, rising slowly.

"Have to go. Have to hurry. Be right back. Forgot my . . . pliers." I powered through the smudgy glass door without look-ing back.

I hit the sidewalk outside and tottered away in my stiletto heels, squinting in the hazy sun. The city was coming to life only sluggishly this Monday morning, but I walked in the shad-ows of the buildings in case any cops were around. I was all dressed up with nowhere to go. I needed a place to read Eileen's file, but I couldn't go back to my underground room until nightfall because there would be employees around during the day. Then I got an idea.

I walked quickly past the seamier blocks of Locust Street, slipped into the first Greek restaurant I could find, and ducked into the bathroom to unroll my skirt and wipe off my lipstick. I popped my sunglasses back on and left the bathroom, heading where everybody goes when they need to read quietly. The police would never look for me there, it was too public. I was there by the time it opened.

The Jenkins Memorial Law Library is frequented by only two types of lawyers in the legal caste system: Brahmins who use it to research the law of another state and the untouchables who can't afford their own law library. This morning, Jenkins contained both extremes, and the best of times and the worst of times regarded each other warily over the marble busts. I avoided them all and crossed the pile rug to the metal stacks in the back where I found a deserted carrel. I settled in, kicked off my high heels, and began to read.

The file was a mess of yellow legal papers scribbled in a childish scrawl. Celeste had apparently conducted only a few interviews with Eileen, and his notes were filled with incomplete sentences: *Grad HS. Cheerl. Drinking. Father in service.* Throughout, in the margins and even across the notes, it read:

apple 35
orange 30
bread 100
Snickers—Fun Size (small) 150
Eggbeaters 150??? (check this)

toast; margarine 80
Baby Ruth—King Size,
*   but only half—?????*

Celeste's calorie-counting was far more meticulous than his record-keeping. It took me a full two hours to recreate his interview with Eileen, which revealed no clues anyway. The rest of the notes were phone numbers in Los Angeles and New York, with names like William Morris scratched next to them. Evidently not witnesses, but film and book agents. Celeste's attempts to sell the story of Eileen's miserable little life. I put the file away in annoyance and pulled out what I hoped would be the gold mine.

The audiotapes. Four plastic cassettes I assumed were the unabridged Eileen. They were unnumbered and unlabeled. I turned them over in my hand. I'd taken a chance swiping them, but so be it, I needed to hear what they said.

I gathered my purse and file from the carrel and prowled around until I found the library's listening booth. It had a heavy glass window in the door and a tape recorder on a built-in desktop inside. I sat down, put on the earphones, and loaded one of the cassettes.

Eileen was giggling at something Celeste had said, and just the sound of it made me angry. That voice—high, careless, flirtatious. And dangerous, cunning. Eileen had murdered a man and put me solidly on the hook for it. I turned up the volume. The interview was in a question-and-answer format:

Q: *Tell me about your relationships, Eileen. The relationships that formed your personality.*
A: *Only the hot stuff now, right? (Giggle, giggle)*

Q: Right.

A: Well, Bill, of course, he wasn't the first.

Q: Kleeb, you mean. Well, who was?

A: Oh, a boy from home. When I was, like, fourteen?

Q: That's young.

A: Nah. Not for me. I was ready.

Q: Who was he?

A: Another farm boy. I just like farm boys, I guess.

Q: Why do you think that is?

A: Big muscles. Tattoos. No brains. (Giggle, giggle) I even got married, once upon a time.

Q: I didn't know that.

A: Nobody does.

Q: When was that?

Barbara Freaking Walters. I tried to concentrate, but it wasn't easy. I struggled to listen to this self-indulgent tripe, but I hadn't slept all night. And I hadn't had my coffee. It was criminal working conditions, no pliers and no caffeine.

A: When I was eighteen. He was twenty. An older man.

Q: Twenty? A regular Methuselah.

A: A what?

Q: Forget it. Go on about your marriage. It's good background information for the character.

A: Do you really think it'll be a movie-of-the-week?

Q: I wouldn't be here if I didn't. So go on, okay? I want to get the tapes to the agent right away.

A: Will I get a copy?

Q: (sighing) I'll make one for you. Just tell the story, please.

A: Well, my husband, he was (unintelligible)—

Q: *What was he?*

A: *He was . . . abusive. He used to hit me, when he drank.*

Q: *Really.*

A: *Uh . . . yes. The loser.*

Q: *Did you ever take pictures of it, like Polaroids?*

A: *No.*

Q: *Did you ever go to the hospital for it?*

A: *No.*

Q: *(disappointed) Well, how often did he hit you?*

A: *Once a week, or twice, for a long time.*

Q: *Then you divorced him. You had to raise yourself up and divorce him, right?*

A: *No I just left him. The lawyers weren't no help. I got the court orders, one after the other, but he just kept comin' back. Beatin' me. There wasn't nothin' the courts could do about it. Half the time the police wouldn't even come.*

My head was beginning to pound. I rubbed my eyes to stay awake. The sadness in her story was lost on me. She was a victim, so she victimized. I accept no excuses for murder. An innocent man was dead at her hand and maybe Bill, too.

I shifted in my chair and my gaze fell upon a Daumier sketch on the wall. A lawyer slipping his hand into his client's pocket or the other way around, but the glass over the print reflected something else. A figure. A man in the library stacks, in a dark suit jacket. He was bent over reading a book. I couldn't see his head or face, but his back looked familiar. I held my head down to avoid being recognized.

Q: *So you never even divorced him?*

A: *Nope.*

Q: You're married to him, now?

A: No. I heard he died. He got shot.

Q: (impressed) Really. In a bar? Or by a gang or something?

A: No, no. A hunting accident. He always drank when he hunted, so did his buddies. Dumb-asses.

Hunting. I flashed on the cabin in the woods. Bill's cold body. Was there a connection? My eyes fell on the Daumier sketch. In the reflection, the hunched figure turned the page of his book. Who was he? Did he recognize me? Was he a cop? I tried to remember the cops I knew who worked plainclothes. I covered my face with my hand, like I was getting a headache, which I was.

Q: Okay, so let's get on with it.

A: It was the courts, you know. They screwed it up. I went to the law clinic, you know, to try to get whatever it's called to keep him away from me.

Q: A TRO, a temporary restraining order?

A: Yeah, that's it. But the courts, those judges, they don't know the score.

The figure had shelved his book and was moving in the stacks now, right down the aisle toward the listening booth. I doubled over quickly and pretended I was coughing.

A: (excited) I don't care, they don't know jack.

Q: Who was your lawyer?

A: At the clinic?

Q: Yes.

A: Just one of the clinic lawyers.

Q: Can you remember his name?

Suddenly there was a hard rap on the glass door of the booth. My stomach tensed. I didn't know what to do. I turned up the volume on the tape player and hoped he'd go away.

A: *Why do you need the name?*
Q: *In case we need to get a release for the TV movie. You need releases if it's real people.*
A: *(pausing) Oh. It was a girl. Uh . . . Renee. Renee something, I think. I'll have to get back to you on that. I don't know where she is now, anyway.*

Huh? What? Renee? Could Eileen's lawyer have been Renee Butler? I couldn't believe my ears. I hit the REWIND button just as the door swung open behind me.

THIRTY-FOUR

s that *you*?" he asked, shocked.

"Is that *you*?" I asked, equally shocked. It was Grady, my lawyer and faithless lover. I wondered fleetingly if these things would always go together in my life. Maybe that was the problem.

"Bennie!" He closed the door quickly behind him, his gray eyes relieved.

"Grady, how the hell are you! Here's a good one. How can you tell when a man is lying?"

"What?"

"His lips are moving."

His brow knit in confusion. "What are you talking about? Where have you been? What are you doing *here*? I've been worried about you."

"Of course you have. That's why you needed consoling the other morning."

"What are you talkin' about?" he drawled, squatting down so that he was eye-level with me.

"What am I *talkin'* about?" I rolled my chair backward, even though he was wearing my favorite dark blue workshirt and khakis. I should've known he'd cheat. Nobody could do that much for a workshirt and not cheat. "I'm *talkin'* about that woman. Was it your old girlfriend? Backsliding, again?"

"Who? I'm not seeing her anymore, I told you."

"Then who answered your phone, Grady? It was morning. You were asleep."

"Was it Sunday?"

"I guess."

His forehead uncreased and he smiled. "That was Marshall. She told me somebody called and hung up. She came by and spent the night. On the couch, of course."

"Marshall?" I heard myself sounding stupid and felt even stupider than I sounded. "She talked so softly, I didn't recognize her voice."

"She'd been upset and wanted to know the truth about you. That's why she ran off, she was worried you might have done it. She thought you found Mark's hidden files, she knew he was setting up his new firm. We talked until late, and she stayed over on Sunday."

"Marshall, huh." My face felt hot. So I'd been wrong to suspect either of them of anything. I wanted off the subject. "What are you doing here anyway?"

"Wait a minute, you were jealous."

"I was not."

"Were too." He grinned.

"Drop it, Grady, and tell me what you're doing here."

"I had research to do, but I couldn't do it at the firm. The cops are all over it. They've got a guard there all the time in case you come back." He grabbed the arms of my chair and pulled me close to him. "By the way, I like this outfit."

"Black leather?"

"Why do you think I ride a motorcycle?" His hands crept to my knees, but I pushed them away.

"We don't have time for that. What are you researching?"

"Nothing."

"Bull. What did you find out?"

"Let's not discuss it now." He leaned close and planted a small kiss behind my ear, but I squirmed away.

"What's going on?"

"Doesn't matter."

"Tell me or you're fired."

He sighed. "The cops found the Camaro in Sam's garage. Somebody called them because it didn't have a resident sticker. They traced it to my cousin and found out he has the same last name as mine. They're trying to prove I helped you get away."

"Oh, no." My heart sank. "Can they?"

"Probably. Azzic called Jamie himself, but Jamie didn't tell him he lent the car to me. He told him it was stolen from in front of my uncle's house."

"Had he reported it stolen to the Jersey police?"

Grady's lip buckled. "No. He can say he forgot."

"A new car?" I felt a wave of guilt. "I should never have involved you."

"That's enough of that," he said, touching my arm. "I involved myself. I love you, remember?"

It only made me feel worse. "They'll pick you up for aiding and abetting. They'll have enough as soon as they ask around Sam's building. Then they'll figure out my disguise, if they haven't already."

"I'll handle what happens with me. What are you doin' here anyway? What are those tapes you're listening to?"

But Grady was already popping the earphones over his

thatch of blond hair. His eyes widened as soon as he hit the
PLAY button.

We stood like strangers on opposite sides of the elevator, at my
insistence. I wanted distance for all sorts of reasons, but Grady
wasn't having any.

"Bennie? What about you? How do you feel about me?"

"I'm wanted for murder and am becoming one with my
sunglasses. We should discuss this subject when neither of
these things is true." And maybe by then I'd know the answer.

He began watching the elevator numbers change. "So
you're going back to that hole in the basement?"

"Sooner or later."

"You sure I can't just stop by to check on you?"

"Too risky."

"Do you have enough money?"

"Now I do, thanks to your continued aiding and abetting."
He'd given me forty dollars, all he had on him.

"Are you safe where you're hiding?"

"Safer than in that booth with you."

He smiled. "How am I going to find you again?"

"You're not, for a while. It's too dangerous," I said matter-
of-factly. I was the boss here, wasn't I? "After we get it all
straightened out, then we can give it a try. Us, I mean."

"Yes, sir."

"Good. I like it."

"You like it too much."

We reached the ground floor. The elevator doors glided open
and a horde of suits shoved their way past us into the elevator. I
moved into the crowd with concern, more for Grady than for me.

"We can't walk out together," I whispered, as we squeezed toward the front of the lobby. A glass wall and revolving doors divided us from a congested Chestnut Street.

"I'll go first." His eyes were scanning the street as anxiously as mine. "This way I can scope it out."

"No. Let me go first, then you follow. Wait ten minutes."

"But nobody will recognize you, Bennie. I barely did. Let me go first. I'll signal if there's trouble."

"No, good-bye now. Take care." I left him by the revolving door, which emptied onto a pavement lousy with lawyers flowing into the building. They were returning to Jenkins Library after lunch, bellies full of corned beef specials. Damn the cholesterol, life on the edge.

I adjusted my sunglasses and was about to swim against the tide when an older woman, caught in the crowd, got knocked off-balance. "Oh, my!" she yelped and she tumbled right into my arms.

The crowd flowed around us, apathetic as trout. I was the fugitive, my job was to run, but I had an armful of old lady.

"My back, my back! Please help me, it went out," she said.

"Okay, it's all right." I eased her to the wall of the building and out of the foot traffic. She felt as frail as my mother, brittle bones in a thin sack of skin.

"My back, I need to lie down. Please." Her face was etched with pain, so I squatted against the granite wall and eased her head onto my tight skirt. Her pink uniform smock said MAIN-TENANCE in a patch sewn over her breast, but she had no nametag. In a world of nametags, the people who clean up after us remain nameless.

"What's your name?" I asked.

"Eloise," she said with difficulty. "It hurts, my back." Her forehead was damp at her hairline, a steely gray, and her hand clutched at my jacket sleeve. For lack of anything better to do, I got down on my knees and cradled her, a lawyerly Pietà.

Suddenly there was a disturbance at the far side of the crowd. Noises out front, on the street, then shouting. The crowd burst into excited chatter and edged back towards the old woman.

"Hey!" I shouted, and bonked a man in the calf.

Out of nowhere came a blast of police sirens, not ten feet from where I crouched. My heart began to pound. Brakes screeched at the curbside. Tires squealed. Orders were barked. Were they after me? I couldn't see anything but a gaggle of wingtips and black nylon socks. What was going on?

The crowd pressed dangerously back toward us. I cradled Eloise, as much for my comfort as for hers. Between the ankles and feet, I could see the white flash of a squad car streaking to the curb, then another. Uniformed cops were hustling from the cars. Leaping out of the first one, his tie flying, was Detective Azzic.

I felt a bolt of fear. My instinct was to run. I felt it in my feet, in every muscle in my legs. Adrenaline dumped into my bloodstream, telling my body to fly. *Go, run. Take off.*

"My back, it hurts." Eloise groaned. "It hurts so bad."

What about Eloise? I couldn't leave her on the pavement, she'd be trampled, and if I got up and ran now, they'd nab me for sure. No. Stay put. The crowd would screen me from the cops. I ducked lower so they wouldn't see my face.

Then it hit me. It wasn't me they were after. It was Grady, and there was nothing I could do about it.

In the next instant, a phalanx of uniformed cops hustled from the office building. In the middle, taller than most of them, was a stoic Grady. His hands were cuffed behind his back, and the cops yanked him along by his elbows. I felt a wrench of pain at the sight. One of the cops dangled his back-pack by a strap. They shoved him into the back of the squad car, and Azzic climbed into the passenger seat in front.

"On your way, people," said one of the cops, dispersing the mob. "There's nothing to see, nothing to see."

Eloise squinted up at me. "Keep your head down, honey. They'll be gone in a minute."

THIRTY-FIVE

Ten minutes later I had my co-conspirator on her feet and was hustling in spike heels down Chestnut Street, trying to blend in with the lunchtime crowd. I looked everywhere behind my sunglasses, eyes sweeping right and left. Only public transportation and cops were allowed to drive on Chestnut Street, making the police cars easy to spot. None were around, but I was still uneasy. I couldn't believe how fast they'd materialized at the library. They must have been tailing Grady. Maybe they were tailing me right now. My gut tensed. I hobbled along with the flow on the sidewalk, my thoughts churning.

So Grady had been arrested, undoubtedly as an accessory after the fact. Either Azzic had traced the bananamobile to him, or wasn't worried if he could make the charge stick and wanted to increase the pressure on me. He would ruin a terrific lawyer in the process, and it was way too close for comfort. They were closing in.

I picked up the pace as best I could, fighting the panic rising in my chest, constricting my throat. I thought of the Eileen tapes. How long before Celeste discovered they were missing? Eileen's folder had been near the top on his desk. It had to be the hottest thing going for him right now. How long before he reported it to the police? How long before Azzic realized I had something to do with it? I was running out of time. The guard would remember my disguise, no problem. *Pliers?* Damn.

"Hey, baby," said a voice at my arm, and I jumped. "How you doin'?" It was a short man with tattoos, and he was leering at me. "You wanna spend some time with a real man, baby?"

Then I remembered what I looked like. An oversized hooker who couldn't walk in heels. "I am a real man, handsome. Now beat it."

I wobbled ahead. There were fewer and fewer people on the sidewalk. The bus traffic had thinned out. Everybody was going back to work, leaving me feeling exposed. I needed to hide, but I still couldn't risk going uptown to the basement. I needed to get off the street before another tattoo stopped me.

A bus steamed by in a cloud of sooty smoke and braked with a hydraulic squeal at the corner stop. Perfect. *Go.* I hustled across the street, grabbed the bus, and fed the machine my fare with a shaking hand. The bus lurched forward, and I groped for the slippery pole, eyeing the riders. There were no cops on board and the faces in the padded seats looked comfortably blank, many plugged into radio earphones. No one seemed to recognize me.

I made my way to the back of the bus and took a seat in the last row, which was empty except for a teenager on the far right in a Raiders shirt. I sat down in the back row, scooted way over against the greasy window on the far left, and willed myself to calm down. Breathe easily, normally. I wiped my damp brow under my sunglasses. I couldn't stop thinking about Grady. Where was he now? In a holding cell? Had he called a lawyer? Who? I couldn't help him or me, except to solve this damn thing.

I fished in my purse and unpacked the Casio cassette player Grady had had in his backpack. He said it would free me from the library and he'd been right. I tried not to worry about him as I unwrapped the long wire, slipped in a cassette of Eileen unplugged, and pressed the itsy-bitsy black earphones into my ears. Now I looked just like the other people on the bus.

I pushed the PLAY button.

Q: Where was this lawyer?
A: At a clinic. I didn't have to pay.
Q: See, you get what you pay for.
A: But it was the courts, not the lawyer. The lawyers there,
   they were good.
Q: So tell me about your next boyfriend.
A: That would be Deron.
Q: (laughing) Deron, huh? A nice Jewish boy.

I listened to this kind of crap for the next four hours, riding around my hometown in circles. Down Chestnut Street, over on Sixth, then up Walnut, all the way to West Philly and back again. The Raiders fan stayed on the bus for two round-trips and he wasn't the only person riding aimlessly, maybe because the bus was air-conditioned. During that time, the back row filled in and emptied out. Riders came and went. Nobody spoke to me or even gave me a second glance.

The day turned to an overcast evening, the tapes ran to

their end, and no other clues announced themselves during Eileen's inane interviews. If anything, the tapes were more significant for what they didn't say. Eileen barely mentioned Bill Kleeb, he was a footnote to her fascinating life story, and there was no mention of any drug use, or of Sam. On the last tape, a jailhouse interview, she told the fabricated story of the CEO's murder as if she had been my dupe, the pawn of a crazed radical lawyer. I could only shake my head. We used to give jail time to frauds like Eileen, now we gave them book deals.

I rewound the tape and listened again to the part about Renee Butler, but learned nothing more than I already had. I played the tape over and over as passengers climbed off and on the bus at the end of the workday, toting briefcases and shopping bags for the trip home.

I hadn't gone anywhere, but I'd made progress. I was narrowing in on Renee, developing the next questions to be answered. What legal clinic had she worked in? I knew every public interest law center on the East Coast and didn't remember any of them listed on her résumé. We'd gotten her right out of Penn Law, so maybe it was the law school clinic, staffed by students.

It could have been. Renee could have met Eileen there. But would she really kill Mark and frame me for it? I remembered our conversation in her office. Maybe her anger with me that day was all an act. The best defense is a good offense. It would make sense, and she would testify against me so she could drive in the final nail.

A siren blared suddenly on my right. Two squad cars came racing toward my bus, which squeaked heavily to a stop. I

slunk down in my seat, my breathing shallow. A middle manager searched my face inquiringly. The police cars screamed
past my window, then tore down the street. A near miss but my
pulse refused to return to normal. The middle manager got off
at the next stop, with a quizzical look back at me. Was he going
to call the cops? I couldn't take the chance. My stop wasn't for
three blocks, but when the manager was out of sight I stood up
and got off the bus.

I had no time to lose. My head down even as night fell, I
hurried down the blocks to my building and strode through
the employees' door acting for all the world like I owned
the place. The Trident gum I'd stuck in the door's lock had
worked like a sugarless charm. Inside, I fumbled in my purse
for the penlight I'd bought instead of the red lipstick at the
dime-store.

I hustled as fast as I could down the corridor, behind the
jittery pinpoint of light. My feet swelled in my heels and my silk
top grew damp as the corridors got hotter and hotter. I slipped
my shoes off and walked through the transformer room, tip-
toeing behind the gray boxes to avoid any maintenance types
still around, maybe an evening shift.

I snuck into my little hovel, closed the door, and switched
on the light. The place hadn't been disturbed since yesterday and the smell of dope was almost gone. Whoever's hiding
place this was had been working harder lately, which was fine
with me. I'm all for American productivity.

In fact, I had a job to do myself. I reached under the bed
for my clothes and changed into a navy pantsuit with retro
bell bottoms, the closest thing I had to burglary wear. Then
I shoved my puffy toes into the heavy black clodhoppers that

said Dr. Martens Air Cushion Sole inside. What was this personal shopper thinking? You'd have to pay me to wear these in the daylight. I laced them up, grabbed my penlight, and went out into the night.

Bouncing along to a break-in.

THIRTY-SIX

Renee Butler's rowhouse was a typical Philadelphia trinity, so called because there were three floors with a single room on each floor. It looked like a tiny brick box with pale white shutters; white flower boxes over-flowed with leggy purple pansies and vinca vines. A women's house, and tonight its owners, Renee and Eve, were throwing a party.

I stole into a dark alley across the street and watched, disappointed. Even I didn't have the moxie to break and enter during a house party. But what kind of party was this? And so soon after Mark's death?

Music floated from the open windows, a syncopated jazz rhythm, not Green Day. Odd. Nobody was dancing, either, and in the windows I could see people chatting over iced drinks. I spotted a waiter through the window on the second floor, serving hors d'oeuvres to guests in shirts and ties. A waiter? What gives? This wasn't the type of party the associates usually gave at R & B. But then again, there was no more R & B.

A head turned suddenly on the first floor. Renee. Her coarse hair was slicked back into a glossy twist and huge silver hoops dangled from her ears. She wore a long dashiki, looking like she'd lost some weight. Suddenly she walked to the window and lifted the sash.

I dodged back into the alley and waited a beat. Except for the party, the street was quiet and still, one of those cobblestoned Philadelphia backways that's too narrow even for a car. I popped out again. I wanted to see what Renee was doing.

She appeared to be chatting up a good-looking man in a suit. Who was he? Who were these people? I heard voices coming down the street and flattened against the building, edging into the alley.

A couple approached, the man holding the woman by the elbow. She was giggling as she negotiated the cobblestones in pumps. When they got closer I could see it was Bob Wingate, dressed in a real tie, with the ever-perky Jennifer Rowland. I turned my head to the darkness to avoid being seen.

So there were other R & B associates at this shindig. Did they know about Grady's arrest? I waited until I could hear the front door close and Wingate's voice had disappeared inside. Then I peered out again.

On the second floor, I could see Eve in a tight tan dress, flanked by a tall man. I couldn't tell who it was because his back was to the window, but when she leaned over to whisper something to him, I caught a glimpse of his steely-glassed profile. Dr. Haupt from Wellroth. Beside him stood Kurt Williamson, the general counsel, with a chiffoned battle-ax I assumed was his wife. Around them stood a circle of sycophants, like corporate ringworm.

Of course. This wasn't the usual associate party. The faces were older, the hair was silvered, and the couples were married. These people were corporate clients. No wonder nobody was having any fun.

"Quiet, please!" someone shouted inside. The music stopped abruptly and the conversation trailed off. Heads turned in the direction of Dr. Haupt, who raised his glass in a toast I couldn't hear. Eve beamed and everyone sipped their champagne. Then I understood. The joint venture must have gone through. Everyone was clapping and Eve mock-curtsied. Only Renee, watching her roommate, barely smiled behind her goblet.

What was going on behind those dark eyes of hers? I had to find out, but I didn't know what to do if I couldn't search the house. I needed a Plan B. I took an inventory of what I knew. Renee Butler was connected with Eileen Jennings and their connection was Penn's legal clinic. If I couldn't find out this way, I'd find out another.

Either way you looked at it, the party was over.

I cleared my throat, squared my shoulders, and prepared to confront my umpteenth security guard in a week's time. I'd met old ones, young ones, black ones, and white ones, and yet was rapidly coming to the conclusion there were too many guards in the world and not enough security. Too many police and not enough safety. How could it be otherwise, when a girl like me was on the run?

I pushed through the glass doors to Penn's law school and confronted my latest guard. This one was a civilian; short, spectacled, and seated behind a wooden dais studying corporation law. A law student, in his second year if he was taking what we fondly called "corpse." He looked up, blinking through thick hornrims as I approached. He wouldn't be the best-looking security guard, but I was guessing he'd be the smartest. Damn. I'd have to find his pressure point. A second-year student? In this economy? Piece of cake.

"I have a problem and so do you," I said, leaning on the dais with a weariness that came easily.

"I have a problem?"

"I'm a partner at Grun & Chase. You know the firm."

"Sure, I know the firm." He swallowed visibly and closed the thick red casebook, squishing his index finger in the middle to mark his place. If it hurt, he didn't show it. No feelings? He'd make a fine suit. "Everybody knows Grun & Chase," he said.

"Of course they do. As I was saying, I interviewed here the other day and, unfortunately, left my résumés and my entire file in the law clinic. You have a key to let me in, I assume."

"Sure."

"Good. Let's do it."

"Uh, I didn't know they held interviews in the clinic."

"Well, they do. They're for clinic students."

"Weird." He cocked his head. His dark brown hair had been buzzed into an old-fashioned cut, from when the styles had names. I was guessing his was The Geek.

"What's weird?" I asked.

"It's summer. I didn't know they did on-campus interviewing in the summer."

Think fast, stupid. "It's not the normal interviewing. It's of select second-year students. Clinic students. I didn't interview you, did I?" I flashed him an arrogant, Grun-patented should-I-know-you squint.

"No. I, uh, didn't know about the interviews."

"They're very hush-hush. We like it that way."

"I don't take clinic either."

"Too bad."

"And I'm not very *select,* anyway, I guess." He looked away, his thin shoulders sloping dejectedly in their Nine Inch Nails T-shirt He reminded me a little of Wingate. I felt momentarily sympathetic.

"Did you interview with Grun?"

"Yes, during the year. But I didn't get a call back."

"How are your grades?"

"Not Law Review."

"Okay, but are they good?"

"Well, they're not terrible." He bit his lip.

"Not terrible?" If this kid didn't learn to present himself better, they'd eat him alive. "You mean they're improving."

"Improving, right." He punched his glasses up at the bridge.

"Do you have some sort of experience? Grun likes that, all firms do. Practical experience, you know."

"I worked at my father's office first year summer and I got a lot of practical experience. Also, I'm a very practical person. I approach problems in a *practical*—"

"I get it. Do you have a job lined up for after you graduate?"

"No," he said. His face reddened as if it were a source of deep shame, which in the law school culture, it was.

"Where are you working now, this summer?"

"Uh, here."

"Even during the day?"

He swallowed. "I couldn't get a law job."

I looked at him and he looked at me. We both knew what this meant. He was about to graduate at least a hundred grand in the hole, with no hope of paying it back. This kid needed help. I almost found myself believing my own scam. "What happened with your grades?" I asked. "Didn't you study?"

"I did, I studied really hard. But when the tests came, I just kind of . . . froze." He shook his head, biting his lower lip again. "Maybe I'm just not good enough to be a lawyer. Maybe I'm not cut out for it."

"Maybe you just don't think well on your feet."

"I don't. That's what my dad says."

"All that means is that you can't be a trial lawyer. But there are other kinds of lawyers."

"But litigation is the coolest—"

"Forget what's cool. What's your favorite course?"

"Corporate tax."

"Tax?" It was almost inconceivable. What was it with this younger generation? Tax, instead of constitutional law? "You actually *like* tax?"

"It's like a puzzle, a big puzzle, and you can put it together and it all makes sense." He smiled for the first time, lost in the beauty and wonder of the Internal Revenue Code.

"How did you do in tax?"

"I got an E, an excellent. It was my only one." He grinned with pride, and I, with relief.

"So why don't you apply for a tax program, like at NYU? Get your master's in tax. You'll do well, then you can slip right into any firm. You'll get forbearance on your school loans and another year to find a job."

"You think I can do it?"

"Of course you can."

"Maybe it's not too late to apply?"

"Not if you do it now."

He beamed. "Then I will!"

"There you go," I said, buoyed until I watched his expression change from ebullience to confusion.

"Wait. Why are you telling me this?"

It caught me up short. "Because I like you."

He eased back in his chair, frowning behind his hornrims. "You don't work at Grun, do you? You can't, you're too nice."

I paused. The lobby fell deathly silent. No one was around. I felt exhausted, suddenly. I'd had twenty minutes' sleep in three days. Maybe, just for a change, I'd go with the truth. I wanted to kick out the jambs, and the kid had a face I trusted, like Wingate's.

"You want the truth?" I said. "I'm not a hiring partner or a hooker *or* a murderer."

"O-kay. What are you then?"

"I'm a lawyer and I really, really, really need to get into that clinic."

"Why?"

"It's a long story. I'll tell you on the way."

He paused, considering it. Then he opened the middle drawer. Maybe he didn't think so badly on his feet after all.

THIRTY-SEVEN

We walked down the glistening white corridor of the law school. Everything was stark and modern, except for the gold-framed oil portraits on the walls, one dead lawyer after another. I trailed behind the law student, whose name turned out to be Glenn Milestone, as he led me through the halls and down the basement to the legal clinic. He unlocked the door when we reached it, and it swung open onto a new office that cost more than its indigent clients would make in a lifetime.

"You swear you won't steal anything?" Glenn said for the fiftieth time.

"Swear to God. And you're not going to tell the cops, right?"

"I swear. I'm going, I don't want to see this." He slipped the keys into the pocket of his baggy shorts and turned away.

"Thanks." I watched him go, then looked around to make sure nobody was watching. The place was deserted, so I went inside and closed the door behind me.

The clinic was set up for the kids to play office in, and I half expected to see toy cash registers with Monopoly money in white, pink, and the coveted yellow. There was a small reception area and I went past it to the hall. Off the hall was a lineup of offices. Each one was the same, with steel desks against the wall and padded chairs in front, but I was looking for the file room. I found it at the end of the hall and flicked on the light.

The files were alphabetical. I went to the J's and yanked out the drawer. The files were neatly kept by the lawyers-to-be, and I thumbed through the Jacksons, Jameses, Jimenezes, and Joneses. No Jennings. I stopped, stumped for a moment.

Renee graduated from law school three years ago, so any client file of hers had probably been put away. Where did the law babies keep the dead files? I glanced around but there were no cardboard file boxes or archives in sight. Maybe they were in the file cabinets, unlabeled. I opened the drawers, one after another, each one sliding out with a smooth sound. No dice. They were all current files, applications for credits and evaluation forms, form complaints, answers, and other pleadings. Damn.

I slammed the last one closed and stood there snarling, my hands on my hips. There must be storage somewhere. No lawyer throws away files. No lawyer throws away anything. I thought about my young friend Glenn. I was having second thoughts about him. How long before he told them about me? Would he betray me? How much time did I have? I left the file room and hustled through the office, searching for a storage room.

I ran down the hall, then checked the closets in the offices. Coats, umbrellas, and backpacks. No luck. Behind one of the offices was a small coffee room. I went inside. A can of Folger's sat next to an abandoned coffeemaker and a cord of Celestial Seasonings boxes. Red Zinger, Ginseng Plus, Sleepytime Tea, my ass. I wouldn't hire a kid who didn't drink coffee. No fire in the belly. I shoved the chamomile aside and opened the closet door.

BIERS BUSINESS ARCHIVES, said the cardboard boxes. Bingo. The same archives we used at Grun. I yanked on a hanging string and turned on the closet light, but it was still too dim. I dug in my handbag for my penlight, got up on tiptoe in my clumpy shoes, and rummaged in the first box. They were dead files, but only the first part of the alphabet. I thought I heard voices outside and waited. Nothing. My heart began to pound as I dove into the middle box, propping up the other boxes on my shoulder.

Hilliard. Jacobs. Jensen. A tiny circle of light fell on each manila folder. Then finally, Jennings. My hands began to tremble as I yanked out the folder, then peeked inside to see if it was Eileen's. Complaint In Divorce, said the papers. It was a draft, and the caption read EILEEN JENNINGS V. ARTHUR JENNINGS.

Yes! I flicked off the penlight. But was it the same Eileen Jennings? I tugged the manila folder from the box and flipped to the back of the first pleading. It was signed, in a neat hand, by the name of the lawyer wannabe who drafted it:

Renee R. Butler, Legal Worker

So Renee *had* been Eileen's lawyer! I fought the impulse to read the file and stuffed it in my purse so Glenn wouldn't see me carrying it out. I felt momentarily guilty for breaking my word to him, but it couldn't be helped. I was about to leave when a news clipping sailed to the floor. I picked it up. The paper was yellowed and the printing blotchy, like a neighbor-hood newspaper:

YORK MAN FOUND SLAIN

A York man, Arthur "Zeke" Jennings, was found dead in the alley beside Bill's Taproom this morn-ing, at Eighth and Main. He died from multiple stab wounds. Police Chief Jeffrey Danziger said the police have no suspects in the murder at the present time.

What? The clipping must have dropped from Eileen's file. I held it in my hand and mentally rewound Eileen's cassette tape. She'd said her husband had been shot in a hunting ac-cident, not stabbed in an alley. What gives? And was Renee connected with it somehow? She must have been.

I heard a noise outside in the hall, then something creaky being dragged. I swallowed hard. Someone was coming in. There was no time to run.

"Who's there?" called a woman's voice, from the clinic hallway.

"Linda Frost," I answered.

"Who's Linda Frost?" she asked, coming into view. A stocky black woman, at least fifty years old, wearing a T-shirt and jeans. She pulled an old cleaning cart with a white bag at-tached, and she squinted at me with suspicion. "What are you doing here?"

"I'm a partner at Grun & Chase, one of the law firms downtown, and I needed some information on a clinic student. They let me in to get it."

"In the middle of the damn night?"

"We want to make her an offer tomorrow, and I forgot my notes."

"Well, they wouldn't be in that closet. The students never go in there. That's old files."

"Oh. I thought they might have stuck them in here. You know, put them away. After the interview."

"You interviewed students here today?"

"Yes. Right."

She put a skeptical hand on her soft hip. "What's this student's name? Maybe I know him. I know all the students in the clinic."

"I don't think you know this one. She graduated a few years ago."

"I been here ten years, come December." She rolled her cleaning cart in front of the door, blocking it, and not inadvertently. "What's the student's name?"

I gave up. I was out of lies. "Renee Butler."

"Oh, Renee!" Her broad face burst into a sunny grin and her distrust melted instantly into warmth. "I know Renee! Well, well, well, you lookin' to give Renee a job? You'd be lucky to have her, yes you would. She's smart, that girl, and sweet as jelly. She helped everybody that came through here and plenty of them needed it, believe me."

"I'm sure," I said, surprised.

"And she's not a snob, that girl, no sir. Not high-and-mighty just 'cause she's a lawyer. Always remembers my birthday, even now. Renee sends me a card, every August the 12th. She's smart as a whip. And strong."

"Strong?"

"Very strong. Come through fire." She nodded emphatically. "She had a bad childhood, you know. Her daddy, he beat her and her momma. She had to raise herself, that child, and she did a pretty good job of it."

I thought of Eileen's husband and the beatings she talked about on the tape. Maybe this woman knew something. "Renee told me she helped a lot of abused women at this clinic."

"She did. She was a hard worker, always went the extra mile." She nodded again, and I began to wonder what the extra mile included. Had Eileen killed her husband and Renee covered it up? And what, if anything, did that have to do with Bill or Mark? The cleaning woman had fallen silent and was looking at me expectantly. I didn't think she knew any more, so I stood up stiffly, closed the closet door, and replaced the Red Zinger.

"Thanks for your time now. I think I'll recommend she be hired. I'd better go."

"What about your notes?" She rolled her cart slowly from the threshold, and I squeezed past it, catching a strong whiff of ammonia.

"I don't need them, after talking to you. Bye, now." I went down the office corridor as quickly as I could without renewing her suspicion.

"When you see Renee, tell her 'hi' from Jessie Morgan, will you?" she called after me.

"Sure."

"And tell her to get her fat butt to the next meeting! I never miss a meeting, I lost twenty-eight pounds in one year and kept off every single ounce!"

I reached the clinic door. "Meeting?" I asked, at the threshold.

"Weight Watchers! She missed last Monday night!"

But I couldn't ask another question. Glenn was hustling down the hall towards me, and with him were Azzic and three uniformed cops.

THIRTY-EIGHT

un. Flee. Go! I turned around and sprinted out the exit
onto Samson Street.

"Freeze, Rosato!" Azzic shouted. "You're under arrest!"

I hit the sidewalk outside at a breakneck pace. My heart pumped wildly. My only hope was to outrun them. I'd always been the fastest on my crew.

"Stop, Rosato!" Azzic bellowed from not far behind me, but I barreled up the street.

SCCRREEEEEEEEEEE! A cruiser siren blared in back of me, joined by others screeching in unison. Even I couldn't outrun a car. I needed to go where the squad cars couldn't. Where? I thought back to my college days. My legs churned faster. My heart pumped harder. Adrenaline surged into my bloodstream like jet fuel.

"Rosato! Freeze! Now!"

I careened around the corner and raced across Walnut Street in the dark, dodging cabs and a Ford Explorer that honked angrily. The uniformed cops were right behind me, I could hear their shouted directions to each other as I darted for the main campus. Students hanging out on the common gaped as we ran by. I bolted past them, the police sirens deafening, then took a hard right up Locust Walk. No cars were allowed on the Walk, it was blocked off by cement stanchions. I'd be safe from the cruisers here.

"Rosato! Give it up!"

I glanced backward. No cruisers, but their sirens screamed close by. They'd be flying up Walnut Street, parallel to me. The uniforms were lagging behind but Azzic was gaining. He reached into his jacket as he ran and pulled out his gun in a practiced motion.

I felt the shock of sheer terror. *Please don't shoot me I didn't do it.* I faced front and put on the afterburners.

"Stop or I'll shoot!" Azzic ordered.

A bystander screamed. I imagined Azzic dropping to his knee and aiming two-handed for my back, so I zigzagged for a few steps, then ran like hell. I tore up the Walk and hit the concrete footbridge spanning Thirty-Eighth Street, taking its steep grade in stride. Charging up the hill with power and muscle and stone-cold fear. It was almost easy after the stadium steps. I ignored the pain in my thighs, the ache in my lungs. Even my shoes were helping, bouncy as running shoes.

One, two, three, breathe. One, two, three, breathe. Keep your knees high.

I reached the crest of the footbridge and streaked full tilt down the other side. The momentum carried me down the hill. I accelerated, surefooted from the stadium steps. My breathing was easy and free, my wind strong. Soon I couldn't hear Azzic's voice anymore. I couldn't feel the strain, I couldn't feel anything. I was running, I was moving, I was gone. Slicing down the blackness like a scull. Running, rowing hard.

Nobody was faster. Nobody rowed better. The night blew cool. The wind gusted behind me. The city was far away, so were the police. The city lights, streetlights, the headlights were pinpoints in the darkness, on the banks of the river. Everything was far away. There was only me, my heart pumping explosively, doing what I'd trained it to do. Sweat poured down my body. I took it up for ten power strokes with energy to spare.

One, two, three strokes, to move the scull. It was a race and I was riding high, a long-legged waterskate, feeling only the speed and the spray. Hearing only the clean chop of the oars as they splashed into the moving water, one stroke after another. No halting, no lurching, just the smoothest race possible, pulling the oar hard and then harder. *Four, five, six.* Rowing fast and then faster.

Taking flight. The creak of the rigging. The smell of the river. The wetness of the spray. The cops were gone. Azzic was gone. *Seven, eight, nine, ten.* I'd finally found the rhythm and I couldn't go wrong.

In the middle of the river, in the middle of the night.

I slumped on the floor, naked and exhausted behind the locked door of my room in the basement. I had stripped off my wet clothes, but was still sweating from heat, exertion, and fear. The room was arid, my lungs burned. I felt dizzy, nauseated. I couldn't think clearly, my brain was a fog. I blinked sweat out of my eyes and tried not to drip on the clinic file as I turned the page.

It was a typical case file, except it was neater. The correspondence file, in its own manila folder on the top, contained only form letters from Renee at the legal clinic and no response letters from Eileen. I tossed the folder aside, not caring where it landed.

The pleadings index held restraining orders against Eileen's husband, filed by Renee. Ten orders in all, with contempt citations when the previous court order was broken. There were fines levied against Eileen's husband, but he must have been judgment-proof. Incarceration orders, too, but he couldn't be found. The record told a story if you could read between the pleadings. The courts couldn't stop Eileen's husband from beating her. She would never be free of him, no matter where she moved, no matter where she went.

Until he was dead.

Had Eileen taken matters into her own hands? Had Renee covered, or even done it for her? Was it possible? I flashed on Renee's childhood and the beatings she must have suffered. There were worse things that fathers could do to their daughters than abandon them. Renee had said she knew the depth of my anger, maybe that was because she knew the depth of her own. And maybe Eileen's anger had struck that same dissonant chord. My head throbbed. It hurt to think. I needed sleep, rest, and food, but I couldn't stop now.

I slapped the pleadings index closed and hunted through the accordion file for Renee's notes. Aboveground there would be sirens screaming for me. Azzic and the cops searching the city. I didn't think anyone had seen me slip into the building but maybe I was wrong. Maybe they were upstairs right now, entering the lobby, finding the staircase down. At the door.

Not yet. Not now. I was so close.

Renee was involved with the murder of Eileen's husband, I just didn't know what Mark had to do with it. Had Mark discovered the truth, and Renee killed him for it? Both men had been stabbed to death.

My damp fingers found notes in one of the folders. I

squinted to read them, but they wouldn't come into focus. I felt light-headed, disoriented. The notes were scribbled in ballpoint on legal paper, apparently notes from another interview with Eileen. I was so close I could smell it. I just couldn't read it. My head was killing me, and the handwriting was terrible. I held up the paper. Renee didn't have sloppy writing, did she? I fought to remember but my brain wouldn't work.

I threw the paper aside and ripped through the file. I felt sick, crazy, almost deranged. Where was it? What was it? There had to be an answer. Mark was dead. Bill was dead. I had to find the answer, I was dead if I didn't. It had to be here. The initial complaint stared back at me from my wet hand. I tore off page after page, scattering it willy-nilly, until I got to the last. The signatures.

There. Renee Butler's signature. It swam before me, teasing me like a fish just under the water's surface. I held the signature page next to the messy notes. I blinked. They were completely different. Renee's script was careful, but the notes were careless. Who had taken these notes? Who else had worked on Eileen's case? Another clinic lawyer? Who?

I ransacked the file, then dumped it onto the dirty concrete floor. A waterbug scurried by but I ignored him, tearing through page after page. The file flew in all directions. I was losing my mind. I found the clipping and read it again, then hurled it across the room.

Think. Think. *Think.* Assume Renee killed Eileen's husband, what did that have to do with Mark? Where was Renee the night Mark was killed? What had the cleaning lady said, just before I saw the cops? And what had Hattie said, about Renee bringing a box of stuff to my house?

I could barely breathe. My brain sizzled. I'd played out

the string and reached the end. I slumped forward, doubled over on the littered floor, a madwoman in isolation. I squeezed my eyes shut and screamed silently, every nerve, every muscle stretched to the limit of fear and fatigue. A silent primal scream. A secret cry of pure anguish.

And then it all became clear. My eyes flew open. I sat bolt upright on my haunches.

It had been right in front of me and I hadn't seen it.

Hiding in plain sight.

Now all I had to do was prove it without getting killed.

THIRTY-NINE

G ood morning," I said into my cell phone. "This Leo the Lion?"

"*Rosato!*" asked Azzic, in disbelief. "What the *hell*—"

"I'm at the federal courthouse. Tenth Floor. Be there or be square." I hung up, flipped the phone shut, and jumped out of the Yellow cab. It was done, set in motion.

I bolted through the doors of the courthouse. The Roundhouse was only blocks away and traffic wouldn't be an issue. Azzic would fly here. I checked my watch: 9:30. I figured I had ten minutes to pull this off, at the most. I rushed into the lobby.

Deliverymen pushed dollies across the polished floor. Lawyers conspired with their clients before trial. Federal employees moseyed by on their way to work. There were no cops in sight, only a few blue-jacketed court security officers talking among themselves near the elevators. I kept my head down and joined the line at the metal detector. It was longer than I expected. My stomach tensed. I glanced at the time. 9:35.

My gaze fell on the tabloid carried by a young woman in front of me. WANTED FOR DOUBLE MURDER! the headline screamed. I did a double-take. It was my own face plastered on the front page. A life-sized pencil portrait, complete with new hairdo. My insides torqued into a knot. If anybody in the lobby recognized me I'd be dead.

I lowered my head. My heart thumped inside my chest. Stay calm, girl. Nobody would expect a killer in a courthouse, especially dressed like I was, in a classic red blazer over a black knit dress, with chic sunglasses. It was the only businesslike outfit the shopper had sent me, and I didn't look like a fugitive in it, I looked like a lawyer. I squared my padded shoulders, arranged my face into the mask of a busy professional, and frowned at my watch. 9:37.

The woman put her purse and the tabloid on the conveyor belt to the right. The tabloid flopped open to my picture. I fought the urge to bolt. Did anybody see it? A court security officer stood next to the belt but he was watching the parade of X-ray images on the monitor. If he looked over he'd spot the front page. All it would take was one glance.

"Miss? Step on through, please," said an older court officer to my left. I hadn't even noticed him standing there.

"Sure . . . sorry," I stammered, tearing my eyes from the tabloid. I walked through the metal detector with the newspaper traveling beside me on the conveyor belt, plaguing me like the false accusation it was. I checked the security officer on the stool, but his gaze remained fixed on his monitor. The woman picked up her paper and other belongings, then went on her way. I exhaled for the first time and nabbed my purse as it came off the conveyor belt.

"Kinda dark for sunglasses, don'cha think?" asked a security officer with a cocky smile.

"Pinkeye," I said. I hurried past him and lost myself in the crowd waiting restlessly at the elevator bank. I checked my watch as coolly as possible. 9:40. The seconds ticked by almost palpably. The elevator was taking forever. I should have given myself more time, built in the delays. Police sirens blared outside and everyone ignored them but me. *Just give me five more minutes of freedom.* I had to get upstairs and deliver the cross-examination of my life. For my life.

Where was the damn elevator? Two lawyers began to complain loudly. One in a three-piece suit seemed to be watching me, trying to catch my eye. Did he recognize me from the newspaper? From somewhere else? I turned away, to the gray marble wall.

Bing! The elevator came and I shoved my way in with the mob as the doors closed. The gleaming Rolex of the man sandwiched next to me read 9:42. It was the three-piece suit, who must have maneuvered for the position beside me. He flashed me a sly smile but I stared at the elevator buttons with apparent fascination. The panel was lit like carny lights, and I sweated bullets each time the elevator stopped on a floor that wasn't mine.

9:43. We were at the ninth floor, with only one left to go.

The lawyer shifted closer. "Excuse me," he said, "but don't I know—"

Bing! Tenth Floor! I jumped out of the elevator, ran past the COURT IN SESSION sign, and slipped into the courtroom. I paused by the doors, slipped off my sunglasses, and scoped out the scene.

The gallery was fuller than the first day. Bob Wingate was there next to Renee Butler, as I'd hoped. The Honorable Judge Edward J. Thompson presided and Dr. Haupt sat stiffly in the witness stand. Eve Eberlein stood next to a projector that cast equations onto a white screen at the front of the courtroom. I hadn't figured on the projector. All the better.

The wall clock said 9:44. Time to go. I strode past the bar of the court and slipped my paper under the overhead projector before Eve had time to react. "Your Honor," I said, "members of the jury, would you please take a look at this exhibit? I think you'll find it serves the cause of justice."

"Bennie?" Eve sputtered. "Is that you?"

"Look at the screen. It's Exhibit A."

Eve whirled around and faced the projection screen. It was the news clipping, blown up larger than life at the front of the courtroom:

YORK MAN FOUND SLAIN

I heard her suck wind before she turned and said, "What are you doing here? I'm in the middle of a trial!"

From the dais, a puzzled Judge Thompson said, "Miss? Miss? Aren't you out of order?"

"On the contrary, Your Honor," I said. "This is my only chance to be heard, and it has to be in court to make the police listen."

"Police? What police?"

I looked around. The courtroom was still. The wall clock ticked onto 9:45. No cops. The jury stared at me, everyone stared at me. My face flushed red. Damn elevators. "Uh, they're on their way, Your Honor."

Suddenly Azzic exploded through the courtroom doors with a squad of uniforms behind him and charged up the aisle.

"You killed this man, didn't you, Eve?" I called out. "You

and Renee Butler murdered him, just like you murdered Mark!"

"That's outrageous!" Eve's pretty features were etched with a controlled fury as she eyed the police. "You killed Mark, not me!"

Azzic stopped at mid-aisle and held back his men with a beefy hand. The gallery wheeled back and forth at the commotion.

"You and Renee," I said. "You killed Eileen's husband together. Don't deny it. Renee confessed. She even gave me her key." I reached into my blazer pocket and flashed the edge of my locker key. It was too big, but it would do.

Eve's face slackened with momentary surprise and her gaze found Renee in the gallery.

"No, no!" Renee shouted, jumping to her feet. "That's not true! That's not my key!" Her hands flew to the neckline of her dress and she fumbled with the deep folds of cloth.

A group of court security officers banged through the courtroom doors. Most of the gallery was on its feet and headed for the exits, flooding the aisles. "What is going on here?" Judge Thompson demanded, but nobody was listening, least of all me.

"She's lying, Eve," I said, playing one off against the other. "She told the cops everything. That's why they're here, to arrest you. You stabbed Eileen's husband to death and you hid the murder weapon in a safety deposit box. Renee wears her key on a necklace, you keep yours on that charm bracelet. I remembered your line from the opinion letter, 'keys to a treasure chest.' I confronted Renee and she told me the whole story."

"No, no, no!" Renee cried. She began to panic and clawed

frantically at her dress for the key. Azzic stood hard as bone, watching the scene in grim silence.

"Order! Come to order!" Judge Thompson shouted, slamming his gavel. *Crak! Crak! Crak!*

"This is ridiculous!" Eve spat out. "I'll sue you for defamation, for slander!" A sneer crept across her lipsticked mouth. She was too smart to incriminate herself, and I hadn't expected her to. I knew which one of them had a heart. I turned to Renee.

"Tell her the truth, Renee! Eileen's husband was your idea, but Mark was all Eve's. The cops have a statement from Jessie Morgan, from the law clinic."

"Jessie?" Renee froze on the spot, her eyes wide and brimming with tears. Her hands ceased her frantic motion and her fingers halted at her neck, encircling her own throat. I felt a pang of sympathy but went straight for the jugular. She had killed Mark and she had betrayed me.

"You planted the scissors on me when you went to my apartment, Renee. You called in your chit with Eileen and got her to frame me for the CEO's murder. You had Eileen kill Bill because he wouldn't go along with it. Say it now. Tell the truth. This is your chance. You don't have to keep the secret anymore."

"No, no, no!" Renee cried out, her face contorted with anguish. She shook her head and began to sob. "It was . . . Eve's idea. I didn't want to kill Mark. He didn't . . . do anything. She said she'd tell . . . about Eileen, what we did. She wanted the firm for herself. The new firm, the money."

I would have cheered the confession, but a wave of exhaustion washed over me, leaving me trembling. My eyes welled up with tears of relief. It was over.

Suddenly Eve bolted past an astounded jury to the judge's entrance by the dais. Azzic signaled to the uniformed cops, who chased up the aisle after her. Security guards clambered over the emptying pews to where Renee had slumped, weeping. Judge Thompson banged the gavel in vain. *Crak! Crak! Crak!*

Azzic fought his way up the aisle and stared at me, his eyes flickering with the tiniest twinge of regret, quickly masked.

I wiped my eyes, self-conscious. "Nice policework, Azzic."

When I looked up he was gone.

FORTY

I woke up lazily the next morning, savoring the sensation of rest and peace. I tugged the comforter to my chin, taking a leisurely inventory: I was safe in my own bed, Bear snored in her favorite spot at my side, and a lawyer banged around in my kitchen. "Hey, you," I called out.

"Hey, yourself."

"Come back to bed."

"I'm busy." There was the *clang* of a pot, then cabinet doors opening and closing.

"What are you doing?"

"None of your business."

"When are you coming back?"

"When I'm good and ready." The tap was turned on, then off.

"But *I'm* good and ready now." I'd been less tired than I thought last night, and this morning I was feeling even less tired than that. Must be the rowing. A useful sport.

"Stop being so bossy!"

"I can't help it, I'm the boss."

"Are not, partner."

I smiled. "Are we partners now? I'll have to think about that."

"Rosato & Wells is fine with me. I know how shy you are."

In the next instant I heard it. A gurgle I could identify in my sleep. My heart leapt up. I hoped against hope. "The paper towels are—"

"I found them," he said, and I snuggled under the covers in delicious anticipation. Life was good. A man with this set of skills was hard to find. I doubted I'd look any further. The aroma of his perfect coffee arrived just as he did.

"Lord, are you rude!" Grady said, naked except for his briefs and the STUDMUFFUN mug I'd swiped from Homicide when I'd sprung him. My fee to be a nuisance. And now it was full.

"Coffee!" I sat up and reached for it thirstily. The first sip hit my tongue. It was my third orgasm in eight hours.

"Drink fast. We have something important to do." Grady sat on the bed and grinned at me.

"More important than coffee?"

"Absolutely."

"What could possibly be more important than coffee?" I was backsliding into Mae West, but Grady only frowned.

"You think I mean sex? No way." He plucked his pants from the floor and pulled them on. "Drink up and get dressed."

"What?"

"It's all arranged. I fixed it while you were asleep." He searched for his workshirt. "We have somewhere to go."

"Where?"

"You'll see," he said, and even Bear lifted her ears, intrigued.

Ten minutes later, I was locked in one of Hattie's pungent

bear hugs, pressed awkwardly into the royal flush of shiny play-ing cards that spanned her bosom. "I'm so happy to see you, so happy," she said. "Thank God, thank God."

"It's okay now, it's all over." I hugged her back as hard as I could. I'd gotten home too late last night to stop in and I wasn't up to seeing my mother then anyway. I'd intended to deal with her after a solid night's sleep, but Grady had made other plans. Without my permission.

"Come in," Hattie said, then stepped back and wiped her eyes on the sleeve of her sweatshirt. "Come in, both of you. She's in her room."

"How is she?"

"You'll see soon enough." Hattie closed the apartment door and shot Grady a look so knowing it made me laugh.

"Have you two been conspiring?"

She smiled. "Me and Grady are old friends, by now."

He nodded. "We grew up not ten miles apart, did you know that, Bennie? Hattie grew up near the Georgia border, and I was born in Murphy, right over the line."

Hattie tugged at my arm. "We had ourselves a nice long talk on the telephone. Now let's go see your momma. She's awake."

Grady took my other arm. "Come on, Bennie. I want to meet her."

I let them yank me along only reluctantly. "Do we have to do this now? What do I say to her? Sorry I sent you to—"

"Say what comes natural," Hattie said. Bear trotted at the heels of her scruffy bedroom slippers as she and Grady tugged me through the living room. "Did you know your momma knew all about Mark's murder?"

"She did?"

"Said you told her all about it, at night." We reached my mother's door, which was slightly ajar, and Hattie pressed it open.

"My God," I heard myself say, the sight was so unexpected.

A soft morning breeze blew through the open screen, billowing through the curtains. The room was bright and smelled fresh, only faintly floral. My mother sat in a chair by the bed, still as calm water, reading a newspaper. JOINT VENTURE, said the headline above photos of Renee and Eve. My mother's hair had been combed into neat waves, and she wore slacks and a pressed white blouse. She seemed not to see me standing at the threshold in wonder.

"Is she . . . *cured*?" I whispered.

"No, but she's gettin' there," Hattie said softly. "Carmella, honey," she called, "see who's come home."

My mother looked up from the paper and her brown eyes opened slightly in surprise. "Benedetta."

Her voice struck a chord, buried deep. No one but my mother called me Benedetta, and I felt the sound reverberating inside me. Resonating within my chest. Calling me to dinner, or from play. To climb onto her lap. Benedetta.

"Benedetta, you're free," she said.

My eyes stung. A lump appeared in my throat. My heart lifted. She didn't know how right she was, and neither did I.

Until now.

FORTY-ONE

Mahogany bookshelves stocked with Supreme Court reporters surrounded the huge, still office. His desk was an English lowboy, bare except for a Waterford cup that held a flock of white quills. Three telephones sat on the various polished surfaces, but they hadn't rung all morning. There wasn't a computer in sight, but there was a box of Godiva chocolates on the coffee table. Next to a kitten.

"She's a cute one," Grun said. We sat together on a couch covered with navy damask.

"And she's already litter trained." I didn't mention she preferred legal briefs. I was pushing my luck as it was.

"She reminds me of my Tiger. She has a similar color fur."

"I thought Tiger was striped."

"Underneath the stripes, she was tan. Brownish."

"Well, she's yours, if you want her. She needs a home now that her owner's on . . . vacation." I didn't tell him Sam was in rehab, since everyone at the firm thought he was at Disney World, switching cartoon allegiances.

"Do you think she likes me?" He tickled Jamie 17 with a

wrinkled index finger, but she ignored him in favor of a black Mont Blanc.

"Of course she does. How could she not?"

"You didn't," he said, more than a bit resentfully.

"I told you, that was before I knew you." We had spent the morning together, with me confessing my ruse as Linda Frost and The Great and Powerful forgiving me, at least after I swore to reimburse the firm for the hooker suit and tuna fish.

"I don't think she likes me. She doesn't pay me any attention."

"She will in time."

"I'm eighty-two, dear. I don't have much time."

"Stop that." I didn't want to think about it. I'd had enough death for a lifetime.

Grun watched Jamie 17 flop over on the table and stretch one furry paw to the pen. "She certainly is a playful gal. Tiger was, too. She was this little when we got her." He held his hands six inches apart. "She liked cream cheese."

"I remember, you told me."

"What does this kitten like?"

"Uh, Snickers and Diet Coke?"

"You're joking."

"Of course." Eeek. "She likes salmon. Only the best for this baby."

He paused. "I must say, I didn't know what to make of it when I saw your note." He meant the one I'd left him when he fell asleep on me in the conference room. It lay crinkled on the coffee table between us, a single sheet of yellow legal paper on which I'd scribbled three large letters: I O U.

"Well, I did owe you. I owed you an apology and a kitten. Now you got both."

"I don't remember the apology. Perhaps you could you say it again. I'm quite old and my memory fails." He was smiling slyly.

"You remember, Mr. Grun."

"Perhaps I didn't hear it. My hearing, particularly in my right ear—"

"All right, already. I'm sorry I thought you were a tyrranical bastard."

"I accept your apology." He tickled Jamie 17, and she batted at him with a floppy paw. He tickled again, she batted again, and she finally abandoned the pen for one of the most prominent lawyers of his day.

"See, she likes you, Mr. Grun. You have to take her. She has no place else to go."

"Why cant you keep her?"

"My dog doesn't like her. She's jealous." Another lie, and it had come so easily. Practice makes perfect. "This cat has no home. She needs you."

"Well. I suppose I'll take her."

"Wonderful!" I said, only partly meaning it. We both watched the cat, me for the last time, but I didn't want to think about that. Maybe I could visit her. In Boca. In December.

"Bennie," he said, "where will you practice now? There's a place for you here at Grun. I'd arrange for you to have a fine office near this one. I have many important clients that need attention and, considering your years of experience, your partnership draw would be considerable."

It gave me pause. A Gold Coast office? A huge paycheck? Blue chip clients and Ivy League associates? It was a no-brainer. "No thanks, sir. I'm starting another firm."

"Understood." He nodded, smiling, as he stroked Jamie 17's back. "You say the kitten has no name?"

"None at all."

"A cat should have a name."

"Why? It's only a cat."

"I'm shocked to hear you say that!"

"It's not a real pet, like a dog. I bet you could even leave it in a car, all day long."

"Never! Cats are intelligent creatures, sensitive creatures!"

"Sorry." We both looked at Jamie 17, who had waltzed over to the box of chocolates and was sniffing at it delicately. Her cat brain was telling her it was Snickers, but it was only Godiva. "So what do you want to name her, Mr. Grun?"

"I confess, I don't know any good names."

I acted like I was thinking hard. "How about Jamie 17?"

"That's a horrid name."

"Sorry."

"*Horrid.*" He wrinkled his wrinkled nose.

"Gotcha."

"I could name her Tiger, like my other."

"No. It's stupid to name all your cats the same thing."

"Quite right. I stand corrected." He nodded. "Her name, it should suit her." He paused. "I have the perfect one."

"What?"

"Think. She's a brown cat. What else is brown?"

Crap? "I give up."

"I'll give you a hint. We both adore it."

"Coffee?"

"No, use your head."

He looked at me, I looked at him.

And we smiled at the same moment.

ACKNOWLEDGMENTS

They tell me my acknowledgments are too long and mushy, but I think a thank-you is supposed to be long and mushy. In fact, I avoid people whose thank-yous aren't long or mushy enough. Life is short. Say thanks. And this is my chance.

Thank you very much to my editor, Carolyn Marino, to whom this book is dedicated. Her professionalism and her judgment are invaluable, and if I could handcuff her to my chair as I wrote, I would. Thanks as well to her assistant, Patricia Gatti, for all her hard work.

Thank you so much to my agent, Molly Friedrich, for her improvements to this manuscript and for her representation. Molly has nurtured me with the devotion of a mother grizzly, but is much prettier, and I am one lucky cub. Thanks, too, to Molly's staff, The Amazing Paul Cirone and author-to-be Sheri Holman. Thank you also to Linda Hayes, for everything she has done for me and my books.

Thanks to everyone at HarperCollins, especially to Jack McKeown, Geoff Hannell, and Gene Mydlowski. As always, thanks to Laura Baker, publicist and bride extraordinaire. Thanks to the sales and marketing departments, and to the trade and paperback reps on the road. Stay safe, folks.

Special thanks to Robin Schatz of the Mayor's Office in

Philadelphia. Robin has answered all of my nitpicking questions for many books now, and for this book smuggled me into the Homicide Division at the Roundhouse, where I met the nicest and most professional group of detectives ever. They talked law and plot with equal ease, and helped me on more than one occasion. They know better than anybody else that *Legal Tender* and its characters are fiction. Thank you very much, gentlemen.

Thanks to Joseph LaBar of the District Attorney's Office, a true pro, and to Susan Burt, another pro, but for the other side of the fence. For superb estates advice, thank you to Robert L. Freedman of Dechert, Price & Rhoads in Philadelphia, my alma mater.

For medical and psychiatric advice, thanks to Dr. Daniel Kushon and Dr. Ginny Galetta.

To the University of Pennsylvania Women's Crew, thanks for letting me hang at the boathouse and act like I still belonged there. To Dana Quattrone of Benjamin Lovell Shoes, thanks for teaching me about Doc Martens.

For managing not to point and laugh as I crawled around their sub-basement, thanks to the building engineers at Commerce Square.

A big bear hug to one Frank Scottoline, an architect who proved very helpful. For research assistance in the clutch and eggplant parmigiana beyond the call of duty, a loving thank-you to Mary Scottoline. Whoever said you get what you pay for never knew my parents. Finally, thanks and love to Fayne and my friends, and especially to Kiki and Peter.

A final thanks to Chuck Jones, and a tear for Mel Blanc.

ABOUT THE AUTHOR

LISA SCOTTOLINE is the *New York Times* bestselling and Edgar Award–winning author of twenty-three novels, twelve of which are in the Rosato series. Thirty million copies of her books are in print in the United States, and she has been published in thirty-five countries. She served as president of Mystery Writers of America, and her thrillers have been optioned for television and film. She also writes a weekly humor column, "Chick Wit," with her daughter, Francesca Serritella, for the *Philadelphia Inquirer*, which have been adapted into a series of memoirs, the first of which is *Why My Third Husband Will Be a Dog*. She lives in the Philadelphia area with an array of disobedient pets. You can visit Lisa at www.scottoline.com.

BOOKS BY
LISA SCOTTOLINE

FINAL APPEAL
Available in Paperback and eBook

RUNNING FROM THE LAW
Available in Mass Market Paperback and eBook

DEVIL'S CORNER
Available in Mass Market Paperback and eBook

DIRTY BLONDE
Available in Mass Market Paperback and eBook

DADDY'S GIRL
Available in Mass Market Paperback and eBook

THE VENDETTA DEFENSE
Available in Mass Market Paperback and eBook

For more details, visit: www.scottoline.com